D0439524

ALSO BY JERRY STAHL

Fiction

Bad Sex on Speed

The Heroin Chronicles (Editor)

Pain Killers

Love Without

I, Fatty

Perv

Plainclothes Naked

Nonfiction

Permanent Midnight

HARPER PERENNIAL

NEW YORK • LONDON • TORONTO • SYDNEY • NEW DELHI • AUCKLAND

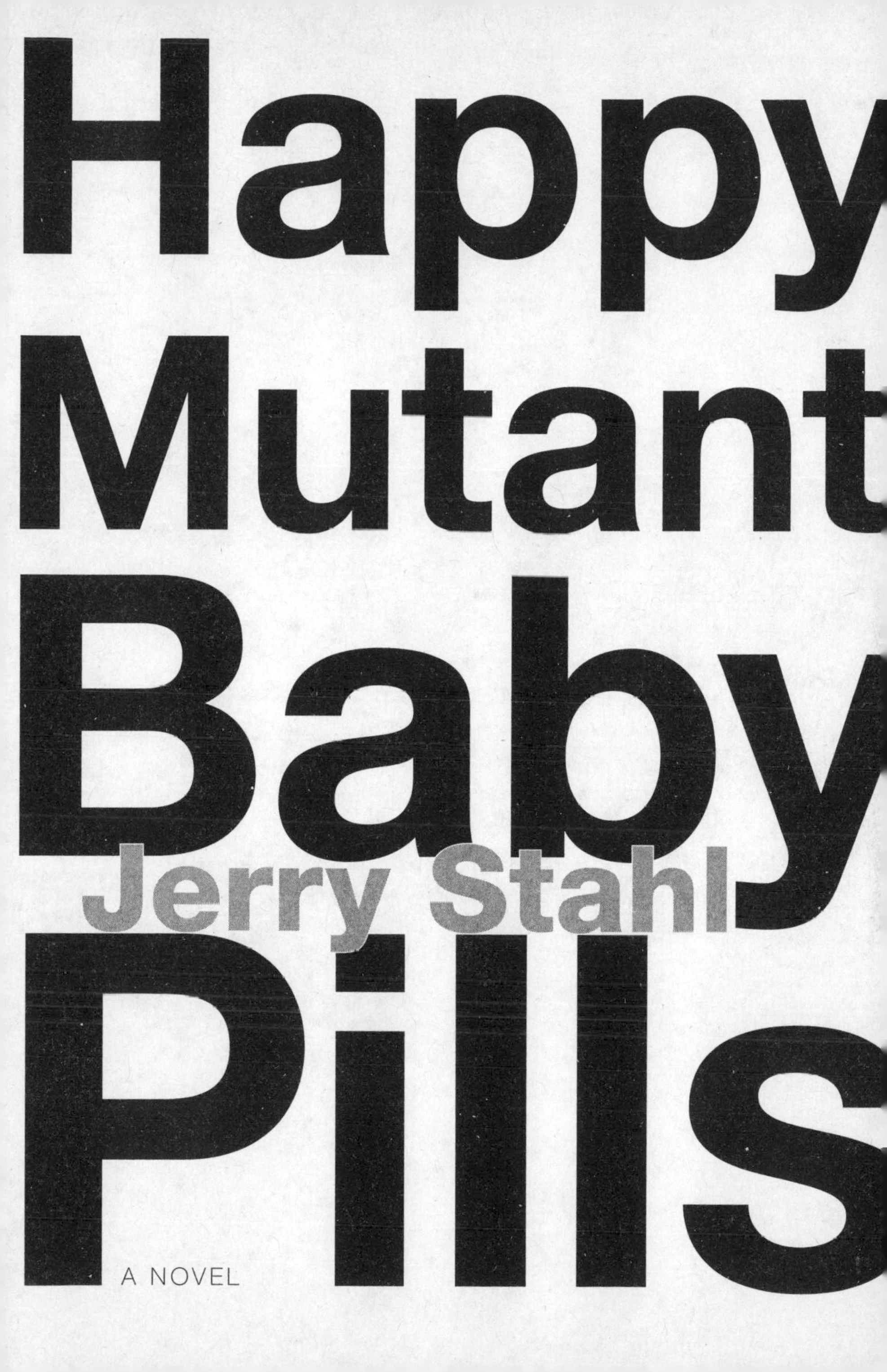
Happy
Mutant
Baby
Jerry Stahl
Pills
A NOVEL

HARPER PERENNIAL

This book is a work of fiction. References to real people, events, establishments, organizations, or locales are intended only to provide a sense of authenticity, and are used fictitiously. All other characters, and all incidents and dialogue, are drawn from the author's imagination and are not to be construed as real.

HarperCollins books may be purchased for educational, business, or sales promotional use. For information please e-mail the Special Markets Department at SPsales@harpercollins.com.

FIRST EDITION

Book design by Sunil Manchikanti

Printed on acid-free paper

Library of Congress Cataloging-in-Publication Data is available upon request.

ISBN 978-0-06-199050-2

13 14 15 16 17 OV/RRD 10 9 8 7 6 5 4 3 2 1

For Elizabeth

People are
too durable,
that's their
main trouble.
They can do
too much to
themselves, they
last too long.

BERTOLT BRECHT

Happy Mutant Baby Pills

Book One

Perhaps all pleasure
is only relief.

WILLIAM S. BURROUGHS

Prologue

Once upon a time, I was a fucking maniac.

Not, mind you, that I have since morphed into the spawn of Mr. Rogers. It's just—how can I put this without sounding like a douche (the eternal question)—there were years so weirdly searing, so down to the bleeding toes of my soul draining, I found myself putting words on a page at a time when I could barely string a series of sentences together, trying to GET IT ALL DOWN, to get it, you know, *right*, so that when things got better—because I had to believe they would, they fucking had to—I would have a digital memory, some kind of record, however short, however unflattering, if not (occasionally) outright embarrassing; something to call up, in trying times, to help me feel grateful, however out-of-control fucked life might seem, that it's no longer as bad as, you know, that . . . (In much the same way horrific drunks whose "friends" video them taking their clothes off on the subway singing "Tiny Dancer," or all-but-raping a mentally challenged cousin in a Burger King, will have that moment, or those moments, preserved for eternity, on hand when needed, to remind them, when things go south, that, if nothing else, they're not as far south as they were, back in the dark days, when they were Elton John–ing or cousin-raping or generally making regrettable spectacles of themselves. (Or sending regrettable e-mails. The worst! How the Internet has provided all new humiliation-delivery systems. Your whole mentally challenged Tiny Dancer party can go viral.)

Until, of course, the banner day—O Gratitude!—when something happens and—like *that*!—you realize the Burger King years were a season in paradise, subway shame a MacArthur grant compared to the level of demoralization you now feel. The particular demoralization that comes from thinking you were out of the woods, and then the woods turn out to be a park, and the park's in front of the Petrified Forest. Which is full of man-eating boars. Who only eat men who look like you. Or something. You get the point.

For years, I couldn't talk, I spritzed. Who knew?

This prologue—for lack of a better word—comprises (compresses?) the febrile spray of what I thought were life's worst moments, PPA—Preserved Personal Archaeology™—jittery hieroglyphics that, when deciphered, fill twenty pages unlike the rest of the book but necessary to it, a borderline-personality palette cleanser for the more traditional narrative to come.

Nobody sets out to write the world's longest cocktail napkin. But Jeez, Beaver, I thought I'd hit bottom. A good place to start a book. But bad place to start a life. The problem, as the great Hubert Selby liked to say, is that the bottom is bottomless. In other words, I thought I was fucked. And it turned out I didn't even know what fucked was.

Your indulgence, then. The waters calm considerably after the opening storm. The storytelling settles into sanity, as sanity itself, by degrees, becomes a far shore, forgotten and unseen, like land itself after years at sea.

(How creepy was that? I used to write greeting cards. Sometimes I relapse.)

I could have just said, after the prologue things calm the fuck down.

But let's start with a joke: *Bad penny, she always turns up.* (I didn't say it was funny.)

This was one of my most popular campaigns, back when the porn business was referred to as "adult films." Not that I'm a porn guy. I'm not. Anymore. I'm the kind of writer you don't hear about. The guy who always wanted to be a writer—who read the backs of cereal boxes as a kid, dreamed of being Ernest Hemingway, then grew up and wrote the backs of cereal boxes.

You don't think about the people who write the side-effect copy for Abilify or olestra ads . . . It's not as easy as you think. You need to decide whether "anal leakage" goes best before or after "suicidal thoughts and dry mouth." I take a ribbing from some of the guys at the office—which, I have to admit, gets to me. They know I've been working on a novel, but it's been a while. I guess I should also admit that the heroin helps with some of the shame I feel about writing this stuff. Or life in general. I'm not, like, a junkie-junkie. I use it, I don't let it use me. And I'm not going to lie: it helps. It's like, suddenly, you have a mommy who loves you. You just have to keep paying her.

Not that life was bad, either. I made a living, and not a bad one, considering. When I got my MFA I thought for sure all I had to do was start writing stories and things would just kind of take care of themselves. I realize now that it probably wasn't smart to use my "craft" to make my living. "Don't use the same muscle you write fiction with to pay the rent," my professor and thesis adviser, Jo Bergy, advised. (Jo writes a lot of YA stuff. Her alter ego/heroine is a unicorn named "Teensy.") Of course I ignored her. I wanted to be a writer! In New York! But gradually, as the years passed, the bar for what passed for writing got a little lower while the pay, occasionally, got a lot higher. Why is that? Why should I be paid more for vibrator copy than my searching and personal novella about growing up the son of a blind rabbi and his kleptomaniac adulterous wife in Signet, Ohio? Sure, I placed a few "chunks" of the book as short stories in the beginning. That's what made me think I could do it. Though why I thought the three free copies from *Party Ball Magazine*, or the two hundred I got from *Prose for Shmoes*, a hipster "web-lit" site out of Portland, was going to make a dent in my living expenses, I don't know. I had some hopeful correspondence from *The Believer.* But ultimately they ended up printing the letter of protest I wrote when they rejected my twenty-first submission. Again, the drugs helped. I feel a terrific sense of shame about my whole life situation. I see other people my age, and way younger (which kills me), making big money doing screenplays, snagging memoir deals based on tweets, and here I am bouncing around from Porn Dog to New Media Guy to Uh-Oh Boy—industry lingo for Side Effects Specialists—aka SESSIES.

And yes, just thinking about this, the knife-in-the-chest regret I feel at chances blown, assignments fucked up, books unwritten or written badly . . . public scenes (more than once involving knee-walking, twice on a plane) when I was, you know, more high than I thought I was, it all twists me up. On smack, sometimes, you feel so perfect, you just assume everything you do is perfect, too. And when you remember, and the remorse kicks in, it's like a razor-legged tarantula crawling upside down in your heart, cursing you in dirty Serbian for being a lame-ass dope fiend who blew every chance he ever had and ended up in the world of incontinence wear and catheters. (Referred to, among pharma-hacks, as "dump lockers" and "caths.") Well, do a little heroin and you can remember the good things. On smack, everything feels good. I would gladly slit my own throat, attend the funeral, and dig my own grave if I could do it all on decent dope. As William Burroughs once opined, "It's not the heroin that kills you, it's the lifestyle."

But we were talking about the good things!

Like, not to brag, it was my idea to refer to the discharge from the rectal area as "anal leakage" rather than actual "intestinal discharge." Which technically (if not linguistically) speaking are two different things. My thinking was—and I said this to Cliff and Chandra, the husband-wife team who took over the agency—my thinking was, bad as "anal leakage" is, at least it's vaguely familiar. Tires leak, faucets leak; it's round-the-house stuff, and we all have anuses (ani?). But discharge is never good. Try to think of one situation involving discharge from your body that is not kind of horrible. Perhaps, hearing about my life and "career," you think *they* sound pretty horrible. Or maybe you're thinking to yourself: okay, he has some problems, he's had a bumpy career path, but he doesn't seem like a heroin guy.

Exactly! It's no big deal! Everybody has their little rituals. Miles Dreek, the other SESSIE, walks in with his spirulina and hemp protein smoothie and gluten-free bran muffin every morning. When I come in, I have my own stations of the cross. I go to the men's room, cook up a shot up in my favorite stall, grab coffee in my ironic *Dilbert* mug, and amble back to my cubicle, where the latest batch of American maladies awaits. Today, for example, is Embarrassing Flaky Patches Day. I watch the moving drama the clients have already filmed, showing a nice white lady with other nice white people in a nice restaurant, and listen to her VO: *It was a weekend to relax with friends and family. But even here, there was no escaping it. It's called moderate to severe chronic plaque psoriasis. Once again, I had to deal with these embarrassing, flaky, painful, red patches. It was time for a serious talk with my dermatologist.*

Here's where I roll up my sleeves. (Well, at least one of them—ha-ha!) From a roster of heinous side effects I start cobbling together the Authoritative-but-Friendly PSE (possible side effects) list. *HUMIRA can lower your ability to fight infections, including tuberculosis. Serious, sometimes fatal, events can occur, such as lymphoma or other types of cancer; blood, liver, and nervous system problems; serious allergic reactions; and new or worsening heart failure.*

I had me at cancer! Seriously. I don't care if bloody images of Satan bubbled up on my flesh, I'd have to do heroin just to stop worrying about the lymphoma and heart failure I might get for taking this shit to get rid of them. That's the dirty little secret of TV medicine spots. We start off with a bible. A Side Effects Bible. Basically a collection of horrible possibilities. Which it is our job to recite and minimize—sometimes by just saying them really fast—other times by finding language that can render them acceptable. Whatever revulsion-neutralizing pap they come up with to help sell it, there is no chance in hell the people who write it would go near the stuff.

Of course, people will tell you heroin is bad. But let me tell you my experience. If you take it for a reason, and you happen to have a reason every day, then it's not exactly addictive behavior. It's more like medicine. Or a special survival tool. For example, there may be a thought that crops up in your head. (We're only as sick as our secrets!) Like how, lately, I have this thing, whenever I see a pregnant woman, especially if she's, you know, exotically beautiful, or has dimples, where I just sort of see her in stirrups, giving birth, sweaty thighs wide open, the doctor and nurses with their masks on, the doctor reaching in, up to the wrists. It's better if it's a female doctor. I don't know why; I'm not proud of any of this. Once there's the actual pulling out of some bloody placenta-covered little screamer, I'm out. I'm not sick. But still I think about—this is really not cool, really not something I want to think I'm thinking about—but nonetheless, what I think about, almost against my will, is how her vaginal walls—for which the Brits have the singularly disturbo term "blame-curtains"—no, that can't be right—will just be vastly . . . open. I remember it from when my ex-wife gave birth to our son,

Mickey. (She left me years ago; now she's running a preschool for upscale biters. And biting's a syndrome now; Squibb R&D has some meds in development. But never mind. Kids' drugs take a tad longer for the FDA to rubber-stamp.) Anyway, I just picture the gape. As riveting as Animal Planet footage of boas dislocating their jaws to swallow an entire baby boar. (The same arousal, it goes without saying, does not apply during a caesarean; I'm not an animal.) But still . . . When my thoughts—how can I put this?—veer in this direction, some non-wholesome wouldn't-want-to-have-my-mind-read-in-front-of-a-room-full-of-friends direction (if I had a room full of friends), I need something to get rid of the thoughts. I need the heroin.

Worse than fantasies are memories. Which may, arguably, qualify as disguised fantasy. Didn't George Bernard Shaw say, "The only thing worse than recollecting the things I did as a child is recalling things I did as an adult"? Or was that Cher?

I actually started writing in rehab. (My first one. I've been in eleven. Or eight. Three in Arizona.) And it was awful. The writing, I mean. Rehabs are rehabs. (Work the steps, help do dishes, share the bathroom with a weeping record executive.) We were supposed to paint a portrait of ourselves in words. I still remember my first sentence: "I AM TAPIOCA TRAPPED IN ARMOR!" Followed by: "Little Lloyd" (that's my name; well, Lloyd, not Little Lloyd). "Little Lloyd has cowered continually, long into adulthood, at the memory of deeds perpetrated on his young unprotected self, scenes of unspeakable humiliation." Which—can somebody tell me why? Freudians? Melanie Kleiners? Bruno Bettelheimies? Anybody?—barge into my psyche at the most inopportune moments. Imagine a big-screen TV that turns on by itself and blasts shame porn to all your neighbors at four in the morning. Like, say, I'll be at a job interview, talking to some wing-tipped toad named Gromes about my special abilities recounting the consequences of ingesting Malvesta, a prescription adult-onset acne pill (glandular swelling, discomfort in the forehead, bad breath, strange or disturbing dreams), when I'll suddenly be overcome with memories of my mother paddling around the house with her hands cupped under her large blue-veined breasts as our record player (ever heard of those?) blared Dean Martin. When the moon hits your eye like a big pizza pie, that's amore! She's high-kicking while our mailman, a long-faced Greek with a nervous twitch, peers in the window. And Mom knows he's there. I'm four and a half, waiting to get taken to kindergarten. Mom's supposed to drive me, but instead she starts screaming over the music: "Why don't you play? Why don't you play?" It makes me anxious. Should the mailman be looking in the window? Where is his other hand? What happened to his bag? I mean, Jeez! Not even five, and I already need a fix.

Well, that's it. Once the Dino flashback kicks in, I'm cooked. Forget the job interview. I'm like Biff in *Death of a Salesman*, grabbing a fountain pen and running out of the office. Except I run straight to the bathroom and pull a syringe from my boot. Minutes later, before the needle is out AHHHH YESS-S-S-S-S-S-S-S, Thank you, Jesus!. The mommy-tits-amore image furs and softens at the edges. Until—MMMMM, lemme just dab off this little kiss of blood—what began as horror morphs into suffused light, savaged memory softened by euphoria into benevolence, into some slightly disquieting, distant image . . . Mom is no longer doing a dirty can-can in the living room, entertaining a twitchy peeper in government issue . . . Now—I love you, Ma, I really love you!—now her legs simply float up and down in downy silence. My mind has been tucked into bed. A loving hand brushes my troubled little brow . . . Heroin's the cool-fingered loving Mommy I never had. But everything's all right now . . . My memory's parked in the very last row of a flickering drive-in, with fog rolling in over all the cars up front. I know what's on the screen, and I know it's bad—is that a knife going into Janet Leigh? But—it . . . just . . . does . . . not . . . matter. It's still nice. Really nice. (Provided, that is, I don't pass out in the men's room, they don't end up calling paramedics, and I don't wake up chained to the hospital bed. Again. In California they can arrest you for tracks. Those fascists!)

And now—oh, God, no! No! Here comes another memory. STOP, PLEASE! Why does my own brain hate me? I'm picking my son up at preschool, and I'm early, and I've just copped, so I go in the boys' room. And—NO NO NO NO!—I come to—you never wake up on heroin, you just come to—to screams of "Daddy, what's wrong?" See my little boy in his SpongeBob SquarePants hat, his mouth a giant O. He's screaming, screaming, and—what's this?—my ratty jeans are already at my ankles and there's a needle in my arm and my boy's teachers and the principal of the preschool are hovering over me like a circle of disapproving angels on the ceiling of the Sistine Chapel and—

And I hear myself, with my child looking on, like it's some kind of aw-shucks normal thing, saying, "Hey, could you guys just let me, y'know . . . just give me a second here?" And, in front of all of them, in front of my sweet, innocent, quivering-chinned son, I push down that plunger. And suddenly, everything's fine. Everything's awful, but everything's fine . . . My little boy's horrified coffee-brown eyes glisten with tears. Good-bye, little Mickey, good-bye . . . My wife will get a call from family services. I'll be leaving now. Hands behind my back. In cuffs. All I remember is the officer's name: Branderby. His sausage-and-pepper breath. I manage a little wave to Mickey, who gives me a private little wave back. In spite of everything. I'm still his daddy. For years afterward, I have to get high just to think about what I did to get high. But it's okay. Really.

It's.

Fine.

Heroin. Because once you shed your dignity, everything's a little easier.

Where was I? (And yes, maybe the dope did diminish my capacity for linear thinking. So what? Let's see you count backward from yesterday to What-the-fuck-happened?) When my boss moved to pharmaceuticals from "marital aids," I followed. (He insisted on the old-school term his father used: marital aids. Instead of the more contempo "sex toys.") We'd been taken over by a conglomerate. I cut my teeth on Doc Johnson double dildos ("For ass-to-ass action like you've never dreamed of!") and Ben Wa balls ("Ladies, no one has to know!"). Then it was up (or down) the ladder to men's magazines, romance mags, even a couple of *Cat Fancy* imitators. Starting in back-of-the-book "one-inchers" for everything from Mighty Man trusses to Kitty Mittens to X-Ray Specs (a big-seller for more than fifty years). When I tried the specs and—naturally—they didn't work, my boss said, with no irony whatsoever, "We're selling a dream, Lloyd. Did you go to Catholic school?"

"Metho-Heeb," I told him.

"What's that, kid?"

"Half-Jewish, half-Methodist, and my mom did a lot of speed."

"Well, lucky you," he said. "Me, I was schooled by nuns. But when I put on those X-ray specs, I swear, I could see Sister Mary Theresa's fong-hair."

While cheesy, this is a serious, high-stakes business. To stay on top of the competition, you have to know what's out there. Like, just now, on *The Dylan Ratigan Show*—What great hair! Like a rockabilly gym teacher . . . too bad he quit—I caught this commercial: *Life with Crohn's disease is a daily game of What if . . . ? What if I can't make it to—* Here the audio fades and there's a picture of a pretty middle-aged brunette looking anxiously across a tony restaurant at a ladies' room door . . . The subtext: if you don't take this, you are going to paint your panties.

Listen. I spent a lot of time watching daytime commercials. I had to. (Billie Holiday said she knew she was strung out when she started watching television. And she didn't even talk about daytime!) Back when it was still on, I'd try to sit through *Live with Regis and Kelly* without a bang of chiba. Knock yourself out, Jimmy-Jane. I couldn't make it past Regis's rouge without a second shot. At this point he looked like somebody who'd try and touch your child on a bus to New Jersey.

Is it any accident that so much contempo TV ad content concerns . . . accidents? This is the prevailing mood. Look at the economy. Things are so bad you don't need to have Crohn's disease to lose control. But worse than pants-shitting is public pants-shitting. Americans like to think of themselves as mud-holders. You don't see the Greatest Generation diapering up, do you? (Not until recently, anyway.)

Junkies may be obsessed with bathrooms, but America's got them beat. So many cable-advertised products involve human waste that you imagine the audience sitting at home eating no-fat potato chips on a pile of their own excretions. *Ad Week* put it on its cover: "American Business Is in the Toilet."

But the real big gun in the BFS (Bodily Function Sweepstakes) is Depends. Go ahead and laugh. These guys are genius. Why? I'll tell you. They know how to make the Bad Thing okay. (Just like heroin!) Listen: *Incontinence doesn't have to limit you. It all starts with finding the right fit and protection. The fact is, you can manage it so you can feel like yourself again.* (Oddly, I used to lose bowel control after I copped. I'd get so excited, it just happened. So I'm no stranger to "manpers," as we say in the industry. They could ask me for a testimonial. Though, in all honesty, if it were my campaign I'd have gone with something more macho. Something, call me crazy, patriotic.

Depends. Because this is America, damn it!

Then again, maybe the macho thing is wrong. Maybe—I'm just spitballing here—maybe you make it more of a convenience thing. Or—wait, wait!—more Morning in America ish. More Reagan-y.

Take two: *America, we know you're busy. And you don't always have time to pull over and find somewhere convenient to do your business. With new Depends, you can go where you are—and keep on going. DEPENDS—because you've earned it.*

Subtext, of course: We're Americans! We can shit wherever we want!)

Ironically, because of my own decade and a half imbibing kiestered Mexican tar, I got some kind of heinous, indestructible parasite. Souvenir of Los Angeles smackdom. For a while I had a copywriting job in downtown LA, five minutes from MacArthur Park, where twelve-year-old 18th Street bangers kept the stuff in balloons in their mouths. You'd give them cash, then put the balloons in your mouth. If you put them in your pockets, the UCs would roll up and arrest you before the spit was dry. Keeping it in your mouth was safer. Unhygienic (parasites!), but on the plus side, visit any LA junkie pad, and there was always something carnivale about the little pieces of red and blue, green and yellow balloons all over the place. Like somebody'd thrown a child's birthday party in hell and never cleaned up.

But now—call it Narco-Karma —I have to give myself coffee enemas every day. Part of the "protocol" my homeopath, Bobbi, herself in recovery, has put me on for the parasite situation. Bobbi also does my colonics . . . She likes calypso music, which I find a little unsettling. Though Robert Mitchum singing "Coconut Water" while I'm buns up and tubed is the least of my issues. Bob knew his calypso. (Check out *Calypso—Is Like So!* liner notes by Nick Tosches.)

Like I say, part of my job is recon. And I'm not going to lie, just thinking about that killer Crohn's copy makes me a little jealous. The subject, after all, was shame. What does some pharma-hired disease jockey know about shame? Did he have my mother? Scooping his stainy underpants out of the hamper and waggling them in his face, screaming she was going to hang them on the line for all his friends to see? (No, that's not why I do heroin. Or why I ended up in side effects. Whatever doesn't kill us just makes us us.)

For one semester I attended the School of Visual Arts in New York City. I studied advertising with Joe Sacco, whose legendary "Stronger Than Dirt" campaign, arguably, sheathed a proto-Aryan superiority sensibility under the genial façade of Arthurian legend. (For you youngsters, the ad featured a white knight riding into a dirty kitchen on a white steed.) White Power might as well have been embossed on the filth-fighter's T-shirt. See—excuse me while I scratch my nose—there's a connection, in White American subconscious, between Aryan superiority and cleanliness. "Clean genes," as Himmler used to say. Tune into MSNBC's *Lockup* some weekend, when the network trades in the faux-progressive programming for prison porn. Half the shot-callers in Quentin look like Mr. Clean: shaved head and muscles that could really hold a race-traitor down. Lots of dope in prison. But—big surprise—the fave sponsors of *Lockup* viewers, to judge by the ads, are ExtenZe (penis size), UroMed (urinary infection), our old friend Depends (bowel control), and Flomax (frequent urination). The Founding Fathers would be proud. Once they hosed off.

You think junkies don't have a conscience? All the snappy patter I've cranked out, and you know what made me really feel bad? Feel the worst? Gold coin copy. People are so dumb that when they buy gold—a hedge against the collapse of world markets!—they think it matters if it comes in a commemorative coin. A genuine re-creation of an authentic 18-something-something mint issue Civil War coin with our nation's greatest president, Abraham Lincoln, on one side, and the Union flag on the other. Worth 50 "dollar gold." Yours for only $9.99. The "dollar gold" was my idea. I don't even know why. I just knew it sounded more important than "dollars." Later, in the running text under the screen (known as flash text in the biz), I misspelled gold as "genuine multi-karat pure god." I think this was my best move. Not that I can take credit. Just one of those serendipitous bonbons you get when you type on heroin. In an effort not to fall off my chair, I'd type with one eye closed, as if I were trying to aim my fingers the way I aimed my car, squinting one-eyed over the wheel to stay between the white lines when the world went tilty.

So now now now now now now what do I do? I mean—shut up, okay?—I did leave out a key detail. Like, how it all ended?

Okay. Let me come clean. (So to speak.) I got caught shooting up on the job. Dropped my syringe and it rolled leeward into the stall beside me, where my archrival, Miles Dreek (can a name get more Dickensian?), found it. And, long story short, ratted me out. I couldn't even plead diabetes, because the rig was full of blood, and everybody's seen enough bad junkie movies to know how the syringe fills up with blood. (Generally, on film, in roseate slo-mo, dawn-of-the-galaxy exploding-nebulae-adjacent scarlet, which—come on, buddy—does not happen when Gramps drops trou and Grandma slaps his leathery butt cheek and sticks in the insulin.) That was my first experience of needles: Grandma spanking Grandpa and jabbing the rig in. Grandpa had it down. The second his wife of sixty-seven years geezed him, he'd pop a butterscotch Life Saver and crunch. Hard candy! Sugar and insulin at the same time. A diabetic speedball. These are my people!

But wait—I was just getting busted. At work. (People think only alcohol can give you blackouts. But heroin? Guess what, Lou Reed Jr., sometimes I think I'm still in one . . .)

I remember, right before the needle-dropping incident, I was just sitting there, on the toilet, with a spike in my arm, Lenny Bruce–style. Suddenly I jerked awake, feeling like one of those warehouse-raised chickens, the kind photographed by secret camera in *Food, Inc.* on some infernal industrial farm, feet grafted to the cage, shitting on the chicken below as the chicken above shits on it.

You don't think they should give chickens heroin? Don't think they deserve it? Well, call me visionary, but if they're already pumping the poultry full of antibiotics and breast-building hormones (rendering, they say, half the chicken-eating male population of America estrogen-heavy, sterile, and sporadically man-papped), then why not lace the white meat with hard narcotics? Chicken McJunkets! Whatever. Give me one night and three dime bags and I'll Don Draper a better name . . . Or I would, if I had a place to live. Right now I have enough to stay at this hotel, the Grandee (an SRO) for a couple more weeks. After that I don't know . . . The guy behind the cage in the lobby looks liver yellow. Doesn't talk much. But never mind, never mind . . . Me being here has nothing to do with heroin. Just bad luck. But weren't we talking about heroin chicken? Believe me, plenty of clean-living junkies would hit the drive-through—provided Mickey D could take those damn other drugs out of his birds. Hormones, antibiotics, beak-mite repellent . . . No thanks! That stuff could kill you.

But enough! Let's settle down and spit out the palette cleanser. It's time for the entrée.

ONE

Christ-Work

I was shooting dope at Christian Swingles, a faith-based dating website where I worked in Tulsa. We didn't have coffee breaks at 10:45, we had prayer moments. With a muffin cart. If you think it was easy doing heroin in that situation, well—you'd be absolutely *right*. What a nest of freaks! The good kind. But I can pray to Jesus with a little smack in me. With a little more I can even believe. Opium of the people, on opiates.

This was the dawn of online dating. So I wasn't cranking out my usual side effects, pharma-copy, gold scams, or sex-toy banter. Christian Swingles was weirder. At least for me. (Not being a Christian.) The genius of the site was that it was about so much more than Christ-loving singles. It was about *a way of life*. The dos and don'ts of Jesus-centric singledom. I'm still afraid if there is a hell, I might go there for this. But let me walk you down the path of perdition. No one starts out in hell; they have to do something to deserve it. You have to put in the *work*.

The owners, naturally, were two Jewish guys. Eddy and Teddy Lifshitz. (They swore their cousin was Ralph Lauren—"The schmuck got Goy surgery in Tijuana, after his name change, and then tells Oprah, 'My given name has shit in it?' ") The brothers Lifshitz cut their teeth on J-Dreemz—the first

Jewish dating site (and ultimately BlackBerry to JDate's iPhone). Just because it was owned by Hebrews, however, did not mean the owners wanted anything less than absolute authenticity when it came to Christ-friendly content. (The brothers strove for equal authenticity in their later ventures: Interracial Daters, Black Love, Cantonese Seekers.) Swingles content was half Bible-dating behavior, half typical faux-dating quiz questions. But the man in charge was the real deal, an actual former air force chaplain named Bobby Bobb.

The silver-haired Pastor Bobb was hired by the Lifshitzes themselves to run the place. (I remember the first time I saw the brothers, two thin-lipped hunched young men who might as well have been wearing yarmulkes and talliths. They looked like they'd just stepped from the Wailing Wall to the "Loving Hall"—the short corridor behind reception, where hung framed photos of successful Christian couples, newlyweds who met in Christian Dreemz-land, and pictures of Jesus: the ultimate Christian single.)

Anyway, I started working for Swingles after I met a volunteer from Prison Fellowship, Chuck Colson's group. (Colson, for you under-forties, was one of the Watergate burglars. Watergate was . . . well, why bother? That's why God made Google. Let's just say it was back when they used to prosecute presidents for crimes. Not for secret bombing or lying the country into war or anything like that. For breaking into a hotel room. Then lying about it. You'll notice, presidents don't break into hotel rooms anymore. The system works!)

After serving Nixon, Colson found the Lord in a minimum security federal penitentiary in Maxwell, Alabama, and decided to spend the rest of his life "giving back." As Chuck put it in his

1983 book *Loving God*, "Though folklore has it that minimum security prisons, like the one I was in, are full of wealthy 'white-collar criminals' doing a few months of 'easy' time . . . well, that's just not true!" Chuck knew what it meant to be down. Chuck was giving back.

How I got to the federal pen isn't much of a story. After getting fired from my last job, when that guy Dreek snitched me off, I was flying from New York City to Pittsburgh, Pennsylvania, for my mother's funeral. I forgot I had a syringe in my sock. Crime doesn't get much more glamorous. Because it happened at an airport, it was federal. (Thinking about it now, I don't actually want to shoot heroin—I just want to stick a syringe in my *eye*.) I didn't even make it to the metal detector. As I was standing in line, shoeless, an adorable, floppy-eared beagle puppy padded over on the end of a long leash.

Had I been paying attention, I'd have seen the other end of the leash was in the hand of some yoked flattop in a DEA T-shirt and reflector shades. (The Jerry-Bruckheimer-let's-hire-Henry-Rollins-to-play-a-DEA-agent look.) Instead, I had my nose buried in a copy of *Naked Lunch*. I know, I know. It's a cliché. But for me, somehow, *Lunch* is always vaguely reassuring, a warm bath for the brain, in times of trouble. Not that times were that troubled. I was going to my mother's funeral. I hadn't seen mine in a decade or two. But still . . . I saw that cute little pup sniffing up to my shoe, and I thought, before I even realized I was a fucking idiot, that the God of unhappy boyhoods had sent a little Snoopy to cheer me up. After which, of course, Snoopy sniffed the syringe in my sock, and no amount of explaining could make Bruckheimer Reflector Shades believe it was mom-grief.

Of course, there's a drug for that too. Viibryd. An antidepressant, a *grief-fighter.* It gets me misty-eyed just thinking about it. The sheer paradox. Listen: *Antidepressants increase the risk compared to placebo of suicidal thinking and behavior (suicidality) in children, teens, and young adults. Depression and certain other psychiatric disorders are themselves associated with increases in the risk of suicide. Patients of all ages who are started on antidepressant therapy should be monitored appropriately* . . . The beauty of *that.* You take the stuff for grief, and it makes you suicidally grief-stricken . . . Mission accomplished! It's the Möbius strip of symptom and relief. I have the condition, I want to get rid of it, so I take the medication to make it go away, and—Pfizer meet *Job*!—inflict upon myself the exact thing I want to eradicate.

Other people have prayers, mantras, affirmations . . . I have occasional side effects. In the case of Viibryd, it's the last few torments that resonate: *Unusual changes in behavior.* Yes! *Disturbing dreams.* Thank you! *Sudden violent thoughts*? Hallelujah! Could anything be more human than unusual changes in behavior, disturbing dreams, and sudden violent thoughts? It's almost reassuring. Viibryd has taken the very qualities that separate us from animals and turned them into . . . side effects.

When I was being led away by the Bruckheimer shades guy, after having my freedom puppied at the airport, I found myself repeating to myself: *Disturbing* . . . *Sudden* . . . *Violent* . . . So what if I'm the only one who knows this is poetry? I let myself murmur, under the stares of other travelers, as the stalwart DEA badged a path through lines of passengers and bulled me through, in handcuffs. He was snickering. (*Disturbing* . . . *Sudden* . . . *Violent* . . . I was also the only one who knew this was prayer.)

DEA shades man sat me in a little room with fluorescents, table, and chairs—very *Law & Order.* He would not buy my grief defense, even after I dragged up my dead mother and marched her out to try and get some official sympathy. He might have bit—I could tell he was on the fence until he jammed my sleeve up (the left, as it happened: my shooting arm) and found a few hundred years' worth of tracks. For some time needles had been hard to get, and it looked like I'd been trying to shoot up with a piano leg. "Unless you got some kinda arm Ebola, lady-pants, you're goin' away. And I mean federal." The lady thing, I was to learn, is something law enforcement types seem to enjoy. Especially the prison guards. Feminization. Maybe that's how they deal with their grief. Maybe we should all be given Viibryd at birth.

TWO

Terminal Island

So, it's two months later, and I'm in the kitchen at Terminal Island, daydreaming about Mexican tar and shoving chipped ham down my pants. That was the thing about kitchen jobs: you could boost some food, then trade it on the yard for party snacks. And the snack I wanted was still tar. I'd gotten clean, by accident, and the worst thing was—worse than kicking in the penitentiary (you want to talk about anal leakage!), worse than the cramps, worse than the knee pain, worse than not sleeping for weeks . . . worse than all of it were the emotions. I was moody as a fourteen-year-old bulimic girl. My nerves were exposed. Every memory had me weepy.

Adjusting the lunchmeat in my starchy, state-issue tighty-whiteys—there were freaks in there who would have paid extra if they'd known where I'd stashed the ham—I suddenly remembered my grandmother's hands. Grandma Essie had acromegaly, which made her hands and face swell to monster movie proportions. (Google Rondo Hatton. The Creeper.) Essie's jaw and forehead were bad enough, but the way her brows puffed out . . . she'd spank me for BO, and it was like being beaten by a Cro-Magnon bluehair. "Filthy, filthy, filthy, filthy, filthy." But, yes, what made me think of her were her hands. Always damp. Meaty. Like the treats between my legs.

See, I don't really want to relive this stuff. Thoughts think themselves. Heroin makes them do it. The heroin knows that if I feel bad enough, if I work myself into a state, then I will do it. It wants me to. (That's what they say at the meetings I go to, "First you take the drug, then the drug takes you." They serve animal crackers and Sanka. But hey! They keep me coming back. And it beats watching *Judge Judy* reruns.)

So I'm standing there in the kitchen, in this acro-lunch-meat-Grandma dope jones, when suddenly the Lunch Boss, this fat ex–Wall Street guy named Sid, tells me I have to mix the "Clear"—this nutrition drink the government has started giving to prisoners, to help meet their nutritional needs. It's really Kool-Aid, except they can't put color in, because then it will look like pruno (that's jailhouse hooch, made from fermented fruit, for you innocents). I don't quite understand it myself, but colored Kool-Aid is banned at all federal institutions. What we do serve, instead, is this Clear shit—colorless Kool-Aid with protein and calcium powder. Except the protein and calcium powder they put in isn't really protein and calcium powder. They added a pinch of Haldol. Not a lot, of course. To taste. Just enough to keep things "low level," in the words of Sid. (Haldol, for you non-antipsychotic meds takers, is the granddaddy of "chemical chains," soul-numbing drugs favored by institutions whose job is to keep actual psychotics from hurling themselves off walls or listening to the voice of Elvis tell them to strangle orderlies. Side effects: *blank facial expression, discoloration of eyes, compulsive movement of jaw and mouth, wormlike tongue-darting, a brown tint aka "shit-eye" coating the vision, erections that last for hours,* etc. Pretty much heaven on earth. And no, I didn't write these. Some other side-effects pro had the privilege.)

We mix in just enough Haldol to keep things "low level." That's what the Lunch Boss said. I was mulling on that when I felt a hand on my shoulder—nothing like Grandma's beef slab—and turned to see the man I would later come to know as Pastor Bobb. For a minute, he let me take in his steel blue eyes, chiseled beak, and white crew cut. The only problem was his skin, which looked like it had been buried for a year and dug up. But somehow the muddied complexion only complemented the impact of his stare. It was either acne scars or battery acid that healed up smooth.

"Son," he said, without so much as a hello. "Are you of the Jewish persuasion?"

"Not me, my daddy, sir."

"Why, that's a good thing. Now tell me, son, how are you, in general?"

"In general, great," I said, raising my voice over the sudden din of an industrial mixer. "I'm in a federal prison making lunch."

Pastor Bobb chuckled as if he'd practiced chuckling.

"Well, I hear you know a thing or two about writing?"

"No disrespect, pastor, but what if I do?"

"If you do," he chuckled again, "then it is that much more tragic that you are standing here with pig meat in your drawers."

"How did you know?"

"Son, I was down while you were still boosting Slurpees from the 7-Eleven."

Before I could respond—assuming I could—Pastor Bobb extended his hand.

"My name's Pastor Bobb. And if you don't mind me asking for a sample, I think I'd like you to come work for me."

"You want some chipped ham?" I was a little disoriented by the whole exchange.

"No, boy, I want me some writin'. Write me a little bit on Jesus. Imagine you're a young buck trying to impress a girl with how much you love the Lord. Run with it!"

He clapped me on the shoulder, then leaned in close and spoke in a low voice.

"You do this right, you won't have to be peddlin' no ham to convicts."

Then he winked, the way people wink on TV shows. Pastor Bobb was one of those people who always acted like he was on TV. And not just because he had his own show. I have a theory that people in America learn how to behave by watching TV. You just pick the character you want and do what they do. Pastor Bobb seemed to have learned from Sheriff Andy on *The Andy Griffith Show.* (You kids, Google. It's Old, Weird America.)

"What would you write if you wanted a little Christian gal to love you for the rest of your life?"

Luckily, one of the Native Americans had just smoked up in the sweat lodge—they had one at all federal pens—and was too stoned to make his way to the canteen. Stoned enough to trade me two balloons for all my lunch meat. It was one of those good deals in life that sometimes happen. There's no rhyme or reason. Unless, of course, it was my Savior looking out for me. Without me even knowing I was saved.

For me, Jesus isn't just the Lord. He's my buddy. He's a pal. I would like to go bowling with Jesus. Maybe go fishing. I bet, if you're like me, you think Jesus would even be fun on a date. You, me, and Jesus. On the roller coaster of life. He is always with us. Because that is what being a Christian is. I love you, even though I do not know you, if you love Jesus the way I do!

Then I signed it: *See you in Church. Your buddy, Buddy.*

Almost as if he knew, Pastor Bobb sent a guard down to collect my effort the second I'd finished. Twenty minutes later, another guard told me to roll up. I'd done nine months on a two-year jolt. But I didn't ask any questions until I found my newly free ass planted in the back of Pastor Bobb's Escalade. Terminal Island had disappeared behind us in the rearview before he uttered a word. "Son," he said, "you have a future in Christ."

THREE

Junkle

Pastor Bobb had me cut my teeth on tests. Simple Q&A. Meat and potatoes stuff.

> **I AM A:** (select gender)
> **MAN** seeking **WOMAN**
> **WOMAN** seeking **MAN**

There were no other options. Gay, obviously, was not on the radar. Even though there was something gay-esque about the weirdly rouge-y male models they used for the "regular guys" in the hand-holding photos that garnished the Dating Q&A. Did couples really walk in meadows? Share ice cream cones? Stroll on the beach? My life had certainly been an aberration, but then, this wasn't Junkie Singles. ("Junkles!" *I just want a man who won't steal my wake-up!*) There was no doubt a gaggle of Christian dope fiends as well. That hadn't occurred to me. Though soon enough it would.

Meanwhile, I was living in a Tulsa halfway house and crafting Q&A in the Christian Swingles Center, just down the street from Oral Roberts University, about which all I know is that its founder used to heal sickly Christians on TV. "Touch the screen, my lambs! Touch the screen!" And once, in the eighties, he climbed a tower and announced to his flock that God would call him home if folks did not send him eight million dollars. He climbed back down with $9.1 million. Because that's how things happen when you love the Lord. He wanted to build a 900-foot Jesus. Who didn't? I certainly didn't wonder about it at the time. What I wondered was what his parents were thinking naming their little boy Oral. Did they even know it was one of Freud's classic developmental stages? Maybe his brothers were Oedipal and Anal.

My first big breakthrough was the slogan. Or tagline, in the vernacular. The *hook*. We'd been asked to come up with something that would capture the heart and soul of what Christian Swingles stood for. I finally hit on *Find God's match for you*. To me, it was horrible. When you thought about it. So horrible that it was kind of perfect. If you couldn't find a match, then, it surely followed, God must not have wanted a match for you. God must want you as lonely, miserable, and hopeless as you probably were in the first place if you came looking for a life partner—or a *life*—at a Christian dating service. I honestly thought the slogan was cruel, but Pastor Bobb said he'd be the judge of that. And he judged it to be perfect.

"Son," he said, "the Lord truly gave you a gift. You are a regular Louis L'Amour. The man wrote nine hundred seventeen books that we know of, and every one was like poetry. Now let's us put our heads together in fellowship."

He pulled me aside, out of ear-range of my co-scribes, so close I could feel his salt-and-pepper mustache against my earlobe. Up close he was minty. But you could smell the nicotine underneath, which made me like him more. When he put his hands on my shoulders, they stank like rancid Pall Malls.

"Lloyd, we need a new mission statement, and I think you would be just the man to help get what we are trying to do here down on paper."

"Mission statement?"

"You know, somethin' that says, 'Come on in!' "

But I should back up. Give you a little more about where I was. I'm no storyteller, after all, I'm a side-effects man. I write the stuff on the little piece of paper nobody reads when they pick up their prescription. I'm good at lists—arranging the bad things on them in such away that the bad of *this* cancels out the bad of *that*, and what could have been scary sounds benevolent. But arranging isn't the same as describing. Or telling a story. Still . . . let me at least set the scene. The Christian Swingles Center was actually in a strip mall, two deceptively spacious floors wedged between a Hoover vacuum outlet and a party supply store. (Into which, during my entire, brief stint in Oklahoma, I saw not one potential partier stroll. Nor did I see much of Tulsa. We lived next to the Oral Roberts campus, walked to the mall.) Outside, cars and sidewalks were clogged with a lot of hefty Christians. The O.R. food was on the starchy side. Maybe that was one way the college administrators hedged against the wanton sex that plagued so many other, secular campuses. If you keep the coeds plumped and the boys logy on carbohydrates, there aren't going to be many premarital sex problems. For all I know the churchgoing cooks mixed Depo-Provera in the mac and cheese, just like the chow boss in the pen.

The only tourist attraction I saw in Tulsa was the Golden

Driller. The Golden Driller is a seventy-six-foot, 43,500-pound statue of an oil worker. Of course we went there to look at his crotch. We being Jay, the natty content manager—who insisted the Driller had been built by a closet queen named Mervyn Phelps—and Peter Riegle, the overall content director and the first real genius I ever met.

You could stand right underneath the Driller and look straight up to where the rig jockey had, apparently, been gelded. Ken doll smooth.

Maybe it shouldn't have been amazing that Jay and Riegle, the two other guys at Church Sex Central (as we sometimes called the place), were stone addicts. (I recognized them, the way addicts do, the way werewolves, when in human guise, are said to be able to smell each other across a crowded train station and recognize their kind.) Jay wouldn't talk about his personal life. Well, not that much. He alluded to "pierogi nights," shared an apartment with his mother, and had—he said—undergone extensive, if unsuccessful, "de-gay-ifying" at a number of Christian enterprises set up to combat "the homosexual lifestyle." About which all he said was "I looked at a lot of pictures of Taylor Swift. Which was supposed to turn me straight but didn't. Though she is adorable."

Riegle, meanwhile, had a wife at home with jaw cancer and a cerebral-palsied 29-year-old daughter they'd raised together and still took care of. He was slightly stooped and had an air of long-suffering dignity about him. (Which, he later explained, got people to trust him. That was just human nature.) But what made him more amazing, actually heroic to me, was something called the safe harbor clause, tucked away in an obscure addendum to the Lifshitz brothers' quarterly report.

I didn't even know what a safe harbor clause was, but you know as soon as you read a couple of sentences what it's supposed to do. Listen: *Any statements in this news release that are not statements of historical fact may be considered to be forward-looking statements. Written words, such as "may," "will," "expect," "believe," "anticipate," "estimate," "intends," "goal," "objective," "seek," "attempt," or variations of these or similar words, identify forward-looking statements. By their nature, forward-looking statements and forecasts involve risks and uncertainties because they relate to events and depend on circumstances that will occur in the near future.*

Something about this doublespeak—how it used English in such a bold and flagrantly misleading way you kind of couldn't help *believe* it—was strangely inspiring. So much more artful than my most sugarcoated "may cause kidney failure" side-effect blather. What the statement said, essentially, was that everything in the corporate report was bullshit; but if you didn't believe it, it was probably because you lacked faith. What made Jay and Riegle even stranger and—to me—more impressive is that they both still believed. Then again, I was never sure if the two of them shared a deep personal faith—or if they were laughing in my face.

"You can't fight Satan single-handed," Riegle told me, his gaze meaningful, though his pupils were pinned to the size of periods in a newspaper from the stuff we'd just shot.

Jay was, as ever, more snarky about it.

"The devil loves the Church, but we're gonna show him the door," Jay said.

"You really believe that?" I asked.

"It's from the brochure I did for newcomers to Pastor Bobb's first ministry, back in Toledo," he said. "But don't ask questions like that. Judge me by my acts. Paul 5:33 or Timothy 3:35. Or Bob 7:11 . . . or something. . . ."

We stood facing the giant Driller, whose enormous but curiously flat package loomed overhead. The three of us had shared a bag of Okie Powder, heroin of a consistency, taste, and potency I had never experienced before. It was the kind of high that came accompanied by painful whistling in your ear. You half-knew you were giving yourself brain damage, but it was so good you figured brain damage was a fair price to pay. As long as there was enough brain left to feel the dope that was doing the damage. We'd driven over in Riegle's Saturn, whose interior smelled like candy bananas, thanks to the air freshener Pastor Bobb kept stocked in all the Swingles cars. We didn't talk much on the way over, until the khakied Riegle suddenly smacked the wheel as we came in sight of the sun-blocking oil-worker statue.

"You know what? It is damn exciting to be in on the ground floor of something. I mean, Christian Swingles," he said, before repeating the words slowly, like they were savory on the tongue. "Christian Swingles. Tell me this is not exciting."

"Be more exciting, Pastor gave us stock," Jay snarped.

Living in Tulsa was a little like still being in prison, except you could send out for ribs. And they had the giant Driller.

"But hey," Jay continued. "Let us all behold one of the wonders of the world." He gazed up in mock (or so I thought) awe at the massive miner. "The wonder being how did the Driller drill without a penis?"

"He's a good Christian boy," Riegle said. "He doesn't need a penis."

Looking at that massive Ken-dolled crotch, we all knew what he was talking about.

That morning I'd cracked the Swingles mission statement Pastor Bobb had asked for. Which turned out to be a little harder than just "Come on in!" I'd been looking for something that showed solo seekers this was the right place for them. That being a Christian single was okay. The subtext being: help lonely Believers out there accept their intercourse-free lifestyle. It took me a while, but I found a way. The words came to me while sitting in a broom closet, rolling my sleeve down after a mid-morning pop. Sometimes it was like that. I'd close my eyes, apply my lay hands to the keyboard, and take a smack nap while the words just fluttered out of my fingers in perfect formation. Like the Lord was moving through me. If there was a Lord. And if people were what he moved through.

It's not easy being a Christian singleton.

In today's anything-goes, whatever-feels-good world, there's a question every unmarried person of faith must face: How to live the way Jesus wants us to live? How to stay pure at a time when, everywhere we turn, it seems some new form of salaciousness, devilry, or outright sin has overtaken our so-called popular media. Temptation is rampant. And those of us trying to live a clean, Christian, values based life can sometimes find ourselves feeling all alone.

Finally, there's a place where young, single Christians can find others who love the Lord just as much as they do. Finally, there's Christian Swingles.

Praise the Lord. Together.

Join today.

I "fellowshipped" on this with Jay and Riegle after fixing again—a special treat for a special occasion!—in a men's room stall in the Denny's down the street from the office, then went back in and hammered out the kinks. Jay lay on top of his desk and dangled one stonewashed jean leg off the end of it.

"There's only one thing lonelier than a horny twenty-eight-year-old Christian," he said.

"Yeah," Riegle interrupted. "A horny twenty-eight-year-old gay Christian."

Riegle, who was tallish and balding, did not always look at you when he spoke. He kept sunglasses on so he could nod off without drawing attention to himself on public transportation, and sometimes forgot to take them off. But just when you thought he was down for the count he'd blurt out something to let you know he'd been there all along.

"A gay twenty-eight-year-old who's so deep in the closet he thinks sex is supposed to smell like mothballs."

"Faith," I said, feeling proud of myself, "can be a trial."

"You mean an opportunity," Jay corrected me. "Man does God's work because God's not doing it."

"Really?"

"Gotcha!" Jay cackled, but in a nice way.

Did I mention Jay's features were so regular he might have been a composite of TV commercial dads? He looked like the friendliest salesman in the Sears hardware department. "You'd never know I was a homo," he liked to say, "unless you asked." He confided that he preferred men of color. "Obama sticks," he called them. Which I found vaguely offensive, but he insisted it was in the nature of an homage. "Someday you'll meet Dusty, and you will see exactly what I mean."

It wasn't the first time he'd mentioned his special friend of color, Dusty. Who sometimes sounded made up, sometimes sounded real. (Later I found out the truth.)

Pastor Bobb either didn't know or didn't care about his un-Christian sexual bent, but Jay said the pastor both knew and cared, believing exposure to all the hetero Christian spirit in the Swingles Center would work magic on his "tendencies," make them "withered as the dugs of Satan." One of the Pastor's favorite, if most inexplicable, expressions.

FOUR

Normal People! Doing Normal Things!

All around us on the walls of the Swingles Content Break Room hung health-bookish posters of wholesome guys and gals smiling at each other with shared faith, eyes unglazed by anything as base as lust. The couples in the posters took picnics, canoed, and sang Christmas carols. They wore colorful shirts. Sometimes, we'd all fix in the office—I'd never done social heroin before Tulsa, but shooting up together was what we did instead of bowling. After hours, Jay, Riegle, and I would amble into the snack pantry and stare up at those posters. The clear, doubt-free, Jesus-loves-me gaze of the believers answered all the questions we might have had about what to write, or how to write it.

The big issue with Christian daters was sin. Old-fashioned sin, like drinking and smoking. But you couldn't just come out and ask, *Do you drink?* At least Pastor Bobb didn't think so. The idea was to appear accepting, when what you were really doing was trying to let your applicants relax enough to hang themselves with the truth. *It's okay, we're just asking* was the tone we were going for. No judgment. Not *Do you smoke?* or *How do you feel about smoking?* but *How often do you smoke?* Give me a medal for that.

The answers were: *Never. On occasion. Frequently. Whenever I can.* Fucking genius. The loveliness of that. *Whenever I can* was Jay's idea. "Don't make it a negative," he explained, "except for believers. Let Satan show his hand."

We went the same route with boozing. *How often do you drink?* Really. What kind of party ferret is going to answer *whenever I can* on a Christian dating site, unless it's Christian Alcoholics? (Which, by the way, is not a half bad idea. One more reason to feel bad about not having money is not being able to immediately invest it in your own brilliant ideas before somebody steals them. *Results not guaranteed for all participants.*)

I wanted to believe there was some guy out there—or some woman—who was going to answer, proudly, *whenever I can* when asked how often they drink. Somebody who *wanted* to come off like a drunk so they could meet somebody just like them. Maybe drive drunk to church together. If somebody picks you after a deal-breaker like that, how could they not be perfect for you? Juiceheads for Jesus. *The Double J's. Results may not be typical, and are not guaranteed.* "No two experiences are alike." Like I say, I would have invested.

We had to wear white shirts and ties to work, but Pastor Bobb was so pleased with my contributions that one day he said I could take off my tie. I said I preferred to leave it on. Pastor Bobb just winked at my pals in Creative, Jay and Riegle, told them to let him know when they de-Jewed me. It was such a disturbing thing to say, I couldn't even say why it was disturbing. I preferred keeping my shirt and tie on because I had learned that the best thing, if you were doing heroin in the normal world, was to blend in. Especially if you were newly released from an institution.

Theoretically, I was supposed to report to a probation officer and take random pee tests. But somehow—well, probably because of Pastor Bobb and his Colson connections (nothing was ever formally acknowledged)—I was spared that indignity.

More than once, I had a conversation with Jay, how it was he could shoot heroin and consider himself a Christian.

"Simple," he said. "It's not a drug when it's medicine."

"Wouldn't it be easy to just get a script for OxyContins?"

"Oxys don't mortify your flesh," he said, combing his long brown hair and then checking his tortoise shell comb for whatever it is people check their combs for.

"Mortify your flesh?" It wasn't that I didn't think I heard right, I just wasn't sure I understood. Or I *thought* I did, but wasn't sure I wanted to.

"The spears that pierced Jesus's side," Jay said, pulling out a syringe and waggling it in front of my nose like a stage hypnotist. "What we're doing is an homage to the suffering of our Lord. It's like being a flagellant, except we're not marching down the street whipping ourselves in some procession; we keep it private."

"That's right," Riegle agreed, putting down the Bible he'd been reading. "My drugs are between me and Jesus. Plus, heroin helps me stay faithful. I'm a lot nicer to the missus and my daughter when I'm opiated. How can you fault something that makes you a better Christian? I go home and change the dressing on Betsy's tumors, then make sure my Liza is tucked nice and comfy in her crib. Liza's a grown young lady. In a crib. You don't think that hurts? You don't think any man might buckle, faith-wise, after the Lord deals him a hand like that? The cancer? The palsy?" His voice grew TV emotional. "Imagine a man seeing his pretty little girl lolling her head, looking up at him with those darling beautiful cow-eyes, not even capable of saying 'Daddy.'" Always a pause in the same place. "Well, I'm okay with it. Heroin and Jesus make it okay."

This was the best part about working on the dating site. A lot of times what we did in the Creative Room was just talk. We could do all the writing we needed to do in half an hour. The days took on a rhythm. At least once or twice a day I'd find myself going back over Riegle's safe harbor clause. It was still remarkable to me. The nakedness of *forward-looking*.

I'd spent so much of my "professional life" trying to find a way to couch scary, nasty facts in some less-than-ball-clutching way. Riegle went one step further, just saying everything was great, making whole-cloth blue-sky projections out of whatever shabby numbers were being disguised as fiscal triumph. I had to admit, I was in awe. To say so much, in such a way, without saying anything. By now I'd memorized it. *There are a number of factors that could cause actual results and developments to differ materially, including, but not limited to our ability to: attract members; convert members into paying subscribers and retain our paying subscribers . . . maintain the strength of our existing brands and maintain and enhance those brands and our dependence upon the telecommunications infrastructure and our software infrastructure. . .*

It was almost mystical. No matter what the subject at

hand—in this case, the flesh-mortifying qualities of piercing your vein with a needle full of dirty opiate solvent—I found myself going back to the safe harbor clause.

Riegle changed the subject—this is how junkie conversations went—to his favorite pet peeve.

"You know what I hate? I hate those movies where people about to fix up shoot a little splash into the air." Here he'd wield his needle, then point it down—not up—and spritz straight into the cotton, right in the spoon. "Waste not, want not. You just know that whoever wrote those shoot-in-the-air scenes was never a dope fiend. 'Cause if you're a dope fiend, you always know you're going to run out. And the last thing you're going to do, if you actually have a rig full of heroin, is squirt some of it up in the air, unless you plan on sucking your carpet fibers later. Which you will. When you need the stuff."

Here Jay would jump in.

"Need 'the stuff'? Oooh, Riegle, I love it when you go all Street Hype!"

But I'd always steal the conversation back. I felt like a little kid nagging his daddy to tell him his favorite story. I couldn't stop.

"Tell me again, how'd you come up with *forward-looking*?"

"You're still obsessing on that? I keep telling you, all quarterly reports have fine print explaining, basically, that being optimistic is not the same as lying."

"But it sounds like such bullshit. It doesn't even try *not* to sound like bullshit."

"Exactly," he'd say, voice lowering two registers by the time he eased the needle out of his arm. "Bullshit is okay if everybody agrees to believe it. That's what corporate reports do. I learned that in law school."

"Wait. You went to law school?"

"Maybe I did, maybe I didn't. Anyway, I'm gonna keep my cotton here. You keep yours over there. I don't have a single disease. I don't even have cavities. But looking at you, no offense, I feel like I could get bad teeth even sitting next to you."

"That's nice," I said. "Thank you."

I tried to play it off as good-natured office joshing, but I'd spent so much of my life trying to "look normal" in job situations—and I *was* normal, except for the heroin—that whenever he teased me I cringed. Not only because I hadn't been to a dentist for the greater part of ten years. The junkie mind-set was perpetual catastrophe. Things made you jumpy. But were you jumpy because you needed heroin? Or did you need heroin because you were jumpy?

Jay (ever-compassionate in Thy sight, oh Lord) always defended me from Riegle's mild attacks.

"Don't listen to Miss Jesus-pants," he would butt in. When Jay got high he liked to put on his Enya CDs, which Pastor Bobb considered devil music. "We're all good soldiers here. No cause for Son-of-Godly snark."

"You know Jay and me were bunkies," Riegle piped up. "In college."

"State College, as in the State of New York. Sing Sing."

The day I found this out, before I could even register my surprise, Jay further lifted the top of my brain off, suggesting we knock over a pharmacy. I had him repeat himself three times to make sure he wasn't kidding. And when I finally did agree to listen, I expected him to punch me in the arm and say, "Gotcha!" Instead, he and Jay pulled up chairs around the snack table and peeled the lids back simultaneously on a pair of Dannon yogurts.

FIVE

Crime Spree

The "job" was simple. Pull up behind a pharmacy in a strip mall on Wiggins and Main and walk in. Riegle broke it down.

"The owner goes to our AA home group. After the ten-thirty meeting on Friday morning, he fellowships until quarter to two. The place will be closed."

"He's got a year on Friday," Jay added, with what sounded like sincerity and affection. "We're taking him out to lunch. So he won't be back till three."

Nobody counted on what happened happening. Though considering the success rate of recovering addicts and alcoholics, maybe we should have. I walked up to the CVS door at eleven on the dot. Only I didn't need the key Riegle'd slipped me. The door was open. The pharmacist, Sy S., was behind the pharmacy counter, open for business, but he didn't look well. I knew this wasn't part of the plan. In the plan, Sy was at his AA meeting. But I could see what happened. Up close his skin shone a little green. He was sweaty. He had his hand over his eyes and he was sitting forward, behind the Plexiglas, looking down. Like he was readying a particularly tricky prescription. I was improvising now. But it felt okay. It felt fine. (That's F-I-N-E, as Pastor Bobb used to say, in his Aw-Shucks mode: FUCKED-UP, INSECURE, NERVOUS, and EMOTIONAL.) At the last minute I decided to turn around, but it was too late. Sy the pharmacist sensed my presence. He looked up, and right away I knew what happened. He was weeping. Red-eyed. It took him a while to register what was in front of him, and when it kicked in he craned his neck sideways like he was trying to bite his own shoulder. The man had obviously relapsed. I couldn't say on what, but whatever it was he'd taken too much of it.

Without knowing I was going to, I crooked my finger and hissed, "Sy! Hey, Sy!" His eyes darted left and right, but he moved forward to the speaking holes in the glass.

"What is it, Sy? What did you take?"

"Vicodin," he said, as though he'd been waiting for the question, visibly relieved that I'd asked.

"What else?"

"Adderall."

"What else?"

For the first time, the glimmer of the man behind the red, tear-streaked face revealed itself.

"Valtrex," he said, and lowered his eyes. "I got the herpes."

"Keep that. Give the rest to me," I said. "Right now."

To my surprise he didn't slam the window closed. But he hesitated, which is when I pulled out a one-year A.A. medallion and pressed it against the Plexiglas like a detective badge. (You never know when you need one; it's as useful as a Masonic handshake.)

"I'm a Friend of Bill. It's okay. I'm going to give them to a hospital. We distribute meds to the homeless."

"They do that?"

I nodded. "When they think you're ready, they'll be sending you to help guys like you."

He handed over the drugs without another word, and then I suggested he should probably open the register and give me the money, so it would look like a robbery and he wouldn't have to explain why big jars of narcotics were unaccounted for.

"What big jars?"

"The ones you're not telling me about," I said. "Come on, Sy. This is just one addict talking to another."

Again, he handed the drugs over without a peep: the stuff he mentioned, plus two jug-sized jars marked Percocet and Ritalin respectively. Up, down, and in between. I could have used a wheelbarrow.

I thanked him. "You're helping *me*, Sy. You don't know even know how much."

"I am? I'm helping you?" He sniffled and wiped his cuff across his tear-runny eyes.

"You're showing me how The Program works," I said. Which seemed to make Sy unaccountably happy. "Now hand over the money. We have to make this look real."

I imagined the shit I'd get from Jay and Riegle when I told them the story. Sy pulled a key from an extendo-chain on his belt and unlocked a drawer under the cash register. From the drawer he pulled out a small satchel. He dumped the satchel out on the counter and handed me four fist-sized rolls of twenties, tens, fives, and ones. I almost wanted to stop and recommend Depakote, drug of choice for Obsessive Compulsive Disorder. (Some patients complain of feeling "fuzzy," a gauze-like patina over vision, and in rare cases a fecal taste on the tongue.)

"Don't tell your sponsor about this till tomorrow." I said. "That's the tradition."

For the first time, Sy looked skeptical. "Which tradition is that?"

"The Thirteenth Tradition," a voice suddenly boomed from behind me. "Put your hands behind your back."

"He made me do it!" Sy whimpered.

I saw the cop in the mirror above the counter, the one customers checked to see if anything sketchy was going on behind them when they got their pills. He answered the pharmacist when his eyes met mine. "I'm not talking to you, Mr. Sydowsky, I'm talking to your customer."

He was a shambling man in a brown suit, with a solid roll of fat over his belt. He held up his badge in one hand and a gun in the other. "Nice and easy," he said.

I complied without a struggle. But I was still curious. "Is there a thirteenth tradition?"

"Sure," said the policeman, pocketing his baggage but leaving his gun-hand extended. "It starts with you have the right to remain silent. You want to hold hands and say it together, sunshine?"

The Shambler walked me to an unmarked Crown Vic, opened the back door, barked the obligatory "Watch your head" familiar from big screen and little, and shoved me in. That was not the last thing he did. The instant my backside hit the ripped upholstery, the officer leaned in, shoved me roughly sideways—my hand landed in something wet—and reached down to unlock the cuffs. Before I could ask why, he slammed the door and disappeared. I sat still for a second. The car smelled like Lysol and Armani for Men. (Pastor Bobb's scent of choice.) I realized there was someone else in the car. Behind the wheel. A sleek, bullet-headed African-American fellow, his right cheekbone sporting a crescent scar. (He resembled Paul Robinette, the handsome, high-cheekboned black assistant DA in the early days of *Law & Order.* Then I saw his name tag and the coin dropped. This was Detective Dustin. This was Jay's Dusty. The mythical Dusty, in the flesh, with a wedding ring and a stare that burrowed into the back of your head. "You still here?" he said.

"What? Am I supposed to—"

"Shut up, Lloyd. You know how this works. Tell us who set up the caper, we'll let you go right now."

He actually said the word "caper."

"Nobody set it up," I said. "I walked into the pharmacy and got a stupid idea on my own."

"You sure about that? I know all about you and your pal Pastor Bobb. None of your buddies, back at Christian Swinglers or whatever, had anything to do with this?"

"It's Swingles. And I don't have any buddies there."

For the first time, Detective Dustin's gaze softened. (It was like watching an *L & O* rerun, except I was in it.) He gave the faintest of nods and spoke without moving his lips, like a ventriloquist. "You passed. Door's unlocked. Get out. Go to Greyhound, Will Call. There's a ticket waiting. Don't make any stops and nobody's gonna stop you."

As I stepped out, I was pretty sure I saw a shimmer, the noon sun bouncing off binoculars in a building directly across from the pharmacy. I could feel the blessing of Pastor Bobb upon me. Or maybe it was the five Percocet I dry-gulped before getting in the car. (*Artificial sense of well-being, occasional hypermania.*) Sometimes the side effects are the only ones you want.

SIX

Riding the Dog

When's the last time you traveled by long-distance bus? Or sat in a Greyhound station? It's not just the home of homeless and runaways anymore. Now it's a family place. The way homeless shelters have become family fun zones. Without the fun.

I had two hours before my bus. There were years when I was two hours late for everything, in the worst days of the worst days. But now I'm the early guy. Which is either vaguely pathetic or commendably responsible, depending. (The more out of control you feel, the more normal you try to act.) I had a yen for Necco Wafers. I don't know why. Retro candies were fashionable. Or maybe, in Greyhound-world, they weren't retro. Either way, I didn't feel like feeding the pay TVs bolted to the chairs in the waiting room. So I just walked around. And saw a row of Necco Wafers at the snack stand, a row of them right beside some Beemans gum and a stack of Chunkys. I got a Chunky as well, because, even though I'd been on a rigorous protocol for my liver and parasites for some time, I did not foresee being able to stay on it now. I'd managed, through my brief stint at Christian Swingles, to keep up with the juicing, and to administer my coffee enemas. (More room for heroin!) But now, with a three-day ride on Greyhound, I didn't foresee any quality enema time—not to mention the prospect of pouring bus-stop java into a hot water bottle and tubing it into my lower intestine in a back-of-the-bus toilet did not strike me as either wise or de-toxy. If I attempted it and the door swung open, I could probably be arrested by Homeland Security for lewd and malicious interstate anal probing. (I didn't actually drink coffee anymore, but I won't lie, the caffeine buzz after bottom-hosing a hot water bottle full of fair-trade joe is not to be sneezed at. It left me flying. The other advantage—you couldn't dunk with a coffee enema. On other occasions, when I'd relapsed on latte, I'd find myself unable to resist purchasing a Dunkin' Donuts Toasted Coconut Vanilla Kreme or some Sugar Glazed Strawberry Munchkins and soaking them in my liquid liver killer as I consumed them. Why coffee should destroy your liver orally and save it anally remains one of the great mysteries of New Age medicine.) So, when I saw the candies, and realized I'd had some kind of yen I didn't even realize—I don't even like Necco Wafers, they're hell on my chalky molars—I took it as some kind of omen. I was actually going to get clean. I'd decided. Now was the time. No ifs, ands, or balloons.

Somehow, gathering my candies and my copy of *Weekly World News*—I believed the *WWN*, home of "Bat Boy," reflected America's primal fear and id in ways new media couldn't hope to, but it's not a point of view I'd want to defend—hope bit me like a werewolf and kept running, so that I felt simultaneously uplifted and infected.

Speaking of the infected, Curt Siodmak, who wrote the original *Wolf Man*, viewed the werewolf as a metaphor for the Jew in Hitler's Europe. Siodmak escaped Germany and landed in Hollywood. Through no fault of the werewolf's own, he'd been attacked by a monster, who in turn transformed *him* into a monster, a good man become hunted and shunned. Why do I know this? Because Wolf Man was the first Side-Effects movie. First the attack—then the symptoms. We see them at the same time the victim sees them. Once lycanthropic serum is in the blood, the effects—as so often happens, pharmaceutical commercial buffs will tell you—reveal themselves slowly, and then all at once. *Bitten by a werewolf? You may experience mild euphoria, feelings of newfound power, sudden appearance of full-body pelt and canine incisors during a full moon. Some patients report disturbing "incidents," followed by memory loss and occasional incarceration. See your doctor if you experience rapid "bulking up," four-legged gait, urge to urinate outdoors or kill and eat people.*

I love that movie.

SEVEN

Daddy Ink

The woman—not a girl, just girlish—was tiny enough to curl up in the bus seat with her legs under her, and from what I could see, where her army jacket had crumpled down and exposed her back, owned a neck and shoulders of such sinewy delicacy that the size of her breasts came as a shock. Perhaps to equalize the impact, between her shoulder blades, in loving detail, was a tattoo of a German shepherd's head, teeth bared, like it was about to lunge, with DADDY inked underneath in Gothic letters.

Maybe the Daddy dog drove people away. You'd think stripper, or ballet dancer, or both. Trouble in any flavor. By the time I found out the story behind Daddy and the big-fanged dog, my heart cracked in a different place than it would have had I found out earlier. The only empty seat, besides this one, was next to the chemical toilet in back. Aside from the prospect of breathing disinfectant and people's private sadness for twelve hours, I knew, from experience, that the toilet door would probably delatch at some point and start banging back and forth off the seat behind it. Off the knees of whatever large liver happened to be occupying it. I liked my chances better with Daddy's girl.

There had to be some reason nobody else would sit next to

her. I had a feeling I was going to find out why. Is there a tribe of fuckups that seek each other out? That recognize the scent of exhilarating desperation that comes from etc . . . etc . . .

When you've written corpo-speak you sometimes lapse into it. Find that it's crept into your brainpan and shaped the patterns and presentation of all your precious thoughts. Or else whole-cloth replaced them. This is an area worthy of intense and unflinching self-analysis. I was just too tired to pursue it. I'd muddle on, as I did through most of life, guided by a vague sense—my personal code—that if I could stay a little farther from the things I dreaded and closer to the things I didn't hate, life might possibly, you never know, almost (these things happen) be okay.

Happiness. Possible side effects may include disappointment, recurring feelings of despair leading to possible long-term hopelessness. Some people report diarrhea and "copper penny" breath while using this product. Call your physician if condition persists.

I saw the stack of greeting cards fanning out of her backpack before I sat down. It seemed odd. But I wouldn't have reached in and snatched them had she so much as nodded at me.

Acknowledgment, however meager, sometimes matters. We're only human. But she offered none. The girl with the shepherd ink kept herself wedged against the window, face pressed into dark glass—it was a night ride—ignoring me completely.

Book Two

Women have a feeling
that since they didn't make
the rules, the rules have
nothing to do with them.

DIANE JOHNSON

EIGHT

You're So Pretty When You Breathe Through Your Mouth

I did not know romance was in the air when I stepped aboard. But the more I looked at her, mouth-breathing, under a dark blue babushka pulled tight over thick black hair that plainly didn't want to stay in there, the more . . . I don't know how to put it, the more her face became beautiful underneath the wrapping. (Even though, feet to the fire, I couldn't say that I'd really seen it.) Became everything I wanted before I even knew I wanted it. Choose your cliché.

I couldn't even tell you why, maybe it was FMD—Film Noir Disease— but I pegged her for a woman on the lam. I didn't even know if people still said "on the lam." But she had that about her, whatever you call it. Running away. On a trip that wasn't planned. Maybe not entirely unexpected—but not planned.

There was something remarkable about her, but I couldn't place it at first. Then I realized—she was sucking her thumb. It was almost shocking. I thought of Carroll Baker in *Baby Doll*. Sleeping in a crib. Wrongly alluring in infantile sex-wear. Sweaty Eli Wallach having his way with her. Or did I dream the sex-wear and crib stuff? As if she saw me staring, she tugged her thumb out from between her teeth. This was when I realized she hadn't been sleeping, she'd been reading. Face pressed into the bus window, over a paperback I couldn't make out. The cover was dark. Then I saw that it wasn't a book-book. It was a bound notebook. Not one of those moleskins, which everybody bought because they thought it turned them into Hemingway. But a generic brand. Its cover some kind of shiny fake. But big enough for her hand to disappear inside. So she could write without her seatmate knowing either what she was writing or that she was writing at all. My future friend did not acknowledge me, so I (quietly) rifled her bag. I wondered if she was "journaling." But she didn't look like somebody who'd use that word. Unless she was mocking it.

The first card had a picture of a respectable suburban lady nailed to a crucifix on the front. Inside was *GET OFF THE CROSS, WE NEED THE WOOD. Happy Mother's Day!* It was unsigned.

There were more like that. Theme cards. All unsigned. A bulldog on the end of a chain, snarling up at a mailman, said *BOUNDARIES. Try some, just as an experiment* . . . Another showed a meadow of wildflowers, in bloom, tinted blue. A barbed-wire fence cuts through the middle of the flowers. *You call it a restraining order. I call it tough love.* The last, another showstopper, had nothing on the cover but Marge Simpson, arms outspread. *You can't get rid of the button-pushers, but you can get rid of the buttons!*

It must have been my chortling—though I'm not usually a chortler—that made her whip around. We were the only two, in the highway darkness of the bus, who had our overhead on. "The fuck you doing?" she said. I saw her entire face full-on for the first time and thought the word "vulpine," though I have never used it before or since. Little black-bagged fox eyes burned out through her black bangs like those of a wary prisoner peeking through the bars of a cell.

"Are these all blank?" I asked her.

She snatched the cards out of my hand without answering.

I didn't react. "No judgment, I'm just saying. You must know a lot of people with issues."

She blew the bangs out of her eyes and kicked her legs off the seat and onto the floor with what was either energy or violence. (I guessed you'd have to get to know her to find out which was which.) The soles of her boots made a sticky sound when she picked them up again after five seconds and folded herself back onto her seat. A smell came off her like carnival mustard, perspired-in leather, and dill. The scent was dark, possibly tainted. And did something to my heart the minute I breathed it, made me have to gasp for two breaths in a row, gave me a jolt in my testes that felt like love.

I hovered, like some kind of zoner perv. When she finally looked up, her cracked-glass green eyes and giant pupils showed themselves then disappeared again, back to her notebook. Our eyes held long enough for me to study the bags beneath hers. Dark blue Samsonites, from debauchery or pain or just staying up late, like some Paris existentialist sandwiching Sartre and Camus in the forties. Of course, I was done. That was it. Those bags were like matching brands that made love and pity impossible to separate. I was not usually a hallucinator. But for one bright flash, headlights flooded the window and I made out words under each of her eyes. *FUCKED UP* under one, *COME ON IN* under the other. (A counselor once told me I was addicted to women who needed help. He sent me to SLAA. Sex and Love Addicts Anonymous. Where addicts relapsed with other addicts in meetings. (A cringe across a crowded room . . .) Where there were women who needed help in ways I had never conceived of. I'd wandered in to experience the miracle of recovery, the terrible joy of "slipping," and the liberation that comes right after both. Until you surrender, if you're lucky, and you remember who's holding the wheel. Let go, let God.)

Go Greyhound and leave the driving to us!

A jingle, for some reason, that reminded me of my all-time favorite pharma-slogan: *At Parker-Stephenson, we make drugs for people who need them.*

I had an empathic moment, as I settled in beside her, where I felt my bus-mate's internal struggle. Could sense her assessing. *He's an asshole, but he's kind of an interesting asshole.* Outside, we passed a neon Sleepy Bear in a nightcap, sleepwalking with his arms stretched out before him. The legendary Travelodge logo. MOTEL—18 MILES.

"I don't send these," she continued, possibly deciding it was less awkward speaking to me than ignoring me the entire ride.

"You don't send them. I get it. Because it is my fucking business, why do you have them?"

"Because I wrote them."

"You wrote them?"

Instant hostility. I was smitten. Another word I'd never used before. Wouldn't go near. Actually kind of hate. Things were changing!

"Why? You don't think I can write?"

Something in my heart smoldered, though it may have been my left ventricle, set twitching by heroin depletion. Or an endocarditis flare-up, fallout from a long-ago case of cotton fever, when a fiber from the dirty Q-tip fluff I was sucking coke-and-dope through ended up in my heart. (My temperature spiked to 105. Nothing a bathtub full of ice cubes couldn't turn right around.) I've always had a dream of finding another soul I could share my life with. Another artist. But greeting cards! Maybe there *was* a benign force that ruled the universe.

Or not.

I asked her how she even got the idea and her tone shifted completely. She spoke almost shyly—"you really want to know?"—in an accent I couldn't place. Maybe southern. Maybe Pittsburgh. I said I did, *I wanted to know,* and she gathered her black-jeaned legs back under the seam-ripped seat and started. Her voice was deep and throaty. Either from whiskey and cigarettes, in which case it was permanent, or maybe it was temporary, from heroin. An opiated croak.

Smack shrinks your pupils the size of pinpricks. Super black. It's like there's an ant hole in each eyeball, right under the tombstone, but you never see any ants. They're invisible. Sometimes it feels like they're crawling into your eyes. On cocaine they crawl back out and burrow under your skin. Coke bugs! But when you're dope-sick, or even just a little *needy*, your eyes go the opposite way. They pie-plate, widen right up to old-school acid size. Except it's not from taking acid. It's from not taking heroin—or whatever opiate du jour you were talking about. Or weren't talking about, in my new friend's case. Because, from the beginning, what she was talking about and what I thought she was talking about seemed to be circling each other. But that voice!

"Like, somebody will ask me how I'm doing, okay, and every time I try to tell them, to really tell them, instead of laying out some happy horseshit, they say the same thing: *Hang in there!* Do you know how much I hate that? How fucking patronizing that is? But it's like I don't hate *them*, I hate *myself*, for letting myself think I could trust them. You know what I mean? Sometimes people even send that card, the one that actually says *Hang in there!* You know, with the picture of the cute kitten hanging on to a branch? It makes me want to puke."

As she spoke she broke a Necco Wafer I'd given her between her thumbs, into smaller and smaller pieces. A feat, I realized when I tried it later, that required a level of tensile power I didn't have.

"By the way, I kind of invented this whole style," she said after a little while.

"Wait. What? *Hang in there, baby*? But I, like, remember them from the eighties. Hold old were you, five?"

I didn't want to call her a liar. I wanted to believe everything.

"Well, reinvented. The concept, I mean. I, like, gave them a new iteration. It's a long story, okay?" Now she sounded hostile again, like she had at the beginning. "The point is, I got ass-screwed out of the credit. Out of the money, too."

Iteration? Ass-screwed? I already loved her vocabulary.

"That sucks," I trotted out.

She glanced—maybe glared—straight up at me through her bangs and spat out her words. "You think?"

There's a special tang to long-distance bus air. Low-end life and death. Human detritus, confined night-stinks, exhaustion, and plain exhaust. Someone had either passed gas in a nearby seat or passed on earlier in the evening and begun to rot.

I turned around and saw no one awake. Then noticed a shiny pair of aviator glasses a few rows back. Facing me. What little light there was, from the passing cars and roadside lamps, flared on and off the lenses. There's something scary about glasses, when you don't see the eyes. Spectacles had a large square shaved head, trim goatee, and—strangest of all—suit, shirt, and tie, not the least bit loosened. When he saw me he crossed his large hands carefully and laid them on his chest, both forefingers pointing up and out in my direction, here's-the-steeple style. A gesture meant to convey something, I was certain, I just wasn't sure what. The bus was a little like prison, where every gesture had to be interpreted. Was that nod from the con with the cross and swastika on his neck meant to convey *Jesus loves you* or *I'm going to hike your legs up and shank you in the shower while I fuck you*? (The latter, by the way, was something no one said to me the entire time I was behind bars. Though I could not, I will be the first to admit, stop dreading it.)

In the slow strobe light of the highway it was impossible to tell if he was deep black or an albino. Just that there was something strange about that square head, and the big face so set and hard that the finger church and the light dancing off his aviators were the only signs of life. The rest was pure dead menace.

My new almost-friend and heart's desire caught me staring and pulled a loose, chewed-on cigarette from her jacket pocket. Flipped it in her mouth. I waited, with some kind of fascination, to see if she was actually going to light up. Then she took it out again, plucked a shred of tobacco off her pouty lower lip and put the cigarette back in her pocket. She started to say something. I assumed it would be about the prince of men I'd just been staring at. But each time I thought she was going to speak, she stopped herself.

NINE

Was I the Creepy Stranger?

Something irregular and beautiful was happening outside. Yellow lightning. Burning veins in the sky. It made me conscious of my own non-burning veins. They hadn't been fed in a while. My seatmate, whose name, I realized, I still didn't know—possibly because I hadn't asked—raised an eyebrow at me, then faced the window. She seemed, on first view, the kind of young woman who didn't care all that much about her appearance. After even a sneaky glance—all I'd allowed myself, out of some sudden flush of discretion—it seemed unlikely those breasts could have sprouted without surgical assistance. But what did I know? I was never one of those guys who drooled over giant bra-stuffers. The truth (possibly more mortifying) is that I was not one who went after any "type" in particular; no, my kind of girl, from teen-hood on, was any girl who liked me.

It's like, we were connected. But not. Had not even exchanged names.

Was I the creepy stranger who wouldn't shut up—or was I acknowledging a deep and unexpected soul connection? And when, exactly, had I started channeling Oprah?

"You saw Lurch, right?" she said. "The creep with the glasses?"

"Hard to miss."

For a second she didn't say anything, then she did.

"Ever think somebody was trying to kill you?" She spoke without turning toward me, just as some hyped-up semi went flying by what felt like inches from our window. The truck had a high-pitched, unsteady whine that faded in its wake.

"Somebody's trying to kill you?" I said over the noise. "Does this have something to do with 'Hang in There'? The kitten on the branch? Your *iteration* of it?"

Now she did turn around. Fast and accusatory. "What? Are you giving me shit?"

Oh man. I *knew* what she said. But maybe I didn't. Or maybe she didn't want to say it just then. Maybe all life, when you boiled it down, was a series of wrong assumptions. Mine anyway. I just didn't want to be an asshole. Anymore. I'd been off drugs for what seemed like ages—at least a day and a half. Drugs made Lloyd feel like an asshole, and Lloyd needed more drugs to deal with that. Especially when Lloyd was trying to say no to drugs. When Lloyd had promised himself he wasn't going to do drugs anymore. Which of course just made Lloyd—*e-nough*!

If she hadn't been there I would have banged the heel of my hand off my forehead. Screamed at myself to shut up or stop in much the same manner that famed TV reverend Peter Popoff smacks seekers' foreheads and yells, "Heal!" when he strong-arms their maladies by letting the Holy Spirit hammer through him.

"So," I said, wading into the sullen silence that had descended after the freak lightning and my apparent misunderstanding about why someone was trying to kill her. (It's the little things.) "Are you suing? Do you have any kind of plan?"

"Plan?" The way she squinched her face sideways made the word seem vaguely degrading. "That's a strange idea. But I *like* strange, if you know what I mean."

"*Strange*," I said, blocking the words with my fingers in the air before I realized the assyness of it, "*when what you want is an adventure you've never had before*. Then you show a photo of some girl face down on a bed, crying."

She sat up straight. "You could do it that way. Or have that same photo with text across the top: *MAKE A NEW MISTAKE!*"

"Wow!" I wasn't normally a *wow* guy, but I meant it. "Did you just come up with that?"

"It's what we're doing, isn't it?"

We weren't touching, but my skin could feel her skin buzzing.

Everything had happened so fast—the whole exchange—we both kind of froze in place, eyes straight ahead. She may have half-smiled. I didn't want to ruin the moment and check. Sex was something you didn't care about when you had dope—and used to kill the pain when you didn't. Kick-sex was fairly uncelebratory. You—if you were a man—came in seconds. And you could come often. Over and over. You just couldn't come much. The operative term is "air popper." It didn't even feel good. It was relief, not pleasure. Like so much of life. (Well, *my* life; a junkie's life.) *But.* With this person I experienced something. Something unfamiliar. Like that weird yellow lightning. Like chemical refineries that flared in the night, toxic birthday candles lighting the sky right and left for miles.

TEN

I Guess This Is What They Call Pleasure

Or maybe . . . *fun*? Is that going too far? It was all such foreign territory. The snappy patter. The out-of-nowhere joy of it! I remembered my championship line from Christian Swingles. (And yes, there's nothing classier than quoting yourself.) *Sometimes we wait for God to make the next move when God is saying, "It's your time to act!"*

This was more intense than sex. More unlikely, at any rate. For the second time, after our "strange" exchange, I found myself cracking open a silence born either of implied intimacy or complete disregard. *Maybe* she hated me. *Maybe* she hated me and wanted to fuck me. *Maybe* . . . you get the picture. The scenarios were endless. And therefore meaningless. So I plunged on in. Where was she going to go? We were on a fucking bus.

"So . . . you invented the cards? Reinvented. Gave them a new look. Whatever . . ."

"I took the concept. Made it more now-ish."

"Now-ish. Right. And some boss-type guy stole your idea?"

"You calling me a liar?"

"What? No! I'm *commiserating.*"

"Exactly. He screwed me. Trust me on that. I got fucked. Nothing I could do." She sounded angry about it, as if somehow I were in on this travesty, and she resented me for it. "Now I just want to go after him."

"To get the money?"

"I just told you. I'll never get the money. I just don't want him to be happy. I don't even want him to be unhappy. I want him to be destroyed."

"What do you want to do to him?"

"I want to fuck with him."

"How?"

"The worst way you fuck with anybody. You can think about it but you'll never guess."

I flashed on "creepy-crawly." The Manson Family's favorite pastime. Imagine it, insane strangers could be clawing at your carpet right now. Licking your sheets. They did all that shit before the corny stuff, like murdering and writing "PIG" in blood on the wall.

There were so many things I could have said, at that moment. Words of caution. Concerned, reasonable words. Because, for some irrational reason, this was someone I cared about. Despite the fact that we'd just met. I hardly knew anything about the woman, but I already knew enough to know there were things I didn't want to know. (In other words, she was a total stranger about whom I was likely delusional; for whom, not to flatter myself, I harbored huge and inappropriate emotional expectations.)

So, out of all the things I could have said, I said the thing that, I hoped, could make her like me. I didn't think it out of course. But that's what I was doing. I said, "Do you know anybody in LA?"

She asked, "Why?"

I said, "Maybe we can hang out . . . So, what did you say your name was?"

"Nora," she said, like she was ashamed of it. "My mother wanted me to be an old lady."

We didn't speak for a while after that. But I could tell she wanted to say something. Finally she put her cold hand on mine and turned to me.

"You were right, what you thought before."

"About what?"

I could tell she was used to guys staring at her enormous breasts instead of looking her in the eye. So I made a point of not staring at them. I was, as of that moment, an eye man.

"About the guy trying to murder me," she said. "You heard right. He's back there, right now. Looking at us. He probably wants to murder you too."

"Why?" I asked.

"Why do you think? Because you're with me."

ELEVEN

Words Made of Cheese and Blood

Think of all the great murders you've seen in TV and movies. The entertaining death you were raised on. Bullets, bombs, knives, arrows. Janet Leigh in the Psycho *shower. Sonny Corleone machine-gun twitchy at the toll booth. The shoot-'em-ups. The throw-'em-downs. The great Danny Trejo in* Machete.

Our entire EIC (Entertainment-Industrial Complex) exists as one giant instructional murder video. And we haven't even talked about the specialty items. The master courses. Gourmet murder shows. . .

I know, I know. I was trying to come up with shit to say to the *CSI* people. I was, niche-wise, the designated "edgy" guy, which meant, in my experience, serving up the comfortable cliché: the most beloved commodity in Hollywood. Safe Edge . . . Don't get me started.

But I'm getting ahead of myself. See, a weird thing happened when we got to LA. We got a little turned around at Union Station. I'd never been there, but I had seen it already, in the first half of a William Holden double bill on AMC. In *Union Station* (Paramount, 1950), the future dead alcoholic portrays a railway cop whom Joyce Willecombe, played by the world's most forgettable actress, tells about the two very bad men on her train. Joyce is the secretary to a rich man named Henry Murchison (Herbert Heyes), whose blind daughter, Lorna, has been kidnapped and held for ransom. The station has been chosen as the site of the drop! (Despair in film noir is always cool.) Why this (albeit slow-moving) classic has not been excavated and remade with Ryan Gosling is beyond me.

Then again, what do I know? I'm no movieland obsesso, just a guy who's killed a lot of time loaded in front of the TV. Now, *pharma* trivia—whole different deal. Ask me anything. Did you know marketers invented irritable bowel syndrome because crippling diarrhea sounded too low-end? (No pun intended.) Or that Lomotil, an early treatment, contained atropine? About which narco-titan William Burroughs waxed eloquent in the fifties as a cure for drug addiction. Though, until his final dose, Big Bill himself ended up in Kansas on methadone—originally called Dolophine, named for Adolph Hitler by kiss-ass Nazi chemists seeking cheap, synthetic morphine for wounded Wehrmact.

I would argue, if I were the type who argued, that pharmaceuticals provide the secret history of Western civilization; and, pharma-copy, my default niche, will someday be recognized as the representational literature of the twenty-first century. Future archaeologists (assuming there's a future) will dig through our detritus and find more pill bottles than books, iPads, or Kindles—life, in America, now being something you treat, not something you live.

What are we now, but our symptoms?

I once had to meet a connection at an all-night poetry slam at Bergen Community College. I had to sit through his "set" before I could cop. Freestyle. That was edgy, too. I know, because he snapped his fingers between lines. The dealer's name was Bondo and he spoke with a questionable Nuyorican accent. Questionable, because I happen to know he came from Akron. I still remember his highlights.

Is the definition of literature "nothing I actually read"?

SNAP!

Would the Bible still be holy if it had been written in bum dandruff?

DOUBLE SNAP!

Hemingway on Twitter. @BIGPAPA. Roof of mouth itches. Loading shotgun. Like I told Fitzgerald, always keep Mama Twelve-gauge cleaned and oiled!

SNAP-SNAP-BOOM!

The next day I wrote a campaign for Prostex that began: *If Jesus had lived to be sixty, even He would have needed prostate relief.* It went nowhere. But did failure mean you couldn't be proud?

TWELVE

Bad Houdini

Union Station had a bang-up ending. I won't ruin it for you. Union Station itself (the train and bus station, not the movie) also starred in *Collateral*, (Tom Cruise's greatest role! He's great when he plays dark!) and some odd bits of *Star Trek: First Contact*, which I saw in a motel room in Tulsa when I had to stay out of the Christian Swingles Office and away from my apartment, for reasons that have long since escaped me . . .

I had no luggage, and neither did my new friend and confidante, the runaway greeting card innovator. She nudged me when the man with the shiny glasses got off behind us. "He's going to follow us," she said. "The man who screwed me owns a lot of companies. He's powerful. He doesn't like trouble. That's why."

"Why what?"

"Why he sent this freak to assassinate me."

We stood and watched the man who'd steepled his fingers at me walk our way. He kept walking, right past us. But Nora only sneered. "He knows what he's doing."

"So do I. I'm going to the little bus riders' room. Try not to get assassinated till I'm done, okay?"

"You think that's funny?"

She went wide-eyed. In all our hours together, I'd seen nothing like this. Since Tulsa she'd been a mask of brunette disdain. Now she was clutching my wrist with two clammy hands. (And they were both hers.)

"Don't go."

"I have to go," I said. Then I quoted myself. Well, my "work." Listen: *Still ashamed to wear a diaper? Imagine the shame if you don't.* (I won't lie, I still love that.) "Seriously," I said, "I have to, you know . . . *know.*"

"The man is in there . . ." she whispered, and made a steeple with her tiny, nail-picked fingers. I turned in time to see the big man disappear into the men's room. "Please, Lloyd."

It was the first time she used my name. I grabbed her and kissed her and she whispered, "Do him. For me."

I quickly let her go. This is the kind of line you hear in movies. The kind that stops you, makes you wonder if it's just a line.

I could tell by the way he was walk-running that Steeple Man really had to go. You don't walk that way unless you've hit the urgent stage. Bad enough to pop sweat. When every step is organ-churning torture. In which case all you care about is removing the ferret teeth from your bladder. Our man could have used some Flomax.

I followed him into the men's room, where the smell of Lysol and piss-cake industrial-strength cleanser was eye-watering. We interrupted an argument between two overweight, older gay guys washing their underwear in the sink. (They might not have been gay; they might have just been friends with a taste for eye shadow.) They barely took notice of us. A man wearing a pimp hat in a Hoveround scooted in a minute after me and *that* got the pair's attention. "Honey," said the larger queen on the left, "you are *so* Herman Cain. So how does one relieve himself in that thing?" Hoveround didn't answer. Instead he tugged his hat down low, hit his toggle switch, and backed out the door. "*Quel snob!*" the second mirror-gazer snipped.

Meanwhile, the large bespectacled man from the bus gave no indication that he sensed me behind him. I hadn't planned on doing harm. I hadn't planned. I just grabbed his shoulder bag out of his hands as he turned to hoist it on the stall door hook. He was too surprised to react. Or not surprised at all. Up close, his skin shone some strange shade of yellow. I thought black albino. Then, Bhopal. Side effects of the gas leak at Bhopal: thousands dead, children blinded, a generation (this got little press) born a strange shade described in Hindi as *vameesa*, which translates roughly as "glowing egg yolk." (Did I think this then, or am I thinking it now? But Bhopal was in 1984, which would have made him twenty-eight, and he might have been twice that. Maybe he was just African American and jaundiced.)

I hissed at my target, going all Jason Bourne, trying to work up an anger I didn't really feel. Even my voice got deeper. "Why are you following us?"

I could hear the foot-traffic outside hocking and scraping by. The sink queens giggled. I made out "That is so old school!" Were they talking about us—me and Steeple in the stall? He'd switched glasses. His eyes darted, rabbitlike, behind yellow aviator shades.

"Take my wallet—just go," he pleaded. "Leave me alone."

Two envelopes stuck out of the slide-in pocket of his backpack. I grabbed them. (When had I become a backpack snatcher? What was *that* a side effect of? For that matter, what was making my hands itch? Was it the cumulative skank of the bus station toilet stall? Had I touched my face? The average human being touches their face ten times a minute. I remember that from *Contagion*, the virus movie with Matt Damon and Elliott Gould. The Dream Team! Would I be sprouting a face rash?) Why was it Lysol smelled nastier than whatever nastiness it was supposed to sanitize?

Inside the envelopes were greeting cards. The ironic kind. The kind Nora said she created.

"It's my mother," the man said, voice higher than I'd expected, making no remark about my presence in his stall. "She has the female cancer. Why are you . . . ?" He gave up and pleaded, "Listen, I really have to . . . you know . . . pinch a loaf here."

He unbuckled and yanked down his pants. Right down to his shiny calves. Why do some men go calf bald? What is that a side effect of? Pants friction? Without thinking about it I pulled out my paper-clipped flash-wad. A fifty in front and back. Nineteen singles in between. (You never know when you have to impress a date.)

"Wait," he said, sheepish, unleashing a dainty fart, his face disbelieving and horrified. "You ain't gonna watch, are you? Man, I had enough of that in Attica, you know what I'm sayin'?"

I knew what he was sayin'. He was about to go penitentiary-style. He *knew how* to go penitentiary-style.

While he was speaking I pulled off the paper clip and straightened one end so it stuck out like a pointy muzzle. Then I poked him in the ear. Right in the hole. I saw Charles Bronson car-prang a Filipino in one of the *Death Wishes*. "You've been following us. Why?"

"Following? Oooof. I don't want to . . . you know, in front of you. I told you, I had enough of that."

He didn't even curse. Maybe he was Christian. Could that be, a churchgoing hit man? Nora said he must have been sent by the man who—

"*Ouch . . . Please!*"

He tried to push himself up off the seat and his glasses flew off. I paper-clipped his eye. To do it I had to think of Nora, her little foxlike face when she didn't think I was watching.

I held my arm out, poised, to poke him again.

"One more time, why are you following us? I don't want to hurt you. But I will." (Jesus, is it possible to talk, when you're about to hurt somebody, without sounding like outtakes from a generic action movie? Is that how we learn how to do this shit?)

"W-why would I follow you?"

I poked him again.

"*Agggghhh . . .*"

"Wrong answer."

Haven't you always wanted to say that? Seriously, is that all crime was now in the twenty-first century—getting to star in your own movie?

Now I saw the tears. He went so weak in the face I forgot how big he was. I stood in front of him, I now realized, in the jailhouse love position. We both noticed at the same time. Crotch to kisser. I backed away, as far as I could. Which was about two inches before my back hit the stall door. "Put your feet up, on the seat," I whispered. "So no one can see." He did.

And then—he couldn't help it. He just—as they say on the Fleet enema box—"evacuated." (In my free time I used to study the competition.)

I'm going to stop now.

There are smells we naturally, maybe instinctively, spare each other.

So just remember one of them.

Aaaagghh.

(Maybe that is the definition of civilization: not shitting in each other's faces.) "I swear," he said, between birth-grunts. "I am not following you. I don't even know you. Now please. May I . . . This is humiliating."

"You just happen to have her cards?"

I heard scuffling outside. The last thing I needed was to be Larry Craiged. Bus station men's room sex makes airport men's room sex seem suave. And I wasn't even a senator.

He acted confused. "Whose cards?"

I pulled out the proof and waved it around. He snatched it and opened it, putting a finger to the bottom under *Birthdays are for forgetting.*

"This is for my mother. She's old, but she's sharp. Still has a sense of humor." He tried to talk normally, but his ear was bleeding and he kept his hand pressed over his eye. I had to give him points for maintaining while he talked. Even with his strangely high voice. "What are you doing, son? I *bought* these. Look, here's another one, for my sister."

He started to reach for the bag and I parried with the clip again. It had a clump of bloody wax stuck to the end. I poked him a little one. A lobe-shot.

"Shit. You doing it again!"

He started to pull his wallet out—slow—like a shirtless perp on *Cops. Look, it ain't a gun, officer!* (And yeah, I know a guy who writes Reality TV dialogue. Don't kid yourself.) With one hand my stall partner managed to open his wallet and slide out a picture of a woman who might have been him in a bad wig, their faces were that similar. Except she was eightyish, massively sucked up, and smoking a cigarette in a holder with the IV drip in her arm. "That's Moms, her first chemo," he said, and chuckled sadly. "Had to slip that little nurse thirty bucks to take a break so Ma could light up."

"Loved her Luckies, huh?"

I grabbed the wallet and checked out his driver's license, visible behind a little plastic wallet window. "Sargent Haddock of Soup City, Georgia."

"That's me."

"Really? Soup City? This has to be a phony. You paid good money for a fake ID and they gave you Soup City?"

"My name really is Sargent."

"What?"

It was as if none of my words had receptors in his head. "My name is Sargent Haddock."

"Just put the fucking picture back," I said.

I could hear Nora's voice in my head. *He's here to kill me.* It didn't seem like it. He didn't seem like the type. But—

Aaaghh. Ooomph. His voice got even higher. "Aw jeez, son."

He tore off some bus station toilet paper—no doubt knowing I'd look away. I waited a suitable time. I didn't want to see any . . . business. Downstairs. I know, I know, I've written everything from dildo ads to *Hustler* copy, but some things, like I said before, how to put this? . . . *I have boundaries now, Oprah!* Everybody's got their limits. I stood there, staring at his shiny tassel loafers (oxblood), not raising my eyes until he spoke. Someone had scratched "DBL NUGGT" at the bottom of the metal stall separator.

"Okay, done," he said sheepishly, wiping himself. When our eyes met again he said, "Do you even know that young girl?" There was some decent, southern softness in his voice. He sounded authentically shocked. I had no answer and just wanted to go.

I saw myself from above, like you read about in near-death accounts. Or on Ketamine. Looking down, I saw a guy facing another guy in a stall. Reality was sinking in as the thrill of helping a girl I might get to love receded.

The stink was stripping the stars from my eyes.

What he said took a while to sink in. Then it steamed me.

"What do you mean, do I know her?" I clip-feinted at his eye and he juked. "Do *you* know her? Or is it like on TV? You get a photo and location and just show up to blank them?"

"Say what?"

"I guess that's part of it, right. Not admitting you're a hit man."

"Son, you—

"Would you fucking flush?" To stay my gorge, I thought of the side effects of Sumetra, a "critical foot-fungus fighter." That was another triumph—giving athlete's foot gravitas. Making it "critical." Some schmuck scratches his toes and he feels like an executive. It's a *critical situation*. Too bad the price of pill-killing the itch was "possible thrush, ringing in the ears, occasional dry eyes, and an inability to tear." There it is. You don't need to scratch, but you can't weep anymore, either. Life's a trade-off.

"Boy? Boy! You're talking to yourself."

I came back from my babbling reverie and there was Sargent the Steeple Man, trying to squidge his pants on (without getting off of the seat). It was like bad Houdini.

THIRTEEN

Bus Station Toilet Killer

Our neighbor one stall over, who sounded like he'd once had his throat cut, kept repeating, "Co'se ah got *me* a phone, suckah. Whatchu think, ah'm talkin' to y'all on mah dick?" I had the feeling he was a white man.

Everything I didn't want to think was backing up. Was I doing this for love? Or was I doing this because I'd started doing it, and it felt even worse to stop than to keep going; because I knew, if I wanted to see her again, I'd have to do it. Because I wanted love. Why did it stink worse after he flushed? Somewhere there was a metaphor, but who had the time?

"Come on, boy!" Words skritched out of him. Like a trumpet player playing a mouthpiece. "Do you *know* her? She could be troubled. I got a daughter myself . . ." His voice trailed off.

I reached past him and he juked. Like I was about to regouge him, instead of what I was really going to do. "Flush again," I said. He did, over his own shoulder, an extraordinarily Plastic Man–like maneuver, without taking his eyes off me. I half-expected an elbow in the mouth, and braced myself. But he just pleaded some more; this man with thighs like barkless sequoias. Now I wished I *had* looked—maybe he was gelded. But what did *that* look like?

Aaaggh.

"Before you showed up she kept staring at me," said the man I'd just stabbed in the head three times. With my killer paper clip. The only weapon I had, which he knew I was crazy enough to use, to draw blood. Even if he knew jiujitsu, he knew he couldn't make a move without a stab in the eye. (At that moment, I saw myself on film. A hard guy.) But that wasn't it. (Of course.) He was not still there because he was scared of me. He was there because he was concerned. Which was much more startling. And weirdly embarrassing. All at the same time. Because he had empathy. For me. It was like the end of *Gandhi*, when Sir Ben Kingsley forgives the man who shot him. "Son. I swear on the eyes of my children, only thing I know about that gal is that we came in on the same dang bus."

"You came to kill her," I said. How much did I want to believe? Need to.

His mouth formed an oblong O, and that's when I noticed the caterpillar mustache. Yellow gray. A little lip-sweater. Forget jaundice. Now I wondered if he was a Jackson White. One of those Jersey Pine Barrens people. I'd read about them. They had yellowy skin.

I think, looking back, that what spooked him was realizing I believed what I was saying. And if I did, if I was *that* off, then there was no choice. He had to just try to get by me. Maybe he *was* trying to get by me. Okay, maybe he was trying to kill me. (Later I found a knife in his shoe. He didn't go for it. But still . . .) He said, "May I be excused now?"

I wouldn't step out of the way. He tried to get by and I whipped up the now-bent but surprisingly unbroken paper clip. I didn't stab him so much as he jammed his head onto the thing. His left temple absorbed the wire. At just the right spot. It just went in, all the way to my fingertips. (I thought, inappropriately, of the phrase "balls deep.") There's always some secret meridian, the one movie martial artists tap to kill enemies with lethal stealth. (Like the five-point-palm exploding-heart technique, or whatever Tarantino called it, in *Kill Bill*. Daddy David Carradine was more upset that the sensei had shown it to his babymama, Uma Thurman, than the fact that she was going to use it against him. Families!)

Remarkably, there was no blood. He just slumped over. But not all the way. Then he coughed softly, covering his mouth—his last gesture oddly genteel, considering what was going on in the rest of his body. In movies, killers and cops always touch the neck to see if there's a beat. I didn't touch him.

I wanted to feel something. I mean, after what I'd done. But really it was like I'd gone from watching tennis on TV to picking up a racket and playing. I'd gone pro. Crossed from the American pastime of watching people killing people to killing someone myself. At least I wasn't just another schmoe in front of the TV.

I took his wallet to make it look like a robbery. *Double Nuggets!* But I killed him for her. That much I knew. Just like I knew this was a thought I never wanted to think again; I needed to concentrate on what this got me—not what it took away. (I'm a murderer? Really? A thought you don't want to think. Unless you're on *Lockup*, on MSNBC weekends. And want to impress the audience.)

I was hooked. And heroin wasn't even the problem. (No, the problem, apparently, was that every line I wrote sounded like a movie trailer.)

Still. They say a jolt of energy rushes from the victim the instant they're killed, right into the killer. A rush supposedly stronger than crank and crack combined. It had something to do with Bordos and the Tibetan Book of the Dead. But I guess I was too dead to feel it.

Does everybody have a dark truth? A thought they don't want to think? That thinks *them*? If you watch the Lifetime network, do you become the Lifetime network?

I stood up and the room began to spin. (It's a cliché, but it happens.) For a second I forgot my victim. *There's* a word you want in your curriculum vitae. Had I gone this far in life without leaving victims? Or was it just that they weren't dead? I braced myself, pressing my hands against the strangely moist wood stall to keep from whirling down.

Had I just killed somebody? The jolt came like the boom after lightning. Count to five for every mile. The stall slammed into me and I got an icy shiver down to my prostate. Maybe this was the alleged death rush, just a little delayed

Still.

It felt good to be crazy for a reason. It felt rational. It was a relief. Almost a perfect moment, in the Hemingway sense, except that, me being me, I had to pee. (I know my liver is "compromised," so my kidneys "do double duty." Ever read a dialysis brochure? *The kidneys are responsible for filtering waste products from the blood. Dialysis is a procedure that is a substitute for many of the normal duties of the kidneys.*) So I did something maybe worse than murder. Not that I intentionally desecrated a dead man's body. He didn't feel like a corpse yet. Later I found out he was a bus driver. Riding back after a run. Deadheading.

Pee-wise, I'd reached red alert. The sweating and panting level. Where you hope you don't run into anybody you know because you know you look insane, hopping by with a wave because you really have to go.

This is when I did have an Out of Body–slash–Reality Crime Show moment. Except instead of looking down from the ceiling and seeing myself, I saw the reenactment, starring an actor who tried to tell himself this was almost like real acting. I imagined the camera on the guy playing "me," then I had a flaming sword of an insight. This is what I was: I was the writing equivalent of a reenactment actor. Were all the side effects on bottles—unexplained emotions, odd physical manifestations—like my own serial novella?

I'd hoped—to be honest—that murder would obliterate lesser obsessions. But it was just the opposite. Instead, murder became the thing I could not think about. In fact—didn't see this coming—I discovered that the only way to banish a truly horrible obsession (to stop perseverating, in the language of the trade) was to find something more heinous to obsess about.

I could not delude myself into thinking that describing side effects or composing medical and sex-toy copy was anything like real writing. Like it was some hipster thing. (I knew what was in the mail: I would lie in bed with my eyes open at feel-like-shit o'clock. Imploring myself. *Do not think about* Double Indemnity! If I closed my eyes, Nora's face would superimpose itself on Barbara Stanwyck's. Except Barbara Stanwyck at least pretended to be love-struck and sultry. Nora was hot by default. She went to the opposite field. She gave the impression there were great secret depths of hotness within her. But she wasn't giving it up. I saw my future and I didn't care. Nose pressed to the glass of love. Trapped outside, then trapped inside.

Another night terror. Was little Lloyd maybe just in love with longing? Just to have an emotion? The right emotion can haul you out of a habit. If you really feel it, just wanting to fuck somebody bad enough to stop heroin makes stopping heroin possible. It's not really planning ahead. It's like Gerald McBoing-Boing drawing a hole, then jumping in it. Does anybody remember Gerald McBoing-Boing? I imagined not just fucking but being with Nora, and that got my arrhythmic heart pounding even harder. More arrhythmically. (Street drugs were different. Nobody needed to publish a list of cocaine's side effects. Wondering if you were having a heart attack was the whole point.)

All this I thought—*feel* like I thought—in a jumble as I banged out of the stall. The Sink Queens had departed. I remember staggering past an impeccably styled Hispanic man, tie tucked between his shirt buttons as he applied blue-black shoe polish to his receding pompadour. When I looked back, from the door, he was washing the black off his hands. I thought, with a pang of compassion, *If it rains, he's fucked.* At least he had a reason to live in Los Angeles.

I was an idiot when I banged into the station's men's room. I was a murderer when I staggered out. (Not that one trumps the other, or that they're mutually exclusive.) Endorphins overwhelmed me. But that might not have been the thrill of murder. That might have been relief from having peed. I'd had to go so badly my knees were shaking. I had to pee a lot. The aforementioned Flomax was indicated, but (occupational hazard) I knew too intimately the things that could happen if you took it. I stopped, tried to take an honest breath, and then heard, in Bill Kurtis reenactment-sequence voice-over: *To his friends he was known as a quiet, determined industrial writer. To the police, and the public at large, he was soon to be known as the BSTK. The Bus Station Toilet Killer.*

FOURTEEN

Nora Funk

It was dusk when we left Union Station: the thirty-eight minutes when LA is actually pleasant. We didn't speak for a while. Until my companion in death piped up. "You know," she said, as if rewarding me with something of herself, "my name is actually Nora Funk. No, really. My father's name was Funk. He was a manic-depressive shit, and this didn't make him any happier. But he'd never change it. Too depressed . . . *'Hey, do you smell something funky?'* Really great, growing up with that."

I was so moved by this, this little bit of human conversation (as if what had just happened hadn't) that I could barely speak. Instead I just held her hand. And I'm not a hand-holder.

For no reason we headed to Spring Street. A long walk, in silence after that. "Did you?" she finally began. But she didn't need to ask. I didn't need to answer. We both knew.

Neither of us looked back. Like Lot and his wife leaving Sodom. Or was it Gomorrah? Either way, neither of us turned into pillars of salt. Though I won't lie, the thought crossed my mind—maybe instant salt pillar was not a bad way to go.

It was only by chance that we ended up at City Hall, in front of which, in a downtrodden not-quite-park area, a hundred or two buzzed silhouettes bumped and hopped around a drum circle. Nora and I strolled past the drums to a kind of public chat-fest—by the City Hall steps—on the subject, it took a minute or to discover, of Middle-Class Debt Forgiveness. At some point Nora had taken my arm. The thrill of her touch dizzied me. The pleasure was almost embarrassing. Yet I felt like I'd be giving up all my power to even acknowledge it. The speaker, a teachery, thin-haired white man, sitting cross-legged in jeans, crocs, and sun hat, kept punching his fist into his hand. "We need to get a plank together, people, or we will squander the moment." The human microphone (as I soon learned it was called) picked up his words. Repeated them: "We need to get a plank together, people, or we will squander the moment."

The speaker waited patiently for the echo to die. Then spoke another sentence. He had a way of hitting certain words, *plank*, *debt*, *squander*, so you knew exactly what the "take-away" was. Not that everybody was taking it away. The mood was one of festive menace. The sky had that chemical pink flush it got sometimes before dark. (I remember reading once that, before the death camps, when Nazis had to just drive around gassing Jews and gypsies in the backs of trucks, with hoses running from the exhaust pipe to the back where the people were, they called the corpses "tarts," because their faces turned scarlet, as if lipsticked, after they died from carbon monoxide poisoning. The sky over Los Angeles at certain times blasted the same quality. Poisoned to death but pretty. When ugly would have been so much more appropriate. And less disturbing.)

Someone in a Noam Chomsky mask under a black zip-up hoodie kept interjecting the words "fuck jerky" into the debt-relief presentation. Eliciting a wan smile from the cross-legged speaker, who said "I understand" in Chomsky-man's direction, and then launched wearily back into debt forgiveness and infrastructure-investment job solutions. The crowd turned and waved their hands angrily in his direction. "Self-censorship is not self-censorship" is how the professor wrapped up. "Why don't we think about that?"

The human microphone repeated this, and Security, a large-shouldered Latina with flat Mayan features, led ur-Chomsky off to one side, leaving him with a pat on the back.

I had not, at that time, even heard of Occupy Wall Street. This was its early days, and I wasn't exactly up on the news. Then the Chomsky guy ran up to me. "Hey, Lloyd! Lloyd the Roid, is that you?"

I recognized the voice. Adenoidal, snarkastic, but kind of pleady and needing-to-be-liked at the same time. With a Pittsburgh accent. "Harold?"

"Lloyd the Roid," he repeated.

Harold was an old side-effects pal and junkie (maybe ex-junkie; maybe, people can change, right?). I'd heard he had somehow broken into TV. We weren't close, but in that moment, I wanted nothing more than to be the person Harold knew. Me, as I was, instead of the new, still uncomfortable, post-murder me.

Harold prattled nonstop as we turned onto Fifth and Main, where the tents looked more ragged and improvised then the ready-mades in Occupy LA. At one time you could buy a human soul on Fifth and Main. Never mind the Mexican tar and fish scales, as old-time crackheads referred to their brain-crusher of choice.

Harold lifted the mask. Without it, he looked as he had

always looked, like a fluey Orlando Bloom. Still talking. (The way he was talking: fast, flicking spittle, mouth loose at the corners, I began to suspect he wasn't ex-everything.) He had theories, too. "No one at Occupy opted for refrigerator boxes. You notice? That's the difference, see? On Skid Row they do what they *have* to do. Back there"—he thumbed over his shoulder, toward City Hall—"those kids do what they *want* to do. Sleeping bags? That's really being down with the people."

"Just 'cause they're getting laid," Nora shrugged, "doesn't mean they're not serious."

I watched her as I had been watching her, wanting to shake her, shout in her face. *Do you know what I just did for you? I FUCKING KILLED A MAN!* After, I might have added, standing there while my victim took a dump. One more thought to block. Along with one I was already wrestling with: were there surveillance cameras in the bathroom? I'd made sure to close the stall door behind me so that, to the casual traveler in need, it just looked like the stall was occupied. I blinked back the memory as we walked together. The questions. The turmoil. Why it was troubling that there was no blood. Had I pricked some life-sustaining cerebral bubble, bloodless and fatal? Did his memories vanish when I paper-clipped his brainpan? If so, maybe I should take a stab at my own.

There was a minute there when I honestly believed I was beyond heroin. I had a reason not to use, because of love. But because of love—when had *this* melodrama set in?—I had done something that made heroin necessary. If it wasn't Shakespearean, maybe there was after-school special potential. Or at least a cocktail napkin, my favorite pre-Reddit content delivery engine.

Harold must have been talking the whole time. But I tuned

back in as we walked away from the enclave of protest and waded deeper into Skid Row. Now, he told us, he was part of the Bruckheimer team. JB maintained a phalanx of consultants, all, he sniffed, "suckling at the teat of show business." At first his floral hard-guy style rang TV schizophrenic. But he made sense. "Ex-cops, ex-DEA agents, ex-coroner's assistants, ex-you-name-its, these guys are all on the payroll. A writer has to write a kidnap-the-baby scene, you bring a guy in there who's done baby kidnappings. Maybe you bring the baby. You have to understand movie and TV execs." He went on, leading us from City Hall around the block, where he flagged over a squat Cholo, who looked right and left and plucked a few spit-sopping balloons out of his mouth. "Showbiz guys just want to be in a room with somebody who was once in a room with somebody real. Whole lot of law enforcement and military bag the government pay grade to come and be experts in Hollywood. Drink with the stars."

"We don't drink," Nora announced. I'd only known her since Tulsa, and I could already tell when she didn't like people by the sneer in her voice when she talked to them. And I heard that sneer when she talked to everybody. Including, half the time, me. We passed a soiled refrigerator box, caved in on one corner, with screams coming from it. No one seemed to care. Nora made as if to stop and I took her arm, not roughly, but not casually, either. Like I knew my way around. Like I was some kind of Skid Row pro.

"Oh, honey, are we protecting me from these dirty men?"

I didn't mind the insults from Nora. Like I say, I had feelings for her. Though not having had feelings for a while, I wasn't sure, at first, what they were.

FIFTEEN

The Usual Motel

I should probably skip the part where we end up in a motel room for three days, shooting speedballs and watching MSNBC. Nora said she wanted to lick Lawrence O'Donnell's forehead. To show him her respect. Harold explained his whole Chomsky "fuck jerky" thing as a way of keeping some levity in the proceedings. The trouble was, Occupy America didn't have any Yippies.

"So," I asked Harold, running bleach through the needle, rinsing it at the roachy motel sink, "you're going to be the Jerry Rubin of your generation? You're not even a ninety-nine percenter. Are you? You must have Bruckheimer money."

"I got a little Fuck You account. Nothing major. Only Bruckheimer has Bruckheimer money. Bruckheimer doesn't ask about my politics, and I don't tell him."

"Then basically you're just being a dick out there. Fucking with other people who are struggling, willing to transcend trendy ironic hipsterism and be sincere." Even gowed on smack I was disgusted. And junkies, let me tell you, aren't disgusted by much. But Harold looked so hurt, I didn't press it. A guy wants to put on a mask and be a douche bag to people trying to change the fucking world and stop corporations from screwing them, who am I to judge? Especially when he's paying for the drugs.

It's not like I was lifting a finger to stop the foreclosure of human souls. Looking interested was part of the dynamic of free drugs. You learned all kinds of things you didn't want to know that way. I once sat and listened to a legless Vietnam vet in a SF hotel sing new lyrics to "The Battle Hymn of the Republic" for three hours, because he was giving me free speedballs. After the "Battle Hymn" he moved to "God Bless America," which in his condition came out "*Gommessamekka*." I had to listen, then sing along, then listen, then sing along some more. And didn't mind a bit. I was bored, I was hoarse, I was losing my family and wasting my entire fucking life, but I was *high*.

So I ignored Harold's public dickishness. Just let it go. I remembered now how my ex-coworker got maudlin when the opiates faded—that he was just lonely, and no doubt self-conscious about a toast-colored lip herpes. The Chomsky faces made him comfy and anonymous among the Occupy Crowd. Where everybody else was in *V for Vendetta* Guy Fawkes masks.

"So, you know Bruckheimer, huh?" Not that was I even semi-interested, but I needed to keep Harold engaged. We had nowhere to stay, besides this motel.

"Yeah, I met him," he said. "Once. I got the call. It was exciting. But I was worried, too. 'Cause I thought it was a *CSI* thing. Back then *CSI Vegas* was super hot, and JB and the genius who dreamed it up—dude was a jitney driver on the Strip, regular guy—were all over the news."

As he talked he turned the red balloons the dope had come in inside out, smearing any residual tar on the edge of his spoon. "They shot the show out of a studio in Santa Clarita, so I figured

I'd have to go to Santa Clarita. Where all the white supremacists live. You don't want to be a black kid wearing a hoodie in Santa Clarita. Up there, Trayvon Martin wouldn't have made the news. They got guys wear white hoods to pick up Bud and chips at the 7-Eleven. But turns out they weren't calling about a *CSI*-type deal; it was something else. So instead of having to suck fumes up the 5 from LA, this one day I got to go to Jerry's office in Santa Monica, a converted airplane hangar with some kind of World War One plane hanging from the ceiling by a wire. The way the place was set up, the Sopwith Camel, or whatever it was, dangled right above the guest waiting area, over a big white couch low to the floor. So low you couldn't turn your head without bumping your kneecaps. Plus you knew, under the Airplane of Damocles, if there was an earthquake you'd be the first to go. The wire would probably snap and you'd be splacked underneath, one of those embarrassing deaths, you know? Like the guy who jumps out of a building and pancakes another guy taking a leak when he lands. Die with a dick in your hands, where's the dignity?"

"Depends whose dick," I said.

"Your own, obviously."

"Obviously." The last thing I wanted was to annoy Harold. I remembered my mission. "So, uh, why were you seeing Bruckheimer again?"

"Well, it was kind of just that one time. And not just Bruckheimer. Michael Bay was there. You know, the *Transformers* guy? *Bad Boys One* and *Two*?"

"All classics," I said.

"Exactly," he said, "Bay wanted to hear about self-heating shaving cream. The kind that gets hot on your face? It's a chemical thing. I guess he wanted to use it in a script."

“And you know about it how? You were a chemistry major?”

“My father invented the shit. He flunked out of dermatology school. Came up with hot gel and sold the formula to Gillette. It was my first techno-copy. Dad made me write it thirty-seven times.” Here he recited, voice dope-froggy like a white James Earl Jones. *“The heat source in the new self-heating shaving cream is a chemical reaction involving hydrogen peroxide and a reducing agent.* A *small polyethylene bottle filled with hydrogen peroxide is placed inside the aerosol can, followed by a propellant. Not only is it safe, it's convenient, and saves more time for the things that matter . . .”*

I chimed in: “Cut to fresh-shaved handsome guy smooching his pretty girl.”

Harold snorted—that's how he laughed. “Go ahead, laugh it up, big shot. I think Bay actually wanted my father. But when he Googled thermal shaving cream he got me.”

Nora didn't say anything. Just sat on the second bed, watching us talk. At first I thought she was sulking. But it seemed more than that. For all I know she was mourning. But I couldn't ask. Something about her kept me off-kilter. From the minute we met, we went from total strangers to sharing some kind of secret life together. So secret, now that I thought about it, even I wasn't sure if this was true, or in my head . . . When she got off on dope, her face softened a little, so she just looked angry. Not sad. But she wasn't talking much now. No sooner was the needle out of her arm than she lit a Tareyton and aimed a she-sneer at us. Nora not saying anything could fuck with you more than somebody else saying something. I couldn't help but admire Harold, his ability to stay chemically oblivious.

"I'm impressed that you remember all this," I told him. "The polyethylene especially. Who remembers polyethylene?"

"I did," Harold said, "and it's a good thing. From that one little question I got in as a consultant. Became a forensics cosmetic specialist. Kind of invented the field. I guess you could say I'm the go-to dye guy. Before *moi*, somebody wanted to stage a death by makeup, they'd cook up some nonsense about arsenic-laced pancake powder, tainted dandruff shampoo, stuff like that. Me, I took it to the next level. Chemicals I used? All FDA approved. That's the kicker. Ingredients are all right there on the Health & Beauty aisle. One time I even came up with the idea for hair tint that gave you scalp Ebola."

Nora perked up. "There is such a thing?"

Harold smiled crookedly. Proud. "That's exactly what Marg Helgenberger said. The victim was normal one day—a week later, his gray was gone, but so was the flesh over his brain. How can you not love show business?"

Nora scowled at me when Harold wasn't looking. When she spoke to him her voice was pleasant. As pleasant as Nora could be when she was trying to be pleasant. "So, Harold, you don't do any actual work work?"

"I don't dig ditches, if that's what you mean."

Harold chuckled again and licked the tip of his needle. I'd never seen anybody do that before, and it made me a little sick. (He had other creepy habits, like lubricating his non-reusable plastic needles with earwax every time he reused them. The last thing I wanted to think about was cars, or earwax, with the image of that bloody paper clip still fresh in my brain. But none of this mattered. Harold had the heroin.)

Somewhere outside a guy screamed in Spanish. Harold

leaned forward and lowered his voice, as though international makeup killers might be listening in to see what he was up to. "You don't think what I do is work? Well, let me tell you a secret. You know what's harder than coming up with cool ways to fuck somebody up via hair and skin care? Trying *not* to fuck yourself up with hair and skin care. Example. Let's say you wanna dye your hair. *Let's go blond, America!* Well, like it or not, you're going to be splashing on everything from Diamino-diphenylamine to Chloro-2-Aminophenol to Acid Orange 24. Stuff's banned in Europe, but over here, thanks to the chemical lobby, you can soak your head in that swill till your brain swells up like a marinated elephant spleen. Won't even take you long. Drip a little red solvent number one in your ear, you'll be aphasic and walking sideways before anybody can admire your new look. Happens all the time. Open secret. Your big health and beauty corpos keep a fund for shutting up folks who just wanted to get their hair shiny and ended up with festering scalp cankers the size of frogs."

He laughed again, while Nora studied him with an expression I couldn't quite peg. Harold laughed a lot when he was high, before throwing up and passing out and weeping about how it had all gone wrong, in no particular order. The man could go catatonic fast.

A few minutes, maybe a few hours later, feeling expansive on smack and Thunderbird, Harold announced he would get me a job on *CSI*. Based, he proclaimed, on my extensive pharma-scribbling experience.

To hear Harold tell it—he was rehearsing what he was going to say about me, in his dulcet, James Earl Jonesy Mexican-tar tones—I hadn't just composed the copy for Restless-Knee Syndrome, I was the brains behind the syndrome itself: the genius who concocted the disease to justify selling a cure. Not true, sadly. Had it been, I wouldn't have been scarfing motel dope crumbs from the likes of Harold. I'd have been spending the Squibb Inc. "naming bonus" on limo-delivered China white and a pharmaceutical-grade girlfriend. (There's no way to exaggerate: RKS marked new and lucrative territory. Restless Knee went beyond branding. It represented free pharmarketeers tossing out TV bait for folks looking for a disease to call their own. Lyrica was a treatment in search of a disease.) In full SESSIE mode, I could feel the copy coming back to me, like a catchy tune. *Some of the most common side effects of LYRICA are dizziness, blurry vision, weight gain, sleepiness, trouble concentrating, swelling of your hands and feet, dry mouth, and "feeling high."*

That's right. "*Feeling high*"! And how much did I love writing that? Seriously. How many people decided their knees were restless just to get *that* feeling? Once in a while we all get to do our bit for humanity, and who knows how many legions of euphoria seekers dove into the as-yet-unsuspicious world of Restless Knee pills thanks to my little hint? I imagined doctors' offices flooded with otherwise healthy—if slightly skeeved—individuals rolling in with sudden, uncontrollable, loafer-throwing twitches in their lower limbs. "Doctor I need help. This dang knee of mine just won't behave itself. It's all, y'know . . . *restless*!"

Given that any promise a junkie makes has a shelf life shorter than a space heater in a bathtub, I wasn't banking on Harold *really* nailing me a *CSI* gig. I would have been surprised had he remembered that he offered. In the meantime I had to sweat through a bout of my own brain-eating Ebola—otherwise known as my immediate future.

SIXTEEN

Fresh Dead Man Shit (Memory Issues)

And yes, yes, I'm trying to tell the story here, but things occasionally wander. Did I mention that I have—what do you call them?—memory issues? No doubt too much bad shampoo had altered my brain chemistry. Forget the tainted heroin, Plexiglas-cut crack, questionable E, and bathtub crank, not to mention all the preteen hallucinogens and booze. Fucking Head and Shoulders has left me linear-thought-fucked and incapable of spinning a straight narrative without veering left and right, careening over the median like a lush behind the wheel on New Year's Eve.

I can say this: not a minute went by when I did not think about the murder . . . or think about the fact that I wasn't thinking about it. (Which is the same thing—the old Guilt-Over-Not-Feeling-Guilty routine.) Here's what lingers: the Lysol and stale urine stink of the men's room. The ear hair and scalp flecks on Spectacles when I stood above him, wielding my paper clip. The odd way he cupped himself, his "manhood," with both hands while he relieved himself. Detail upon detail. Enough to drown a man in memory if he wasn't careful. But was it guilt? Was it remorse? Well . . . no. It's too late to try and look good, Father. In truth, what I felt after murdering was about what I felt before murdering. Only more.

Does that make sense?

If not, let me, as famously popular and charismatic two-term president and former Screen Actors Guild snitch Ronald Reagan used to say, restate and reiterate. What I felt was a niggling, occasionally-more-than-niggling—okay, *gnawing*—sensation that I had risked Death Row, retribution, and eternal damnation for killing an innocent man out of my new companion's fantasy and paranoia; that I had smelled fresh dead man shit; that, in fact, Steeple Fingers had no connection to Nora whatsoever, let alone the intention of taking her life. And all of it, all of it, was too brutal and soul-soiling to let rise to the surface of my brain. So, naturally, I kept it down, weighted with carefully arranged anvils (well, actually heroin) on the bottom of that roiling cesspool that passed for consciousness.

As for my Greyhound date—she and I didn't speak about the murder. Until the next one.

SEVENTEEN

Pre-Occupied

We had, Nora and I, initially decided not to take a place, but to live with the Occupy people, down by City Hall. It was easy enough to find a tent. People were donating, so there were piles of them. Finding space beside City Hall proved less difficult than boosting canned beans from the local Ralphs. Our neighbors were a wan and truculent Korean gent called Viper and an almost translucent, puppety-voiced white girl named Partyeleanor. (I had to ask her twice, and she insisted this was the name she was born with.) Despite the edict banning all drugs from the Occupy site, Partyeleanor seemed to be imbibing her share of party-grade methedrine, a lapse that left her incapable of not talking. When she met us, like most meth-heads, she did not so much initiate conversation as aim whatever monologue was already spewing out of her mouth in our direction. (And would, no doubt, continue spewing after we departed.) The subject of her rant—actually the subject of most people's the night we arrived—was Scott Olsen, the Iraqi War vet who had just taken a gas canister to the head, courtesy of the Oakland Police Department. Partyeleanor filled us in about Scott Bergstresser, "uniformed Satan," the cop who—she kept repeating—shot the tear gas projectile that hit Scott Number One's head.

She ended every sentence with a little up-trill, so that even, say, "Dogs have four legs" sounded like a question: "Dogs have four legs?" It was something you got used to. After five minutes of Party, I tuned out and found myself meditating on the vicious brown nicotine stains coating Nora's fingers, and her curious habit of dining almost exclusively on canned tomatoes and varietal jerky.

Our first night downtown, doing some supermarket boosting on Alvarado and Eighth, I watched Nora pore over the small print, back-of-the-label information on a package of faux baloney. What was she looking for? "GMOs," she informed me, without looking up. "The food lobby paid off Congress to pass a law saying companies do not have to put on the label whether their shit is genetically modified or not. Fucking agribusiness? I'm telling you, this soyloney causes birth defects they don't even have names for." She put the non-lunch-meat lunch meat back and we moved to the dairy aisle, where she grabbed a half gallon of 2 percent, wielding it over head. "The growth hormones? In cows?" I thought she was going to smash the carton onto the floor in protest. A trio of Cholitas pushing strollers stopped to stare, as if this skinny white girl were some kind of in-store entertainment. Everything about Nora was scrawny, except, as mentioned, her breasts. (And why do I keep mentioning them? What is that about?) What impressed me was that she owned breasts of such girth, they made no attempt to *not* look artificial. When she ranted, they bobbed up down under her T-shirt like fat, drowning babies. The way she fumed at me, anyone would think I had personally hormoned the offending livestock, and saw to it their tainted issue made its way into pregnant women and children. "Babies in Arkansas are being born with cartoon kidneys, from genetically modified corn in baby food. The fucking food lobby—agribusiness is worse than Nazis. But what's the alternative? Breast milk's full of paint thinner, termite killer, and toilet deodorizer. And that's just the good shit. They've done secret tests, at NASA, and found rocket fuel in there. At least Hitler just murdered Jews—he didn't foul the world so that nature could do it for him."

"Not technically true," I said, even though I knew I shouldn't. "Mengele experimented on babies. He exposed them to all kinds of chemicals."

"Well, fine!" she shouted back, even though the manager, a largish red-faced man with a clubfoot, was now marching lopsidedly up the aisle toward us. I recalled—Fun Fact!—how the Nazis, before moving on to Jews and Gypsies, exterminated babies with clubfeet. Though Hermann Göring himself had a clubfoot, he claimed it was the result of a bear-hunting accident.

"At least Mengele bothered to experiment," Nora snapped, cutting off my own unpleasant thoughts. "Monsanto doesn't even do that. They just put the crap out there. What do they care? The money they're not making on deformed toddler hearts they make on patenting seeds that have existed for two thousand years. More than two thousand small farmers in India kill themselves every year. You know why? Because mighty Monsanto bought off the Indian government—not just the prime ministers, but the supervisors and mayors of tiny villages. Now they send thugs out to tiny family farms and shut them down unless the farmers pay piles of rupees for the privilege of planting the same seeds that their grandparents and great-grandparents and their grandparents' grandparents' grandparents used. Oh, and did I mention that Obama appointed the former VP of Public Policy at Monsanto to run the FDA? Change you can believe in!"

This might have been the most sentences my kind-of girlfriend had strung together since I met her. Her passion was impressive, even if, deep down, I had a feeling the real source of her anger was something else entirely. True, she had righteous indignation over Monsanto, but the rage boiling inside her—that sprang from a whole other hell.

Nora was still ranting while I guided her by the arm way from the approaching manager. Steered her toward a case of hot chicken roasters in aluminum pans. "The world's fucking brutal, baby, but right now we have to—"

"*Chickens!*" She eyed the trays as if they were personally offending her. "Forget the chemicals Tyson farms pumps into hens, forget the fact their feet are glued to the bottom of their cages."

The three Cholitas, still following us, laughed and elbowed each other. All three rocked super-tight tops that showed the spaces between the buttons they barely managed to button over their solidly stout torsos. (I could not help wondering, why is it Latinas can be ample enough to show visible stomach rings and still be absolutely sexy, while the same sausage heft on non-Latinas, specifically white women—call me reverse racist—looked desperate and fat?)

"Are you fucking listening?" Nora hissed. "If the hormones in these chickens don't cause a five-year-old girl to sprout pubic hair, the aluminum in those pans will make sure she's half senile by the time she's thirty."

This time I didn't bother to plead, I grabbed her arm and

frog-marched her out of the store, aiming—I hate to say it—a sheepish, shit-eating henpecked hubby grin toward the shoppers who'd stopped to stare. Better to have security think I'm dickless than pat me down for canned goods.

Once in the lot, I stopped smiling fast. "Do you realize I've got two cans of those tomatoes you wanted in my pants, plus the Fritos? You can rant or you can steal, but not both, okay? Nora? You with me on this? Come on, I need to hear you say it."

She eyed me patiently, waiting till I finished. "Corn's the biggest GMO, you know? When genetically modified corn was fed to pregnant rats, baby males were born with testicles that kept changing color. And females with mature uteruses that usually prolapsed."

I gave up. "Bet you can't eat just one, huh?"

"This is funny to you?"

"Nervous joke," I said, checking over my shoulder. "Just keep moving. If a rent-a-cop finds sardines in your pants, they can still arrest you a hundred feet outside of a store."

Her glare let me know the esteem in which she held me.

"For Christ's sake, Lloyd, what are you thinking?"

"You really want to know?" We were out of the danger zone, so I relaxed a little. "I'm thinking about octopi."

"Octopi?"

"You know, your octopus shows mood by changing color. Made me wonder about those male rats. Maybe they have mood balls."

"If they're lucky," she said, without sounding mad about it.

"I'm just saying, baby, you advertise those on an infomercial at four in the morning, people would phone in their credit card numbers, I guarantee."

"You're so funny," she said. "I got a can opener, so I can eat the canned tomatoes now."

Again, I had to ask why.

"Bisphenols. The plastic they use to line the cans."

"What, you like the texture?"

"Mmmm," she said, tossing the can back and sliding a whole tomato down her throat. "It's like licking porpoise belly. If porpoise gave you birth defects."

I couldn't believe that managers hadn't come running.

"Just three servings is enough to mutate frontal neocortical development—and let's not even talk about genital development."

"Jesus, we're back to that?"

My discomfort had no effect on her. We were standing before a botanica advertising "natural remedies" for "*impotencia*." A woman inside stared at us like she knew something horrible but wasn't going to share. I turned back to Nora, who was busy explaining.

"You know about anogenital distance, right? Bisphenols significantly increase the space between anus and genitals."

"Baby taint? Is that what we're talking about?" I felt a buzzy discomfort in some organ I couldn't identify, but still wanted to rip out and beat with a ball-peen hammer. My mouth had gone dry as melba toast.

Now I wanted the manager to come. A rent-a-cop. An irate shopper, anything to interrupt us.

"Anogenital distance," Nora announced, as if stating the name of a dignitary at a state dinner, "happens to be an indicator of neurological development."

Digging deep, I peered directly into her feline eyes.

"I still can't believe I found a woman who can talk side effects. Do you know how hot that is?" Nora didn't respond, so naturally I kept talking. "Anyway, I thought this was a GMO thing, not bisphawhat-the-fucks."

"Bisphenols, GMOs—they're just the delivery system. The source is always the same. The one percent. Who profits from lax regulations? By putting mutagens in tomato soup?"

This was Nora: bursting into political rage after boosting dinner from a supermarket—two minutes from the supermarket. It's a nice sensation: being annoyed and terrified and in love at the same time. Like loving oysters even though shellfish send you into anaphylactic shock. "So," I said, feeling dickish without doing anything to stop it, "there is somebody who makes money off kids with defects and learning disorders. I'm guessing that's a growth industry. There is some secret creepy spread sheet that calculates the market value of challenged toddlers. First it was Baby Einstein. Now it's Baby Hawking. That's the magic of capitalism."

"There's value in every child, though it may not be what you think it is."

"I can't tell if you're speaking like a Catholic or a sideshow operator."

"You'll see what I am."

Here she glared at me. The sky had turned the color of pale dirt, the smog taking over. We'd moved down Alvarado half a block, beside a bus bench where a muttering crone plagued by hair crust had set up camp with a shopping cart full of cats. In matter-of-fact fashion, she yanked up her blanket skirt and relieved herself heartily at the curb. Nora might as well have been watching *Masterpiece Theatre*. She beamed at the crust lady and her splashing, horselike gush. But I was still nervous about walking out of the store with unpaid items. I have always been a terrible criminal. That's why I got straight jobs to pay for . . . what I needed to pay for.

Nora—who seemed, oddly, to blossom the more dire things got—had that golden aura around her when she shoplifted. Like Robert Duvall in *Apocalypse Now.* Lieutenant Colonel Bill Kilgore. Remember when Martin Sheen sees him, strutting around, talking surfboards, with Vietcong shells exploding all around him? Nora had the same aura of seeming protected—if not from bullets, then at least from the mullahs of shoplifting.

I was the one who'd sweat through his clothes. Nora couldn't have been more relaxed—for her—as if it were normal to stroll around and chat with stolen goods in our crotches, as if there were no risk whatsoever of some seven-dollar-an-hour Police Academy washout humping out after us with a cell phone and plasticuffs. (Even though, on some level, a little time in supermarket jail might have been preferable to hearing tales of baby taint.)

We were still using heroin, but smoking it now, so it was more like health food. Besides which, heroin could calm you down but it couldn't cure neurosis. I was once caught shoplifting at a bodega in the Mission, in San Francisco. The owner, originally from Juárez, pulled a machete from under the counter and swung it, nipping the tip off my middle finger and sending it flying into a jar of Slim Jims. The owner chuckled sourly. "Thanks for the tip, *pendejo.*" I was too stunned to feel pain, but not too stunned to appreciate the joke, or the calm in his mild, raspy voice. (On the plus side, the free oxys I got at SF

General made it all worthwhile. So worthwhile I almost considered asking El Bodega Man to slice off another tip.)

There was no danger of macheted retribution with Nora. We'd strolled around the corner like regular people. But wait! My fucking memory! I mentioned the Depakote thing, right? Way up top? Second or third chapter? The whole I-had-a-breakdown backstory? I also mentioned that we'd stolen a Prius? (Didn't I?) Well, not stolen, exactly . . . More like stole-slash-borrowed from Harold.

See, Harold preferred a Prius for scoring, since most cops—undercover or uniformed—were unlikely to profile a white man in a white Prius with a "Vegans Do It Organically" bumper sticker as a heroin buyer. (Or so he theorized.) The one time he got pulled over, Harold insisted he was cruising the hood to look for his little sister, who'd said she had taken up with a man named "Loco" on Alvarado. "Is that a balloon in your hand?" the cop wanted to know. "Oh *this*? I don't know what it is, officer. A Mexican fella just came up at a red light and asked for twenty bucks. I didn't know if he was gonna shoot me or what. I didn't even know he stuck the balloon in my hand until just now. Why the hell is a man like that selling balloons on the street? Is there a party or something?" Harold swore the UCs looked at each other and said, "We can't arrest the asshole for being stupid," and let him go.

Harold also swore he didn't mind the "dumbasses" and "morons" they yelled after him when he left. "Fuck do I care? I used to have the black Cadillac, wear the shades, do the whole look-at-me-I-wear-black-and-think-dark-thoughts-'cause-I'm-the-real-deal junkie thing. Now I go for the normal. I'm a dope fiend in Dockers. Less hassles."

Harold babbled a bit when dope was in the same room with him. He was shooting the stuff we copped him on Fourth and Bonnie Brae in return for the car. (Well, sort of. It was a loose deal. A junkie deal. By definition half-assed.) The dealer was a freckled and orange-'froed African American named Red. He shorted me the bonus bag on a seven-for-a-C-note. But it wasn't my money, and I wasn't going to argue with a young brother who picked his teeth with a steak knife. (For that matter, I wouldn't argue with an old white lady who picked her teeth with a steak knife. Well, I'd probably argue *less*.)

Harold babbled some more, wept briefly, and passed out after fixing, toppling sideways in slow motion on his motel bed. Nora slapped his face a couple of times. It seemed more precautionary than hateful. Then again . . .

We slipped the dope out from Harold's left sock, the same place he kept it in our SESSIE days. Nora fixed after Harold keeled over, then me. We only had one needle, and after we both lied that we'd never done this before—of *course* we'd been tested!—we both got well. (Nora geezed discreetly, somewhere between her legs. Which, I confess, got me hotter than all the porn in China.) After the dope was gone, we "borrowed" Harold's car keys and headed out.

EIGHTEEN

"You Can't Do a Gangster Lean in a Prius"

I pressed the button to start the hybrid, adjusting, as usual, to its unearthly silence and spine-crushing mobile ashtray-like designer comfort. Once driving, as was the local custom, I eased sideways and low in my seat, steering left-handed. Nora elbowed my elbow off the armrest. "You can't do a gangster lean in a Prius."

"You're right," I replied, and recited another slogan I would never sell. "*Prius. On the right side of history, on the wrong side of cool.*"

("Let the words pass through you. You are but a vessel . . ." This is from the inspirational how-to-write self-helper *All the Letters in My Keyboard Spell God* by Dover Dannerson, an ex-SESSIE turned bestselling inspirational scribe. Which in itself was a kind of inspiration, considering that Dover, not to be catty, pretty much ran on Adderall and Xanax, battled a baker's dozen of sexual harassment allegations from his time at Squibb, and lived with his parents.)

"Harold is definitely not cool," I say to Nora, again taking in the comfort-free Prius, from sacro-punishment seat to toilet-seat blue dashboard plastic.

"Cool is a fascist construct," Nora says, surprising me, once more, by speaking in the voice of someone I hadn't met before, though I'd been with her for a while. Someone educated. Maybe an autodidact. Borderline literary/political or totally schizophrenic. Something delicious.

Comfort-wise, the Prius was about on par with our tent, there on the back lawn of LA City Hall with all the others. Despite the media bullshit about patchouli—code name for retro pot-smoking hippie scum—I didn't smell any. (Not as much patchouli as I smelled when I used to have to ride the bus into Hollywood to the methadone clinic, and the Catholic girls in plaid skirts going to Immaculate Heart got on in five-packs. In Asia, you may not know, they use patchouli for snakebites and fly repellant. But the Catholic schoolgirls weren't repelling anything. The flies and snakes were on board, staring hard at newspapers and billboards, trying not to look pervy, foaming over all that plaid-skirt jailbait.)

Our second night, after sundown, a political tweaker named Spang had a teach-in on American foreign policy, going from John Foster Dulles and his secret ties to the Nazis to the current paramilitarization of domestic police. "*What we saw in UC Davis were storm troopers, Obama's Brownshirts!*" I was impressed by how many Occupiers stuck around to the end. The way Spang licked his corner-cracked lips, picked his skin, and halted mid-sentence to clutch his chest, he had to be feeling the side effects of something. Maybe not even the sides. Something, in any case, that really agreed with him. Despite the flaky lips and jitters. *"Arming domestic police forces with paramilitary weaponry will ensure their systematic use even in the absence of a terrorist attack on U.S. soil . . ."*

This resonated, even if it came by way of Spang. ("Ideas," as playwright and human breast milk aficionado George Bernard Shaw once opined, "are not responsible for the people who embrace them.") It was, after all, the same with pharmaceuticals—nobody makes a pill nobody takes. R&D, manufacturing, drug trials to see whether the shit kills you or makes you shit uranium—fuck all that! The heavy lifting is creating the need. You want to sell restless-knee medication, you have to convince people they have restless knees. "Oh, look, Doris, my leg is jiggling!" The cops needed Oakland to start jiggling so they could march out the cartridge launchers ad and Cairo body armor.

I could have told all this to Spang. Instead I listened to him, and a revolving roster of other speakers, until sunup. Nora had other plans. She had blossomed in the outdoor political context. Gone, when she wanted to, from taciturn to eloquent. I thought maybe she grew up in a commune. She thought Occupy was like being homeless with tents and a library. The day Scott Olsen got shot in the head by a gas cartridge, we watched the YouTube of him being carried out on some Spanish lady's iPhone. Each viewing of the travesty refueled the viewers. Only Nora wasn't interested in some viral video. She was, as she said, "interested in the virus who pulled the trigger."

It wasn't long after the news of Scott Olsen's brain injury that she pulled me aside and dragged me up to the City Hall steps. Talked low during the General Administration meeting. "Scott Bergstresser."

"What about him?"

"We got his address."

"Jesus." I played it jokey, but not. "So you're going to SF to take him out?"

"Don't have to."

"Good," I whispered. "I mean, we already committed—"

I stopped myself. We'd never actually discussed . . . the thing. She leaned over and grabbed me by the shoulders, as close to an embrace as we ever enjoyed. Nora wasn't a snuggle-bunny. But everything was changing. (The tent, by the way, seemed to fire her up; inside, our first night, she spread herself open and slapped her clit like she was punishing a puppy while I slid in and out of her from behind. She liked to expose herself while facing the other way, as if she could let one part of herself out of the cage as long as the other part didn't have to know about it. A woman of dimension.)

More on that later. If I remember. For now, as we headed north on Alvarado in the Prius, toward Sunset Boulevard, Nora studied my eyes. Deciding, I sensed, if she could safely peel off the next layer of whatever it was that separated who she really was from who she acted like. "Don't think of it as murder," she whispered. "Think of it as Occupy Death."

"Occupy Death? Wow. You are wasting yourself on greeting cards."

She regarded me a moment—was that pity in her eyes or disbelief?—and continued. "What I'm saying is I don't have to go up north to do it. He totally has a girlfriend in Echo Park he's coming down to visit."

I tried to play it off. What surprised me, more than the fact that she could possibly know this or that she'd said "totally," was that Bergstresser would be going to Echo Park. "He's a cop. Doesn't seem like the type who's into . . ."

"Unless he's gassing them," Nora said, twisting her lip in thought, considering something, and then letting it go. Letting me know—or so I psychically surmised—that she'd made the decision to trust me. "His girlfriend," she went on. "She's one of us."

"Which us?"

"OCI—Occupy Counterintelligence. There's a Shadow Assembly."

"Wait. You're saying Occupy has spies? Moles? You mean you brought us there on purpose?"

Wheels within wheels! She ignored the question. "It's not formally structured. If someone wants to work counterintelligence they just do. My friend Susie is a sex worker."

"And Officer What's-His-Nazi thinks she's his girlfriend?"

"Why do you think they call it work? She's donating her talent to the cause. Doesn't matter. The house is on Echo Palk Boulevard, way up the hill from Sunset. Catty-corner to a coffee shop with outside tables. It's called Fix."

"Of course it is. So we do the latte thing and case the place. As soon as we pull this little Prius over and get some money. Any ideas how we do that?"

"How do you think?" I thought I detected an eye roll, but it was hard to tell with Nora. She had bangs. Sometimes they covered her eyes, sometimes they just film-noired her. She eased a

Citibank card out of her panties and flashed it at me. I wanted to lick it. "We're giving the banks a chance to balance their karma, do something good."

"Whose card is it?"

"A man named"—she tilted the card to read—"Askew. Lester."

"Les Askew. Cool name. Kind of Jim Thompson-y."

"Fuck Jim Thompson, what's cool is Mr. Askew wrote his PIN number on a piece of paper and stuck it in his wallet."

Nora blew bangs out of her eyes. Waiting for my reaction. I knew, by now, the best reaction with Nora was not to have one. Except this time she was grinning. A first. One gold tooth I fell in love with on the spot.

"Cash is good," I said. But what I was thinking, what hit me all over again, was how I'd killed a guy in a bus station toilet. That had to make the crime more suspicious. I knew I'd have to change my appearance: no doubt they had Homeland Security cameras hanging from the roof like bats. I'd be on a dozen of them. If anybody was looking. Going into the men's room right after the big man in glasses who never came out. Why hadn't I gone blond already, or bought a hat?

When I turned right onto Sunset, toward Echo Park, Nora curled her legs up underneath her on the seat, exactly as she'd done the first time I saw her, on that Greyhound bus. I felt like I'd known her longer—was it years or days?—and simultaneously like I didn't know her at all. (I know, I know . . . But sometimes you just have to embrace the cliché.) I was still sitting on a million questions. The first one being, what were we going to do when we got where we were going? The second—well, the second wasn't a question. More of a reminder. As in, "Nora, this isn't some four-eyed old man in a train station toilet we're talking about. This is a violent, violent, presumably sociopathic, Occupy-hating tool of the state, doubtless armed to the teeth with Homeland Security–funded paramilitary gear." (Not that I was some para-gear head, but the online outlets since 9/11 were amazing: army-navy stores on steroids, with fun and hard-to-get items like backyard minesweepers, stand-alone DVR systems with four digital wireless cameras and five-hundred-gigabyte hard disk drives, beef jerky that could last through the apocalypse.) Of course, it wasn't the arms or psychopathology I was chewing my gums about. It was the needle they inject you with for cop-killing.

Do you ever feel like you know too much about the wrong things, not enough about the right ones?

At a red light on Sunset and Echo Park Boulevard, a Mexican girl crossed in front of us, wearing low-slung capris pants that strained at the seams over her Marilyn hips. Mexican Marilyn had both arms around a skinny boy with a six-inch pompahawk. They mad-dogged us and then the boy grabbed one of his chiquita's butt cheeks to let us know he could. Nora slid her eyes my way and shrugged. "Some guys like 'em assy."

It was so not the kind of thing she said that I had to laugh. As I did she bent forward and tugged her forever-slipping-off sandal-strap back up her ankle. She had the dirtiest feet I'd ever seen in my life. Something, to my own weird surprise, I found not repulsive. Was I now, on top of murderer, SESSIE, and ex-Christian Swingler, drifting into foot-sucking territory? Some toe-sucking *This little piggy went to market* action? Is that how it worked? You toppled one barrier—did one thing you'd thought you would never do—and soon you were committing all manner of formerly unthinkable acts with routine frequency? After murder comes shrimping?

Does life turn us into what we are or keep us from ever having to find out? I guess it depends on the life.

NINETEEN

Prayer of Affirmation

Just for today, help me not be who I really am.

TWENTY

Temporary Blonde

So this is life. Driving in a junkie's Prius with Nora to find Deputy Sheriff Bergstresser, virally loathed tool of the state. We arrive at eleven in the morning. Nora tells me to turn around, park facing downhill.

"Done this before, baby?"

"Don't call me baby."

Along the way from Occupy, she'd changed into a platinum blond wig and black men's suit pants. (I mean the pants were black, not, necessarily, that they were pre-owned by African Americans. Though who knows?) Over this she wore a green-on-white Lilly Ledbetter T-shirt. I'd slapped on aviator shades and a thrift-store trucker hat that read "RODRIGO LEAF & TREE," providing, in Echo Park, a level of camouflage a stick-bug on a bare branch would envy. I promised myself I would dye my hair. Later I actually did, peroxide blond, and it was a big mistake. Once I was blond, I looked paler and vaguely pedophilic. My peroxide-stripped hair revealed a rat-tongue-colored scalp beneath. Which I'd never noticed before. That or the peroxide had peeled the weathered flesh-tone top layer off my scalp. Whatever the reason, I had that lives-in-a-subway-tunnel look. One of the Mole People. So I ended up just wearing the hat I got in the first place. Like the other Rodrigo employees or the other hipsters wearing their hats.

In my East Side get-up, I kept thinking of Tom Clancy, how he appears on his book covers in uniform. With his own special insignias. The admiral of that nuclear destroyer they give you when you sell enough right-wing fantasy porn to have a staff and put them in paramilitary-wear, like L. Ron Hubbard and the Sea Org staff, or Anthony Scalia in the Supreme Court robes he designed himself. Epaulettes!

I imagine Admiral Tom going to bed at night doubt-free. Maybe sharing a bunk with Rush Limbaugh. Modern-day J. Edgar and Clyde Tolson. Who gets to be Jack Ryan tonight? *I'm tired of being the president—I want to be lassoed and rode like a teaser pony!* The mind wanders when what's in front of it requires avoidance for the mind to function. And . . .

When you can't forget, there's heroin . . . (When there's no heroin, you can't forget.)

Book Three

Don't threaten me
with love, baby.
Let's just go walking
in the rain.

BILLIE HOLIDAY

TWENTY-ONE

Party Time

We had time to kill. So to speak.

Nora knew the car the deputy drove. A cherry 1968 Dodge Charger, sky blue, convertible. Rear bumble stripes.

"What else could he drive?"

She sounded defiant, as though it were common knowledge that, after a hard day felling veterans and Occupy types, serial law-enforcement canister launchers all tooled around with screaming headers and a forty-year-old 440 Magnum under the hood.

I kind of wished Jay and Riegle, my Christian Swingles crime buddies, could have been here to help set up the play. It seemed like another lifetime, the day we tried to take off that pharmacy in Tulsa for oxys. No muss, no fuss. Of course, it was an utter and complete debacle. But still, someone had my back.

Nora was a different kind of crime partner. I had no idea what her background was. I had a variety of details. Some conflicting. What I didn't have was a particular truth. One minute Nora might have been the Ma Barker of movement vengeance. The next she might have been off her meds. Or on them. Sylvia Plath with ankle tats. Strange, deep water. With skin of beautiful and toxic near-iridescence.

It started to drizzle. One of those peculiar LA mini rains where the sun keeps blaring, so the raindrops feel inappropriate. Evidence of something gone off in local nature, like when you see a coyote on your street at two in the afternoon. Just standing there. Staring. Supposedly, daytime sightings meant the coyote was rabid. Same with skunks and raccoons. But I never took it that way. It was more likely we were the diseased ones, and the fucking animals just weren't going to pretend otherwise anymore. (Sometimes a coyote would just *be there* when you opened the door of your house. They didn't even bother to bare their teeth. They didn't need to. It was enough to just let us know they were waiting.)

We were headed for the coffee shop Nora knew, but I wasn't sure I needed caffeine. I was having waking flashbacks, in the form of hallucinated surveillance videos: Spectacles's purpling face as he expired, atop the toilet, his mouth formed in a final, soul-curdling O so close to my face I could breathe his Scope. Reliving the moment, I reenacted my lethal paper-clip move in my head, with quivering thumb, quivering digits, the way guitar players, or idiots who want you to think they're guitar players, will run their fingers up and down an imaginary neck as they wait in the checkout line in front of you, or doze next to you on a plane. Then again, the finger-moving is (or can be) a form of practice. John Coltrane, according to his wife Alice, holed up in his upstairs room in Philadelphia for eighteen hours at a pop, composing and rehearsing with just his fingers, no horn, reinventing his instrument without actually playing it. It did not occur to me that I was rehearsing.

TWENTY-TWO

Fix

At Fix, when we finally got there, I could barely make out the fair-trade coffee list, because the image of my victim's large-pored cheeks and shiny glasses overlaid the words. I brain-sprayed men's room murder details over everything. My victim's pleading eyeballs gazed up at me from rows of blueberry muffins and chocolate croissants. B-movie psychosis.

I went with Zoka from Seattle. Brew of the day! Nora ordered an iced triple Americano into which she ripped open and dumped an aquarium bottom of NutraSweet.

She must have been dumping her ninth packet when I asked her about it.

"Sweet tooth?"

"Aspartame. Donald Rumsfeld's cash cow for Searle." She gave a little half smile without looking up. "You should really know about excitotoxins. The side effects are amazing. Like mad cow but faster. Turns your brain to mush and fumes. The shit's illegal in Europe but Americans can't say no. Better a cerebral hemorrhage than cellulite thighs." She raised her eyes and took in the legion of tattooed Hollywood creatives. Wallet chains clanked on chairs when they got up to plug in their Macs, grab more coffee, or talk out a scene. Inked up as they were—and they were all inked up—only Nora had that German shepherd, baring its fangs. Daddy's girl. That was Nora's and Nora's alone. I watched her watching them until she suddenly turned to me and said, "What do you make of this scene, anyway?"

"Are you crazy?" I took a scalding gulp. "Living in Echo Park, banging out cool-ass webcasts, maybe being in a band?" I let my fingers lightly drag across my mouth, as if touching the great delight of the life I was badly describing. "Wiping soy foam from your near-beard after a sunset latte . . ."

"Is somebody just a little judgmental?"

Ooof! She was right. Who the fuck was I? King of Anal Leakage? In this world of alienation, was my dirty secret that I just wanted to belong? To be part of a tribe. Corny McCornball. The problem is that the junkie tribe is a whole other category. Even though, here in Echo Park (gentrified gang-land, more or less) I now owned the requisite face fur, my people were fiends, not hipsters. I could have been pigment-free at an albino-convention. It wouldn't have mattered. This was Hollywood. These people wanted to be "in the room." I never set foot in a room I did not want to crawl out of immediately. Because, call me sentimental, just being human feels like a front when what you are is a two-legged need machine.

But hey! The great thing about being a junkie? (Or a degenerate gambler, or drunk, etc.) It shrunk ambition down to manageable doses. Heroin made for mindful and effective ego-management. "*God, just let me get through the next five minutes. . . . God, don't let the fucking security guard wake up. . . . God, just don't let that skeek with face sabs have* AIDS. The problem now—heading into the coffee shop (which actually seemed pretty cool, half inside counter, half metal tables on a fly-plagued patio)—was that I was low on junk. Which has its own strange side effect: unwanted awareness. Now erupting like some kind of mind-acne all over my brainpan. So that it hit me, hard: I'd capped a stellar career in side effects with random murder fueled by irrational attraction to a total stranger. A realization, I won't lie, that made me half wish I'd gone the wannabe screenwriter route myself. (And why did I assume the caffeinates were wannabes? Was it too uncomfortable to imagine that other people in the world were actually accomplished and happy? What the fuck?) True, even if you were successful in show business there was always somebody to shit on you. If you worked in SESSIE-land, you shit on yourself. If, you know, you had pretensions.

Anyway. The thirteen keyboarders I walked by might well have been tapping out big money cutting-edge studio plums. But—don't let me get a swelled head—under the glitz, what these young successes really craved was some quality high basic-cable rotation, like, say, my nonstop Crohn's disease and adult diaper patter. Maybe it wasn't as cool as a Johnny Depp *Thin Man* remake but my stuff ran at two in the afternoon in Omaha, during *The Ed Show.*

Walk a mile in my veins!

"Lloyd?"

Nora's elbow snapped me out of my shame spiral. "Lloyd! Stop muttering." She plopped her bag on a chair at the far end of the grungy fun-terrace. Through some fly-infested poplins we had a view of the "girlfriend's" place, a powder-blue bungalow up a flight of crumbling concrete steps from the street, flanked by palm stumps.

Nora sat down and knocked back her triple Americano. "Can we get back to excitotoxins? Drink enough Diet Coke during pregnancy and, if you're lucky, your baby's just going to be mildly brain damaged. If you hit the jackpot, new Mommy's going to have the lungs of a retired mineworker. And baby's going to be born with Mermaid Syndrome."

"Mermaid Syndrome? That sounds nice." I was glad to be thinking of anything besides bus station toilet death.

"It's lovely," she said, grabbing my cup of Zoka and slurping half before I even touched it. "Newborns come out with their legs fused, like a mermaid's tail. Hence the name. Oh, and they don't have kidneys, but, come on, do babies need kidneys to be adorable?"

I snatched my coffee back and slammed it. Fair-trade heroin would have done more for my opiate receptors, but I needed something.

"For Christ's sake, why do you know all this?"

Nora ignored my query and pointed through the buggy poplins. "Let's focus, okay? There are ground-level windows, which means there's a basement we can sneak in through if Susie forgets to leave the front door unlocked. I don't like going in the back, because it just looks shady."

"Wait, you've done this before?"

Again, she ignored the question.

"Neighbors notice somebody who's walking around the back of a house instead of knocking on the front door or going straight in. The idea is to look like it's no big deal. We're just popping in for a visit. Nothing to make good citizens suspicious."

"Unless there's screaming, right?"

"Like you do when you're dreaming?"

The thing about Nora, she could say the most vicious things, but there was a matter-of-factness to the delivery that made you think she wasn't being vicious at all. She was just being . . . herself.

I had just finished my second "Zucotti Park": Bruschetta, Gruyère, Tomato, and Green Olive Tapenade—when the Charger pulled in. He had the top down. A roundish ex-jock with a crew cut and a Harry Reems seventies porn stache. His was the same sandy color as the one the Brawny Towel Man used to have, a couple of years before the Koch Brothers purchased Georgia-Pacific. A deal that also snagged them Dixie Cups and Angel Soft toilet paper. *Because even an armadillo is softest on the bottom.* (No, they didn't use that one, either.)

Nora had slipped a Nikon out of her purse and worked the telephoto. "He's *that* guy," she said. I borrowed the camera. Took a picture of her that was really a picture of the little blue bungalow. Though I don't actually know if there was any film in the camera. Holding a Nikon is one way you can stare at something without anybody noticing. Because you are a *PHOTOGRAPHER.* (People see you shooting with an iPhone, you're just somebody shooting pictures with an iPhone.)

"What guy, my newly blond friend?"

She reached out and slapped my bicep. Such as it was. "The guy who rolls up the sleeves on a short-sleeved T-shirt. To make his muscle bigger."

"He could be Brawny Man's little playmate," I said, "Li'l Brawny. Your friend must be thrilled."

"Like I said, she's a professional." Nora shrugged and adjusted her own blond wig. I didn't know if she'd like that I liked the look. She looked at me straight on, in the eye—such directness, in most people disconcerting and rare, was normal for her—and announced in a voice throatier than usual, "When this is over, I want to fuck you till your face collapses."

(I'm a sucker for romance.)

Nora took back the camera. Then I paid and dropped my usual inappropriately big please-love-me-because-I-hate-myself tip. Even though it was just a take-your-bagel-to-the-table kind of place. If the bill was ten, I liked to tip five. Even if all I had was eleven. There's a logic to this, but who wants to hear it?

Not Nora, apparently. Making sure no one was looking, she scissored two fingers into the tip jar, removed the five I'd just dropped in, and replaced it with a single. "Your heart's in the right place, but we don't want them to remember us."

Then she slipped a fork up her sleeve and off we went. No one looked up from their Final Drafts.

TWENTY-THREE

Burned Baby Toys

The deputy had found a spot right in front of the blue house, right behind a Prius. We ambled toward it, across the street. The Prius was the same color as Harold's. "Wait," I said, "is that ours?"

"Not yet," Nora replied.

Stress, as always, made me a tad addled.

Nora pulled out a compact—that was a first—and checked her lipstick. But really she was looking behind us.

"Nothing suspicious," she said, dabbing away.

"What's suspicious is he got a spot right in front of his house. We had to drive up and down five times and we're still half on red. It's almost like somebody was waiting, just so they could pull out before he pulled in."

"Lloyd." She stopped in the middle of the street to stare at me. Her expression one of pained compassion. The kind you might give a mentally challenged man who tried to impress you with long division. *Two into two equals November a hundred and five.* "Maybe somebody took care of that," she said gently.

All I could think to say to that was "Jesus, what movie are we in?"

Nora took my arm and smiled a big fake indulgent smile

as we stepped, arm in arm, over the cracked curb toward the fifty or so stairs that wound upward from the street. She spoke through the faux smile, her voice low. "Did you ever think maybe Occupy was a setup?"

"Like Wall Street wanted to call attention to themselves for being white-collar thugs?"

"Like somebody wanted an excuse to crack down. To justify all the armor girdles and bulletproof Plexiglas shields. Everybody thinks it's either *Star Wars* or *Spaceballs*. They miss the iconic subtext."

"Iconic subtext? Watch your step. I think somebody's clocking us from the window. Curtain just closed."

"That's my friend. Closed halfway means living room. Full closed, bedroom." She paused, as if deciding whether to continue or to shut up and just head up the stairs for some afternoon Manson Family action. "It's obvious, once you know. Instead of helmet, face shield, and vest, think hat, lace veil, and fur coat. The whole assemblage is classic femme fatale. Real-life black-and-white. You've got phalanx after phalanx of riot cops tricked out as husband-killing noir heroines. Instead of perfume in atomizers, the ladies have pepper spray."

Here we were, chatting at the lip of the abyss. Well, *another* abyss. They came with such frequency now they'd started to seem like potholes. We stopped by the Prius, talking in the street next to the car after coffee, the way they teach you in the LA handbook.

"So," I said, partly to prolong the conversation, partly to put off going up those steps, knowing that when we came down—if we came down—life would be massively re-twisted, once again. "You're saying everybody screaming about the police being paramilitary is missing the point? They're not fascist puppets, they're militarized transvestites. You're serious about this?"

"Not completely. But read *Vineland*. Thomas Pynchon thought the whole counterculture was cooked up by Nixon, so that Quaker drunk could have an excuse for a domestic crackdown."

"Thomas Pynchon? You've read Thomas Pynchon?"

"Let's just go, okay?" Nora wiped a brown wisp of hair that had drifted south, from under her wig. I saw the fork still lodged up her sleeve. No doubt she had other things up there. Metaphorically and otherwise. Or maybe it was just silverware. For all I knew she was planning a picnic. Before I could freak myself out any further, she discreetly handed me the plastic gloves and we headed up the stairs, careful not to turn our ankles in the weed-cracked concrete. Taggers had tagged the tree stump.

The house was a classic run-to-shit LA bungalow. Rusty porch swing, sagging chaise lounge. A blue recycling bin spilled empty Bud cans and Domino's boxes. Approaching the door, we heard the sounds of what, on the covers of romance novels, used to be called "torrid lovemaking." If part of romance involved screaming "filthy whore" and "cum bucket" from the bed of passion.

A frayed throw rug and lawn furniture graced the living room. But we didn't stop. I followed Nora, who walked into the low-ceilinged bedroom like she'd been rolling up on humping policemen her whole life. "One thing I hate," she whispered as she tossed Bergstresser's balled-up jacket off a Barcalounger and scooped up his Taser, "is a guy who needs to degrade women to get off." With that, we stepped into the bedroom, her friend Susie flipped the deputy sheriff off her stomach, and Nora Tasered his penis.

It happened that fast. The deputy stiffened like a cartoon cat, then curled double as if fried. For a second he stayed fetal, mewling through tears. The women just stared at him. I almost felt sorry for the man. It was awkward. Bergstresser wasn't big so much as bulky, made more so in contrast to Susie, a weed-thin Asian with a pope's hat bouffant that seemed untouched by the action.

The deputy's eyes appealed to me, as the other male in the room. "Scum," Nora muttered, and I felt both women daring me to offer guy-to-guy succor. I resisted the urge, but will not deny a sympathetic squeeze at the law enforcer's high-pitched squeals.

I didn't realize, before this, that Tasers could make you bleed. At least they made a penis bleed. Bergstresser, naked, was just another white man, in his case your basic jock-run-to-seed with a Drill Instructor vibe that played too old for middle-aged paunch. The man's fear-shriveled organ. (In that condition, you couldn't call it his *manhood* or maybe you could. It was more like Porky Pig's tail. Freshly shellacked.

"Let's do pepper spray," Susie said. There seemed no great affection between her and my new life partner. Just two professionals being professional. No small talk. That or they were longtime lesbian lovers, and I was no more than a patsy in some homicidal eroto-political getaway. God knows what they'd do to me! I was as aroused as I was terrified. (Pretty much the norm with Nora, even solo.)

Nora stepped back to let Susie, walking and putting her

jeans on at the same time, get by her. Why were all the women I ever met experts at sprinting and dressing?

"Probably good you just get out of here," Nora said. Susie scowled, saying nothing. Just hopped and shimmied her feet through the jeans into her no-logo Cons—Converse All-Stars with the insignia ripped out. (Which, I admit, I didn't quite get—since the brand was completely recognizable as what it was, even without the branding. What would Naomi Klein make of it? The *No Logo* logo. Unless that was the point: so you could have your consumer props and reject them too. As long as the shoes were stolen, you weren't technically contributing to sweatshop culture. Now that Chuck Taylors were being manufactured by Chinese wage slaves who had never heard of Chuck Taylor.)

Susie's ribs showed through a baby tee, under non-augmented breasts. A contrast to Nora, who was so politically on point it was hard to imagine how she would have decided to go mega-rack. Not everybody starts out radicalized. Even "Cracker Barrel" Ed Schultz was a hard-charging right-wing radio host until 1998. Now he's a backbone of MSNBC and a progressive Rush Limbaugh body double. Miracles abound!

Reassembled, Susie tugged on polyurethane gloves and bent over Bergstresser's pale, sweaty paunch. Dazed now, the man's mewling took on a babylike quality, like a nervous infant dreaming of sweet mommy milk. Everything about him was pink as opossum skin. Not that I'm some country boy: possums hang around under houses in LA like grubs under rocks. And surface at night. Sometimes I'd hear them on the porch, clawing at the screen. The ones I'd seen never played dead. Perhaps they were too intrigued with the sight of me, playing alive.

Holding her breath, Susie removed the barbs from the deputy's bleeding organ and then wound the wires back into the Taser Nora still held in her hand.

That's when I saw the hardware on the floor, under Bergstresser's pants. "Don't tell me the guy wears his Death Star gear around the house?"

"That's not his, it's mine," Susie said.

"What, you hang out at a police supply store?"

"Yeah, it's called Amazon." She held up each item as she ID'd it. "MTW-800, military-grade black stun gun 6.8 million volts, rechargeable with flashlight, $28.99. NYPD tactical-support SWAT vest, $19.98. Rothco black VenTec tactical goggles, $9.89. Schampa CoolSkin balaclava, $6.98 used. Tactical SWAT helmet, $9. Everything you need to get your domestic paramilitary on. The sick fuck probably never had to leave his house."

Susie and Nora exchanged some kind of private smile. Susie licked her lips like a hammy porn star, but Nora ignored that, too. She was all business. "Leave me the party gear" was all she said.

Susie smirked. "*Mais oui*, bitch."

I had no idea of the history between these two. And I had no idea how to ask. I didn't know Nora well enough for anything about her to be called secret. All I knew about her was what she told me. Nora seemed to keep her history, as she did her personality, on a need-to-know basis. Being a habitual, unregenerate babbler, this was a trait I admired mightily. I myself had become a habitual spritzer of personal history, a boundary-blind serial confessor, in the manner of those who've stumbled out of (or into) lives of addiction, gabbing with others of their ilk, transforming every exchange, in or out of twelve-step meetings, into some competitive bout of one-downmanship.

My logorrhea made me nervous. So did global warming, and I didn't do much about that, either.

(In every apartment, home, or cell I've ever occupied, I had the same message to myself taped up over some sink: "SHUT UP ABOUT IT.")

What had I done in the bus station? What was I doing now? Over the years, in my capacity as SESSIE, I had found myself reading books of quotes and epigrams. "Self-delusion is the key to happiness." —Voltaire. That kind of thing. I kept them in the bathroom. (Bathrooms, for a junkie, are like church.) These comprised a kind of insight-lite, unearned wisdom in ADD-friendly chunks. Tweet-sized, it turned out.

Standing there—in a strange house, with a strange woman, watching her torment a strange man who, it now occurred to me, might not even be who we thought he was—it further occurred to me, *This was my life.* I heard skittering under the wooden floorboards and hoped it might be opossums. The babies were adorable. Cuter, for my money, than baby raccoons. Though they were probably rats.

Man! The only pictures I'd seen of the deputy sheriff, he had his face mask on. (Who knew how cute he was?) Which prompted me to mull on yet another gem from my toilet-side *Book of Wise Quotations*: "Murder is born of love, and love attains its greatest intensity in murder." Attributed to Hemingway. By way of Werner Herzog? I couldn't remember. They were both, in their way, heroic confections. The kind of people you want to believe in. Them being them makes us feel better about being us.

Though I'd spent more lost hours curled up with *Morning Joe* than *For Whom the Bell Tolls.* A book, if you know a bit about Hemingway, that always seemed kind of stagey. *Manly mannish.* The Papa movie I want to see is the one about his third son, Gregory, a she-male who—legend has it—bled out in a woman's jail in Florida after a sex-change operation, wearing a party dress. By some accounts he'd actually changed his name to Gloria. Just so he could get back at Daddy when he died. Who wouldn't?

TWENTY-FOUR

Taser Happy

How to put this? I began to love everything I didn't know about Nora; in my experience, the second, deeper phase of, really, pardon my melodrama, "falling for somebody." Loving the things that don't add up, the missing years, the hinky bits. Which, if you are a stable, non-turmoil-driven type of human, makes no sense. Is actually *disturbing*. But you didn't see my dream-date rejigger that Taser gun. Like a pro. See, there are so many things to be addicted to, why pretend you are addicted to dope? Come on! Why be so limiting? What dope fiends are really strung out on are situations. Generally, bad ones. Painful ones. Ones that, with no solutions that aren't awful, can only be endured. And only with heroin. Create the need, supply the solution. That way dope is not just a habit. It's a survival tool . . . Then again, maybe the core addiction is talking about addiction. Narco-narcissism. A habit that's no fun for anybody.

After Susie shuffled off, Nora opened up about the niceties of Tasering. "Each time you fire, you have to wind up and repack the electrode wires. That's the downside, and you have to stick in a new gas cartridge each time." In another era she might have been describing how to bake a cherry pie. But not in this one.

Just then the deputy sheriff started to make noise. He'd been still, aside from his nasal mewling. I'd forgotten he was any more than furniture until Nora barked at him. "Shut it, pig-ass!" Then, brightening, she continued: "Susie left her panties."

I hadn't noticed, what with the armory of Amazon paramilitary accessories on hand to admire. (At what point, pardon my sidetrack, had civilization decided to sell face-scorching chemical sprays in the same venue as organic baby powder? How did the world get so wonderful so fast?) Nora shoved the noticeably damp skimpies in the deputy's mouth and then stepped back to Taser him again.

"I know, I know," she said. "Theoretically, I should be hitting him with gas canisters. Poetic justice. But gas canisters have a nasty habit of releasing gas. Not so great in a small room. So I went with Taser."

"Nora," I said, hearing how ridiculous the question sounded even as I uttered it, "you're not really just a ripped-off greeting card writer, are you?"

"Is anybody just one thing? I got the idea at Occupy."

"You're telling me you didn't get the idea until we got to LA? That wasn't your plan all along?"

"I'm not telling you anything. You're hearing things."

She was right. What I was hearing was that I had somehow ended up with a mysterious junkie waif with iffy greeting card credentials who might have been black ops. What were the odds?

"Anyway," Nora said, "I still have something I have to do. I mean, the main thing."

"What's that again?"

Changing the subject, she read from a square of print stamped on the butt of the Taser. "The purpose of the non-lethal weapon is not to inflict pain; it's to avoid confrontation." I restrained myself from saying I liked the writer's style. Another doomed DeLillo with a day job.

"Mission accomplished." Nora aimed me one of those dark half smirks that, for her, passed as a smile. Then she slipped out the fork she'd been keeping up her sleeve, stretched toward the cop, and planted it in his ribs. "Okay, he's done."

I thought about the coffee shop across the street. Imagined the legions of writers, paid and otherwise, who'd never even been bitch-slapped and were banging out action movies, thrillers, mysteries, violent crime fantasies of every stripe. Yet here was real-life terror: not just the muffled screams, soilage, and writhing of the shocked and re-shocked policeman, but the screaming in my own heart—which always beat faster the less heroin it had been fed—while I watched, and wondered, as the bard said, *What the fuck?*

Listen. Some people play sports and some people watch them. We grow up, here in America, watching death. Our favorite form of recreation. Death-watching. Violence-savoring. All Nora and I had done was turn professional. Join the big leagues.

I closed my eyes, and when I opened them the dark wood grain in the walls had begun to quiver. Nora shoved the panties deeper in the deputy's mouth and zapped him again, on his testicles. This time, mysteriously, there was no blood, just instant, jellyfish-like puff. He breathed through his nose with what sounded like tremendous effort.

"Did you know octopi express mood by changing color?"

"Yeah," I said, my voice astonishingly normal, at least to me. "It's a hormonal thing."

"I don't think this is hormones," she said, raising a hot pink faux-lighter in front of her and spraying an orange stream in the deputy's open mouth. The pepper juice hit his gums with a soft sizzle.

This time I had to pull away. If he sneezed we'd both go blind.

Later, when Officer Pike went skunk and sprayed non-violent protestors at UC Davis, I remembered Nora's prescient spritz. At the time, all I said was "Jesus, baby, you're giving him the combo platter."

Nora wiped her eyes. "Tasers are more nineties. Like billy clubs. Rodney King shit. But I'm sentimental. And don't call me baby."

"My bad. Do people die with Tasering?"

"Down south. Mostly. Hang on." I loved watching her concentrate, the way she chewed her lip, removing a bushy metallic claw from the deputy's ballooning testicles, rewinding the connector wire. The deputy convulsed briefly, collapsed as if he'd had his plug pulled, then re-convulsed.

I looked away again, talking just to talk. "What do you mean, only down south? You mean, like, in the ball area?"

"Close. I mean in Texas. Some naked freak named Eric Hammock got shocked twenty times by cops in Fort Worth. He died in custody." She fiddled with those bushy claws on the end of the Taser wire. "In South Carolina, Maurice Cunningham was Tased nonstop for two minutes and forty-nine seconds. Died of cardiac arrhythmia. Law enforcement always blames PCP, but the real blame is the Taser. He just lasted that long 'cause of the shit he was on."

I hadn't realized the deputy was listening. That he could even hear. His face went slack, then he seized, then he went slack again. His pube hair had stopped smoking and he'd wet himself. He smelled like a burned baby toy.

"Pork roast," Nora said, with no humor whatsoever.

After that we just stood there. Finally Nora broke the silence. "Sometimes I want a cigarette."

I grunted agreement. I really wanted to ask how she'd become a Taser pro. But it seemed, I don't know, wrong to keep chatting. Nora leaned over the deputy's face and whispered, "I don't want to talk about that. What I want to talk about . . . what I want to know? If I put a Taser to your eye, told you I'd pull the trigger unless you got on your fucking knees and sucked my partner off . . . what do you think you'd do?"

Another eternal question.

But was it *political*?

The deputy sheriff writhed. He moved only his head as Nora eased him off the bed. Onto the floor. Giving him the chance to crawl.

"All right, then, deputy, do a knee-walk." To my horror, he started toward me. A lost manatee. Outside, an ice cream truck tinkled. The street echoed with a tinny, brain-scraping "To Dream the Impossible Dream." Followed, inexplicably, by "Take Me Out to the Ball Game."

"Now who's the filthy whore?" Nora said. "Does that turn

you on, Officer? Does it? Pussy-ass bitch! You like hearing that?"

The little yelps from his throat had gone all Blue Angel-y. I'd begun to worry about neighbors. "We have to get out of here. Somebody's bound to, I don't know . . . We should probably—"

"Right," Nora said. "We should dress him."

"Dress him?"

She nodded toward the stack of paramilitary gear. "Technically, you'd say accessorize. I'm not talking about clothes."

As far as I was concerned, the whole situation had begun to curdle. "Nora, look at the guy, okay? His balls are the size of grapefruits. I can't tell if he's crying or his eyes are bleeding. You really want to—"

A knock on the back door stopped my whinging. "Hold that thought," Nora said.

"You're leaving?"

I was already paranoid. Now my paranoia had a scenario. The thought that she might leave and I'd be caught flat-footed with a sack-damaged cop and a Taser in my hand was more than I could handle.

Nora saw the look in my eyes and stopped. "Jesus-Pesus, relax, would you? We're almost done."

"We're going to have to move the body." I tried to keep my voice even. But my tongue got sockish, the socky feeling accompanied by sensations of dread and suicidal ideation. *I react, therefore I am.* I was so weirdly crazy about this person—but she scared the living piss out of me. At what point had true love become indistinguishable from a death wish? More importantly, when would I stop repeating the question?

"More like manipulate than move," Nora said. Then she corrected herself, playing idly with the officer's left ear. "Just help me pose him."

"*What?*"

She put a finger to her lips—the one that just touched the riot cop's scarlet lobe. She sniffed and twisted her lips up in calculation, like a sommelier putting on a performance. "Wait a minute . . ."

"Now what?"

I thought she was going to say something, make a pronouncement. Instead she left the room. Marched to the front door, singing like a housewife in a fifties TV show. "Coming!"

Alone with our captive, I felt a sudden sense of connection. We were, after all, two guys. The bond of manhood, such as it was.

For no reason beyond not wanting to keep staring at the deputy, I kneeled and picked his pants off the floor. Felt for the wallet. I saw him flinch. Doesn't matter if you're wide-eyed or in the depths of a shock-induced fear coma. You see somebody going through your shit, you react.

"Don't worry," I said, "I'm not going to steal your plastic and charge some dope rims." I thought of the Prius. "On my car it wouldn't matter."

What I did, in fact, was check out his driver's license and his Fraternal Order of Police card. Both of which bore the name Oswald Jesus Fernando Pessoa. Confirming the suspicions I couldn't admit I had.

"Jesus, you're not even *him* . . ."

Not only was our fried friend not from Oakland, he wasn't even a real cop. He was LATP. Los Angeles Transit Police.

But I couldn't focus on that. Couldn't quell the stomach-clutching suspicion that, for the second time, I let myself be lured into a murder or, in this case, at least a Guantánamo-esque kidnapping. (Could you call it kidnapping when you didn't take the victim anywhere? Is there a different name for that? Forced babysitting, with a side of imprisonment and torture? *Oh man.*)

I could feel the panic flip a switch in my mind. Heard my brain click into Pacifica Radio late-night discussion mode. Strangely, I never thought philosophically, except in panic situations, when reality was so brain-explodingly fucked that my mind began broadcasting some mash-up of Noam Chomsky, Alan Watts, and Gary Null, product of the countless nights I'd staggered through insomnia, letting KPFK in LA, WBAI in New York, or KPFA in San Francisco marinate my waking nightmares. Listen, it's Alan Watts: *Are men merely two-legged empires, dumb with exceptionalism and brute entitlement? Or are they fury-driven juntas and jihads, mobile terrorist cliques intent on destroying everyone who isn't them? Is self-hate just narcissism with its pants on backwards? Or is narcissism just fascism made personal?*

Watts liked to say he was a Buddhist who liked double martinis. Enough gin and anybody could be one with humanity.

TWENTY-FIVE

Sunshine and Buttercups

Without heroin, even sunshine and buttercups felt oppressive. And this—where I was now—was hardly buttercuppish.

Voices from the next room brought me back, over the muffled groaning of the shocked drooler in front of me; I felt the damp puke-inducing suction of my hand over his mouth. His lips pressed into my palm like pallid suckerfish. I thought my stomach was going to suicide out of my face . . . Have you ever been alone with a man you've just seen shot with something? Who isn't dead but isn't moving much? Who's just . . . sort of . . . *there*?

Nora popped back into the bedroom, waving a pamphlet. "Jehovah's Witnesses, look!" She read from the cover. "'All Suffering Soon to End.' I don't know about you, but *I* feel better!"

She handed me the pamphlet. Cartoon seekers stared earnestly off the cover, walking into a bounteous cartoon valley. "I could have talked to those kids all day. I love their suits. But we've got work to do!"

What kind of woman could savage a man with 150,000

volts, then turn around and talk theology with thin-tied visitors, come to make known the wonder of Jehovah's love?

My kind, apparently.

It all happened fast after that. I managed to get the tactical vest, riot helmet, and utility belt onto the weirdly buff but porcine naked body. Our guest did not seem to spare himself pies or barbells. I had to tell Nora that he might not even be Bergstresser after all. That, in fact, his name was probably Pessoa. But as soon as I opened my mouth, Nora cut me off. "Can you smell those scorched pubes?"

Hoping she wouldn't say "I love the smell of scorched pubes in the morning," I mumbled noncommittally, "Not really."

Nora sniffed again. Instead of quoting Coppola, she said, "Well *I* can. I wouldn't get near that pus nest without a Neosporin bath. Unfortunately all I have on me is Purell."

"That's okay." I played my manly card. "Purell is like rubbing penicillin on your hand. It doesn't actually do what you think it does."

"It covers the smell better than penicillin."

I couldn't argue with that.

Nora helped me yank the jumbo baloney arms and legs through the straps of his bulletproof vest. Our friend was not exactly lively, but he wasn't catatonic, either.

"He may be in a shame coma," I said. "I think I've seen that on *Law & Order*."

"You watch that crap?"

"Just for the commercials," I lied. Why tell her I needed to go numb sometimes, when drugs weren't enough? With enough narcotics, you could learn things from Sam Waterston's eyebrows.

Another fun fact! A while back, some DIY-ers attempted to Taser themselves, following the Internet-touted belief that it was a kind of at-home ECT. Do-it-yourself electroshock. For those seeking all the well-known benefits: relief from severe depression and a sense of baseless and short-term-memory-challenged well-being. Ironically, electroshock's possible side effects were small potatoes compared to what could happen on its pharmaceutical cousins. What they used to call "chemical chains": your stelazine, your thorazine, all the heavy 'zines.

There was some power drooling, involuntary twitches in hands and feet, even the odd bladder control adjustment—but no suicidal ideation, no sudden anger. (And if drooling, twitching, and pissing yourself don't make you suicidal, then you know you're cured.)

I realized I was babbling, but she seemed interested.

"I swear, if somebody had the money, I'd advise them to invest in an infomercial and sell home ECT kits."

Nora raised her eyes from our friend on the floor. She adjusted her wig and dabbed foam from his mouth with Susie's panties, after she had yanked them out of it.

"You're serious?"

"Why not? I once did a promo for an electroshock clinic. It was a testimonial from a 'satisfied customer' on the other end of the treatment."

"A real person?"

"Well, sort of. I lined up a perky 'actor-impersonator' type. She had that sort of early Goldie Hawn fizz." I made my voice girly and gave her a sample: "*I won't lie, I thought ECT was just something from* The Snake Pit, *but then I heard my sister-in-law say it worked for her . . . Now I feel like life can be joyful again. Thank you, Dr. Mason!* Then her kids come on, four, five, and six, all blond, in matching sweaters and holding hands. They chime in, in unison: *Thank you, Dr. Mason, for giving us back our mommy.* Then a big hug, and out. Cute as hell. Mason was the crook who ran the place. The kicker is, he wasn't even a doctor."

"Even if he was, I can't believe any program would want electroshock as a sponsor."

"Right you are. None did. The fucker's check bounced, too. He tried to pay me off in Ultrams, these non-opiate painkillers they sell online, which actually *are* opiates, just really shitty ones, so I just took his car. Bent fuck like that, he's not going to go to the authorities."

When we were done paramilitarizing our friend in law enforcement, Nora tapped me on the shoulder, and when I turned just clamped her hands on my shoulders and her mouth on my lips. Pressing hard. I was so far from thinking about sex at that moment . . . but at the same time, in a room with Nora, I was never *not* thinking about sex.

I had kind of killed for this woman. Not kind of—who am I kidding?—I'd offed a man in a public toilet. (Looks good on any résumé.) And now we were in a room where the only panting was coming from a riot-geared nude law enforcer.

But what did I know? Once again, I wanted to say something, that I'd seen the wrong name on the cop's driver's license. But before I could, there was that clamp action. Mouth to mouth. I needed to say something anyway. It was eating at me.

"Nora, listen . . ." The words jerked up hot in my throat and out of my mouth. Projectile verbiage. "We need to talk." How many times had I heard that from a woman and cringed? (Whether in real life or on film, it's never good.) An Obama bobblehead by the bed looked at me like it knew everything. A judgmental bobblehead.

"Throw me down," Nora croaked.

"What?" (You never know when lust will strike. It's like epilepsy.)

"Throw you down where? Here?"

By way of answer, Nora yanked her T-shirt over her head. She raised her arms, exposing half-moons of sweat. For some reason I had to fight the urge to jam my face in her armpit. Good fucking God, was everything a drug when you didn't have drugs? I wanted to breathe her fumes like they were carbon monoxide coming out of a '73 Camaro and I was in a garage trying to off myself. In a *good* way. Sometimes—and I don't know why this is—you can be strung out like the proverbial lab rat, and not have heroin for a while, and not even notice. Then, just when you think you're out of the woods, you get the first twinges, the first skrank in the back of your neck. The first judder in the bowels. At which point you'd shoot shoe polish in your eyes, if it brought relief—or plunge your face into the armpit of a woman you were insanely crazy about. Just because you could. And it might block out the looming pain. Don't ask me to make sense. It was all just happening.

"Come on, damn it!"

Nora stripped fast, inches in front of me. I kept glancing over her bony shoulder at the pie-eyed "policeman" on the bed. He'd graduated from grasps to grunts. The ascent of man. I didn't want to look at him. I didn't want to think about him. Mostly I didn't want to inhale him. He'd had some kind of *release*. (Did I mention this already? It's not something you forget.) It smelled like he'd shit beef starch—another reason I took the Nora underarm plunge. I'd never done one before. (I've since learned it's a "Euro thing." Your Euros love their odors.) But at that moment, surrounded by heinous sensory input, my face did my thinking for me. The last image to scrape my eyeballs was my own mouth, open wide, like a thirsty dog's, reflected in the black Plexiglas of the deputy's riot helmet. Then blackness. Not damp, dank, pungent blackness, like you might expect. More air freshenery. Aluminum-silicate dry and deodorized, chemically floral blackness. Not that Nora was particularly hygienic, but she used five deodorants, all packed—in retrospect—with enough aluminum to make her brain crunchy. (I'd seen on the Discovery Channel how, when they did autopsies on the brains of dementia sufferers, the scalpel literally scraped metal aluminum bits. Cerebral fallout from a lifetime of Reynolds Wrap, aluminum pots and pans, and the aforementioned super-dry deodorants. They might have had crunch-brain, but damn it, they smelled like Glade!)

Nora grabbed me by an ear and yanked my head out of her pit.

I raised my eyes and saw she wasn't looking at me. She was staring past me, at the mirror, while the policeman quivered sporadically.

She squeezed my ear in one hand while the other snaked between her legs. What I saw, when I think about it, stuns me to this day. But wait . . .

That boyish waist, those enormous breasts, her pale, blue-veined sweat-shiny eggshell skin, and that one double nipple-ringed nipple. *Why two-in-one?* I wanted to ask, but didn't. I still wanted to ask about the German shepherd ink, too. The daddy thing. But not now. Never *now.*

Our captive stayed propped up, limp, against the bare double mattress. Over the blond pouf of her wig my eyes caught his. His look of dumb animal pain hit me like some strange passion-accelerant. I grabbed Nora and half pushed, half fell over the scrote-scorched victim, onto the bed above him.

With her left hand, just the forefinger, Nora tugged up the top of her slit, exposing a purply clitoris so large I wondered if she might be a hermaphrodite. It was shocking, hot, and *National Geographic*–worthy all at once. With her right hand, she began slapping the marshmallowy protuberance, as if it had disobeyed her, accompanying each smack with a moan so stark and personal I felt like I was eavesdropping.

To keep my skull from imploding, I stared away from Nora, to the law enforcer. His Plexiglas visor was raised, and as I locked into his cowlike eyes, I felt myself flooded with a weird affection. Not just for him, but for the squawking grackles outside, for the irritating one-song warble of the ice cream truck, for the whorls in the bedroom wood, which formed eyeballs that regarded me like they knew things . . . Just wanting Nora—wanting something that wasn't a drug—was such a novelty, such a world-changingly unlikely circumstance, I was afraid to breathe for fear it would all turn out to be some near-death hallucination. (A junkie, on some level, lives his whole life as a near-death experience.) But I looked again, and it was real.

Biting her lip, Nora stopped slapping herself and grabbed my hand, exposing herself completely, using me to rub her slick SeaWorld clitoris. When she mumbled, I knew she wasn't speaking to me, and I didn't care. I don't even know how I ended up inside her. Somehow I just was. Only—how to say this?—it did not feel like fucking so much as swimming. I'd never encountered a hole so capacious. She began touching herself again, yanking her sex upward, squeezing her yawning slit tight as she alternately thrummed her circus clit and tugged it with abandon. When I started to actually move, she whispered huskily, "Don't!" She just wanted me to hold still while she worked herself around and above me, her intensity and focus more beautifully obscene than whatever frantic faster-harder I'd imagined. Just holding there, not moving at all, scorched me more than anything in my life. And when I thought I couldn't get harder, Nora let go of herself, rubbed her sex-soaked hand in my face, smelling faintly of dirty soy sauce and iron, then reared back and, with no warning whatsoever, reached past me and backhanded the semicomatose cop across the face. And did it again. We went from zero to cop-smacking and fucking at the same time. The whole thing—I don't know if it even counted as sex. It was some other dimension, I sensed, that could have gone on with me or without me. I was along for the ride. Which, had I had an ego, might have stung it. But ego was gone. There was a sizzling in the back of my skull. Until, in a voice that might have belonged to a talking animal, Nora screamed, "*Yes-s-s! . . .*" and the officer, or whoever he was, made a noise like a man swallowing a can opener, pitched forward, spat blood on both of us, and died.

After that, things got strange.

Book Four

In my fits of optimism,
I remind myself that my
life has been a hell, *my*
hell, a hell to my taste.

E. M. CIORAN

TWENTY-SIX

Mrs. Santa Claus Has This to Say About Fellatio

"We love death!" was the first thing that Beatrice Ender, the executive in charge of *CSI Vegas* said to me. "But it has to be creative!"

She certainly had a creative beehive—the likes of which I hadn't seen since my days as a young pornster in the *Hustler* mailroom, where Ohio blue hairs stuffed dildos into plain brown boxes for shipment to eager consumers. (Neighbor ladies, where I grew up, used to say, "Guess who just got their hair did!") Combined with a largish frame, apple cheeks, and contagious good humor, her do also made her a ringer for Edie the Egg Lady from *Pink Flamingos*. Except, of course, that Bea wore a smart pantsuit, sat at a desk, and probably banked a million a year, while Edie occupied a playpen in nothing more than fat-biting girdle and triple-F brassiere, and lived for her eggies.

Thanks, apparently, to Harold's ridiculous restless-knee buildup, I was invited to make the drive up the 5 to Santa

Clarita Studios. Nora insisted she wanted to come with. We didn't talk much on the way up. Instead, we listened to Rush Limbaugh, with whom she was slightly obsessed. "I mean, dope fiends used to be cool, right? Lenny fucking Bruce? Billie fucking Holiday? Chet? Keith? Bela Lugosi? Lassie?"

"Lassie?"

"You didn't know? The poor pup needed a bang of cortisone, coke, and morphine before every show. She was like a little Judy Garland. After two seasons she OD'd and they had to get a different collie. But fucking *Limbaugh*?" She sighed and sniffed. Wiped her nose. Somebody needed her medicine. "That douche bag should have his junkie license revoked."

"Are you serious?"

"What? You like Rush? You're a dittohead?"

"No, I mean about Lassie."

"Fuck yeah. You ever hear of the Tour de France? In the fifties, before Lance Armstrong and doping and all that crap, there was even a popular needle cocktail for American riders called *la Lassie*. The recipe showed up in all the gossip magazines."

When we arrived on the Santa Clarita lot, Nora announced that the air smelled like fat lady's feet. When I didn't respond—what was there to say?—she added, defensively, that she wasn't being "sizeist," she just knew the smell, because her grandmother used to beat her with her Indian moccasin, then shove it in her mouth for "sassing off." "Tasted like White Shoulders and cat piss."

"Nice."

I have to admit, I was relieved when Nora said she'd wait

in the car while I went about my business. “I’ve got AC and my book,” she said, holding up her copy of *Phoolan Devi, Bandit Queen of India*. Her new heroine.

Minutes later I was ushered in to meet Beatrice by a fawning intern in a plaid wool shirt with Necco-Wafer-sized tribal earholes. Leaving Nora sitting there left me with a mild tingle of dread, but I had other concerns. Even though he had insisted, had sworn up and down, I still felt compelled to ask Harold, the last time I saw him upright (Mexican tar takes a toll), if I could really talk up the jiggly leg syndrome, if he had really laid some track. He’d be pissed about the car, but a balloon of chiba would make him un-pissed pretty fast.

I hardly felt comfortable claiming credit for an entire disease financed and generated by Big Pharma. Then again, this was show business, and credit was a malleable concept. Somehow, having a disease under your belt felt like a real plus, *CSI*-wise, even if it wasn’t one that couldn’t actually kill you—unless you restlessly kicked somebody who kicked you back, perhaps in the throat, crushing your larynx and impeding your ability to breathe until you died writhing on the linoleum like a goldfish plucked out of the bowl and dropped by a sadistic five-year-old. Harold, who claimed he knew the ins and outs of the TV world—due to some sketchy service in the consultant trenches, and of course his Bruckheimer connect—suggested I go even further. Harold suggested I bring up my fetish days. Back in the dawn of the 1-900 era, I had a gig as fetish wrangler, cooking up come-on ads to entice men to shell out for phone sex. (*Two dollars for the first two minutes, five dollars every minute after.*) The numbers were part of the draw. 1-900-*NUN-LOVE*, etc. . . . Creativity will not be thwarted!

People in the business, Harold swore, loved to be in a room with somebody who'd actually done something, somebody who'd "been there," somebody "real," somebody who'd even sat next to somebody real. For a while, in the nineties, writers started getting fake jail tattoos. Spiderwebbed elbows, inked-on teardrops, a broken line around the neck with "CUT HERE" Gothed in beneath. Nothing better, in a meeting, then being able to say you'd been "down." Everything that would have screwed you for a job as bank teller could get you hired on a show.)

Much to my surprise, Harold was kind of right. The friendly exec producer and I hit it off. During the interview, Bea was fascinated by my past. In spite of myself, I went on to tell her about my stint doing "erotic" copy, banging out fake sex letters for *Penthouse* Forum: *Dear* Penthouse, *One day, when my girlfriend and I were hiking, my face got stuck in a chain-link fence and my pants came off. Next thing I know, Cathy picked up this long stick* . . . and so on.

Porn and mayhem were subjects Bea warmed to. At first it was strange, say, talking vaginal chainsaw crimes with this sweet, rosy-cheeked older lady. Before our chat, I had no idea how sexist—or classist—I apparently was. But why shouldn't Mrs. Claus be able to chat about fellatio?

"What does it say," Beatrice wondered, after we'd polished off a pot of green tea and a tray of chocolate rugelach,"that our entertainment is so murder-centric? Murder *is* our prime-time porn. What you were doing was no different than what we do—just a matter of adjectives. There has to be a story, of course. But the dirty little secret is, people love seeing other people die. Blood spatter is the new money shot. That's why *Dexter* is so hot. I mean, we always react with horror to the idea of Aztecs killing a virgin, slicing her heart out, and offering it to the gods, but what do *we* do, show after show? We just have more advanced technology—and different gods—but that's not necessarily progress."

What could I do but agree? The great thing about heroin is that it's a great enthusiasm generator. So that, when Bea leaned forward over her desk, revealing her ample senior gal cleavage, and asked if I had any "special experiences, stuff that might make a good episode," I didn't hesitate. I said, "You bet!" I said, "Absolutely!" I said," I've got a ton of shit!"

"Good shit?" I think it tickled her, talking this way.

"Well," I said, excited myself to hear what was going to come out of my mouth next, "how about Adult Babies?"

"Excuse me?"

"You know, infantilism." It was her resemblance to Edie the Egg Lady that inspired the idea, but I thought it better not to mention it. I adored Edie, but people are funny about comparisons. I once had a girlfriend who told me I reminded her of Michael Richards. I could not have sex with her after that. I kept waiting for her to scream out "Oh, Kramer!" or "Fuck me, Kramer!" Or, as Marlon Brando claimed Ronald Reagan pleaded just before their first tryst (using a different name, of course), "Come on, Kramer, *just put it in an inch!*"

So I didn't mention Edie. But I did find myself, at ten in the morning in the thrumming heart of *CSI* headquarters, expounding on the finer points of manpers, big-boy pacifiers, and milk-play to a woman of a certain age I'd barely known for half an hour. But already wished could have been my mother.

It was the milk-play that got to Bea. She seemed to want to

press me, literally, and—after the rugelach ran out and she had the tribal-eared intern haul in some bear claws—suggested we move to a couch. Bea kept eating, crumbs kept getting stuck to her lip gloss, and I kept sweating in that acrid way you sweat when panic—however distant, however benevolent—begins to take over. It was hard to imagine that she was being flirty. I chose to believe that her chief interest indeed was a potential episode subject. Despite the way our thighs touched on the couch. We were so close I could actually feel Bea's heat. Which had me sweating on the left side of my body, *underneath* the sheen of panic sweat already there. It occurred to me that I was perspiring in two distinct emotional flavors. And I wondered if maybe Grissom could solve a crime with sweat-taste.

Thankfully, my potential employer interrupted my bad idea. "So, you've had some experience, have you?"

"Excuse me?"

"What we need are details, dear."

"Well," I began, keeping my eyes fixed on a photo of Billy Petersen that was glaring down from the wall as if to say, *Where else could you be paid to be creepy*? "There are men who like to be nursed, usually powerful, important types. Their thing is finding women who can, you know, put them in diapers, spank their bottom, breast feed them."

"Breast feed?"

I explained, as best I could. "You've got your drinkers and your stinkers."

Bea's eyes shone, a little glazed. Surely I hallucinated that she had licked the shiny nub of her bear claw before she nibbled it. "Ooh, this is good. Do tell."

"Well, not to get too technical, your drinker's focus is up

top. Mommy's milk. They, you know, suckle. Your stinkers prefer when Mommy goes south. They make a mess, Mommy changes their diaper."

"So . . . they could find a grown man, in a diaper . . ."

"With diaper rash," I threw in, and thought she was going to wet the couch cushion. Bea pressed a button I didn't even see. Tribal Ears padded back in. Stopped in the doorway and snuck a look at me. "Andy, get everybody in here." When Andy padded back out, Bea eased sideways a little more on the sofa. "Lloyd, I think we may have got something delicious here."

Her hand on my thigh was not even surprising.

"You must have had such an interesting life . . ."

In fact, my interesting life was waiting for me back in the Prius. Or so I hoped. I had this sinking feeling Nora would wander off and do something majorly regrettable. But I couldn't think about it. Not then. Intros were made to the staff: three preppy writers who looked like they were about to cry, plus a director who rattled off his name and credits with a sharky glean in his eye—no doubt confusing me with someone who could possibly help him. I went a little overboard elaborating the ins and outs of baby-men. "The big thing is thumb-sucking—look for a groove over the thumbnail!—or, more obviously, a tell-tale reek, from full-time Depends aficionados."

None of the writers said much. The way they stared, I realized they had no idea who I was. A couple of the writers, I realized, must have thought I was some kind of Dirty Diaper Fetishist, a Spokes-Perv, here to plead for some network respect. The third writer seemed weirdly beaten. But when the director, asserting his territory, said the whole thing sounded far-fetched, I dipped into the factoid pile and marched out a few of the ones I'd laid on Bea. I later learned that the Writers Guild allows one "outside writer" a year, and potentially, I was it. Naturally, the director had a girlfriend he wanted to lay the gig on. Everybody wants to look powerful. Especially guys who don't have any power.

Anyway, I was semi-obsessing on Nora, what she was doing back in the car, if she still *was* in the car. I was hoping she hadn't wandered into anything fatal, while at the same time I had to focus on sealing whatever kind of half-ass deal I could come up with here. To my surprise, Bea chimed up before I had to tap dance. "I think Lloyd can bring something fresh. To the show."

It happened so fast, I was almost disappointed I didn't have a chance to talk adult babies again. I was feeling chatty. Maybe everybody likes to be an expert once in a while. But no such luck. Before you could say pervin'-for-dollars, I had a job.

When I went back to the Prius, Nora was gone.

TWENTY-SEVEN

Nasty Klepto

Two hours later, I found Nora in an empty soundstage, sitting by a pile of bloody towels, fondling a discarded Hoover attachment with what looked like a human heart clogged in the business end. (Speaking of Aztecs.) A single spot from a ceiling beam lent her a dramatic, almost Pietà-like intensity.

She waggled the vacuum cleaner tube at me as I approached. "How cool is this?"

"For Christ's sake, it's a prop."

With this she stood up, wrapped the heart in a scrap of towel, and put it in her pocket.

"What isn't, baby?"

We made our way through the lot, past a pair of faux bomb victims moving their face-gauze aside to chow down on tacos. No doubt a special, special episode, Nora said, miming the universal TV announcer guy voice. Nora wanted to stop and grab a bite, but I balked.

"Why not? They can afford it," she said.

"I know they can. But I can't afford for that fucking heart to fall out of your purse. For no apparent reason, they kind of gave me a job. And I don't want to blow it 'cause I showed up with a kleptomaniac."

"Like they'll miss it."

I held her arm lightly—but firmly—as we passed by the food truck.

"You think those are cheap? How do you know they're not using it in the next scene? How do you know the prop master doesn't live for the chance to discover something missing? So everybody can be a suspect and he gets to look like there's a reason he has a fucking job?"

"*Prop master*? It's all sex with you, isn't it?"

I waved to Bea, who saw me passing by with Nora. She motioned us over, but I gave her a little wave and kept going. Then I realized she was waving to the woman behind me, an ex–assistant coroner who had popped her head in during the meeting and introduced herself. I couldn't remember her name. She was the actual forensic expert, a woman who'd been to an actual crime scene. She told a story about finding a woman with a shoe inside her, a Brooks Brothers topsider, and I'd zoned out. I kept walking.

The whole thing with the baby-men and the script I was supposed to write and Bea the Exec Producer's manicured plump but lovely hand on my thigh . . . All I needed was for the fake heart to fall out of Nora's purse. To end up in *CSI* jail. I don't know much about job interviews, but I know it's much easier to look enthusiastic on heroin. Looking responsible is a whole other can of pharmaceuticals. And I did not happen to have them.

We stopped for a second while Nora dug the car keys out of her purse. (Literally a shopping bag, from Vons. She saw Cat

Power carrying one in *Spin*.) The heat in Santa Clarita was so intense it looked like the ground was quivering. I wished I'd worn underwear, but the last time I remember seeing any they were somebody else's, in a Spanish laundromat—Ola, Lavandería!—spinning in a dryer window. Stealing wet clothes from a dryer is the safest way I know to get yourself a fresh wardrobe. Guaranteed clean. Most folks like to stroll outside for a smoke rather than sit there watching their shit spin. Tweakers excepted, of course. Tweakers will sit down in front of a dryer and keep pumping quarters in the slot just because it's deeply entertaining and cheaper than cable. It's what their brain *wants* them to do. (The way crackheads carpet-mine, speed freaks spin dry when they're spun.)

"Can you imagine working here?" Nora said when I finally got her in the car. "All you have to do is think up a bunch of really weird shit and write it down."

"I won't have to think it up. I'll just have to remember it."

"Oooh, listen to you!"

We'd parked in the sun. The seat of the car felt like molten lava. It didn't bother Nora but had me grabbing newspapers off the floor to slide onto the seat and stave off second-degree ass-burn.

That was when I saw a pair of burly guys in tight blue shirts making their way toward us and decided to just start the car.

"Nora, don't turn around. Just stick the heart somewhere nobody can find it."

"What?"

I hadn't noticed the iPod buds in her ears. She didn't have an iPod two minutes ago.

"Nothing," I said, easing up the aisle of parked cars and

pickups, rolling down the hill from Santa Clarita Studios—not, you know, fast; we didn't want to look like people trying to make a getaway after a heist. Just a Normal Couple in a Normal Car so we could head back to the 5, a Normal Freeway. Ideally, unobstructed by authorities. I didn't know if there was a line beyond which studio security couldn't arrest you. It was not exactly like Steve McQueen and Ali McGraw making a run for Mexico in *The Getaway.* All I knew was if you made it a hundred feet from a supermarket, security couldn't touch you.

When we were safely back on surface streets, no one authoritative in the rearview, I started speaking again. "I knew this three-hundred-pound dealer, Mexican cat, who used to dress up in diapers and let his girlfriend use him as a couch. He'd be on hands and knees, pulling balloons of tar out of his socks, while she'd be up there in a polyblend nighty reading *Variety.* I guess she was an actress."

"So . . . the guy had some kind of bowel problem?"

"Of course not. You're missing the point. Homeboy was an adult baby. He liked to suckle *mamá* and wear Depends. But for some reason he also found it relaxing to act like a human end table. Among friends, I mean."

It took a lot to rattle Nora, but she was, in this instance, at least mildly perplexed. "Why are we even talking about this?"

"Because you asked," I said, trying not to grind my teeth while being blown sideways as I passed a double-wide, nearly sideswiping an Exxon truck and hurtling us both into a fiery, Michael Bay inferno. "I have to give them an adult baby treatment."

She just looked at me.

"A treatment. Like an outline. Make up some cool murder stuff, make up some gangster nappy freak, and find a way for the CSIs to solve his murder."

"Then you write the script?"

"Ideally, yeah."

She thought for a moment, rolling the window down and putting her face out of it. "Then maybe we start working."

"On the script?"

"On the murder part."

Did you ever meet somebody who either had no sense of humor or was never serious, you couldn't tell which?

I'm not saying Nora was a liar. I'm saying she didn't always tell the truth.

So, back in Harold's apartment . . . No, wait. I should, I suppose, tell you what happened to Harold. I keep wanting to, but at the same time I don't want to dwell. Part of me just wants to say we now had his credit cards, not to mention his car. Leave it at that. But how we got them probably does bear explaining.

"He's not doing too well" is what Nora said when we walked in and found our junk-friendly host lying facedown in the little place between the bed and the wall. This was a day or four ago. She'd wrinkled her nose and taken off her T-shirt. Indoors, she preferred to go shirtless. "He smells a little dead."

"Harold just does this," I said. "If he were dead, he might smell a little better."

"Then let's trick him out, Mr. Forensics."

"Trick him out how?"

I knew where she was going, but I don't have to tell you I didn't want to go there.

"How do you think? We do him up in diapers and baby bonnet, get some little crack ho in here . . . you know, a real strawberry, make him go goo-goo ga-ga. See how it plays out."

I sat down on the twin bed closest to the door, suddenly tired. Not from driving sixty miles, or pitching to a producer, or stressing over groceries and dope, but from the effort of not thinking about everything I'd done—that *we* had done, Nora and me—the stuff that happened but that we didn't talk about. The effort of suppression is taxing enough, but when it's married to an effort not to admit that you're suppressing anything—to having to deny that you're in denial, so that you can't really admit that you're denying anything, you just, I don't know, banish the shit you don't want to think about from inside your head altogether. It's like holding down the handle on a toilet so the toilet keeps flushing. It doesn't work. At some point, inevitably, even if the handle's down, nothing's flushing. In fact, just the opposite.

But the effort can take it out of you.

While we were arguing—or *I* was arguing—over the wisdom of spending the evening shoplifting Depends and petroleum jelly, not to mention a baby bonnet—assuming we could even find one big enough for a big-boy junkie in the immediate vicinity—Nora stormed into the bathroom and slammed the door.

TWENTY-EIGHT

Super-Nutritious Celebrity Placenta

I checked on Harold—still numb but no longer drooling. Maybe beyond drooling. I didn't want to know. We'd decided to keep him that way, happily semicomatose, until whatever happened happened. Not knowing what else to do, I turned on the TV. I didn't want to watch TV. Who did? But I was in a motel room and there was a television. So I turned it on and, after a bit of fuzz and blur, there was January Jones on *The View* talking about placenta snacks. Made from her newborn baby boy's placenta.

"Animals eat their placenta. Why shouldn't people?"

Whoopi Goldberg made a silent-movie "shocked" face. January joined in the audience's laughter. Unfazed. "I call them happy pills. I've got a placenta encapsulation specialist. He cleaned, cooked, dehydrated, and ground my baby's into perfect capsules. I was working again, with my old body, less than a month after my baby was born."

Which is when, without thinking about it, I dropped to my knees and started studying the floor to see if we'd dropped anything. Carpet-mining, not to get technical. The nagging side effect of crack use. But in this case—me being a garden-variety heroin enthusiast—a more methodical pursuit. We'd run out of drugs and I was scouring the floor to see if we'd dropped any. This is when I saw the big faux leather bag under the bed. I didn't recognize it, but then, in this kind of motel, you were bound to find all kinds of things. If you were non-germaphobic enough to actually get down on the floor voluntarily. As opposed to involuntarily, or Harold Style: facedown and fancy-free on the moldy carpet.

I yelled, "Nora! Hey, Nora, I found something!" But she was still in the shower. The bag was out of reach. I had to move to the other side of the bed and reach past Harold, who didn't seem to mind. He might have done something in his pants, or else he hadn't changed them in a while. Maybe both. (Old-school hopheads swear a layer of filth "keeps the high inside." But mostly, when you're jonesing, your skin hurts. Water hurts. Plus, junkies are busy guys 'n' gals. Who has time for hygiene?) Anyway, I knew from experience you could bend Harold like a pretzel and set his face on fire and he wouldn't mind. Worse than breathing Harold, I had to breathe that rug. God knows what nasty, fucked-out, sex-twisted monstroids had shed skin, barfed, farted, fornicated, wept, shot up, or all six simultaneously on the floor in a fiend palace like that.

Anyway, I pulled out the bag, unzipped it a little, stuck my hand in, and screamed. Loud. Due to skracking pain when a mousetrap snapped and nearly took a fingernail off. Not that I minded the pain. I was too excited. Anything worth rigging a mousetrap to protect was bound to be good. Drugs? Money? I ripped it off and went in. And what treasure, you wonder, did

I find? Let's just say it was so surprising I took the time to dig a pencil stub out of the motel desk drawer and write it all down. Of course I had no paper, so I had to unwedge the "CHECK-OUT BY NOON" card from its frame on the door. It had been a while since I'd been the kind of diligent scribe who walked around with a notebook. Even when I did, I wasn't exactly jotting down ideas for haikus. I wasn't jotting down anything, except the occasional phone number, or smudged out *WHY?* Which is why I stopped carrying notebooks at all. But forget all that. When I saw what was inside I wanted to inventory. Not because the contents meant something, but because, at first, they didn't. Basically, it was a bunch of products with no outward relationship to one another.

Roundup weed killer, Phisoderm face wash, Clearasil acne cream, Gatorade, Rust-Oleum, Diet Coke, and Axiron testosterone enhancer. (The latter boasting my all-time fave product warning: *Discontinue if you see signs of advanced puberty in a child.* (Unless, you know, you want to speed things up. Then Ax-up, tiger! Turn that tweener into a teen!)

Before I could complete my inventory, out popped Nora, one towel wrapped beneath those breasts of hers and another around her wet hair, lending her a Cleopatra look. A ridiculously buxom yet dainty Cleopatra. When she saw the open bag in my lap she stopped. "What the fuck are you doing?"

Before I could answer she got a crazy expression on her face, then whipped the wet towel off her head and across my face. I could handle the towel smack, but the crazy scared me.

"Jesus Christ, Nora!"

"Fuck Jesus Christ. What the fuck are *you* doing, going through my shit?"

"*Your* shit? I found it under the bed." Then I picked up the Roundup. "What? You boost this? Weed killer?"

"Not just weed killer. The CIA used Roundup in Colombia against the FARC, when the radicals were making money taxing *coca*. Monsanto directions say don't spray from more than ten feet up. Glyphosates are not good for humans. From that high, it drifts onto other crops: beans, corn, coffee. Food and subsistence for whole villages are wiped out. But you know what's worse? CIA mixes it with Cosmo-Flux. An adhesive, like? Makes the shit stick to leaves. Except it doesn't just stick to leaves. It sticks to kids. Who can't wash it off 'cause they can't use the water. You want know what happens to babies marinated in CIA herbicide? Check Operation Phoenix in Vietnam. Now Monsanto's going to make sure we eat it, too. Varietal GMOs."

I waited patiently, until she was through. "So that's a yes? Why are you stealing weed killer?"

"I'm not planning on selling it."

"Then what?"

She didn't explain any further. Instead, she moved closer. Let the second scrabby motel towel drop to the carpet. Then, naked—be still my heart! (she owned the last of the Seventies *Playboy* bushes)—reached into the bag with her eyes still on mine and grabbed the first incongruous product her hand fell on. Axiron. She broke the seal, pulled out a blister pack of twelve pills, thumbed out a couple, and popped them in her mouth. I could see from the empty slots that she'd already gobbled a few. I like to think I'm fairly unshakable. But this shook me.

"Nora . . . What are you . . . ? I mean . . . you wanna tell me what you're taking?"

She dry-swallowed without making a face, like a professional. Had no problem talking. "What do you think?"

"I think you're fucking insane. That shit's not gonna get you high. Not to mention the fucking side effects. You're not supposed to even touch anybody after you've held a pill in your hands. You have any idea what it can do to your reproductive system?"

"As a matter of fact," she said, smiling—there was that gold tooth again—"I do."

"Sure about that? They don't put everything in the commercials. If that stuff came near a baby girl, she'd be menstruating by five. And it does things to fetuses the Discovery Channel won't even show."

The smile got brighter. She actually giggled. A total first. "I love that you know that, baby."

Nora thumbed out another pill and rubbed it over her belly, making an X. Then she dry-popped that one, grabbed the Rust-Oleum, snatched the pillow off the bed, yanked the pillowcase away, and bit the lid off. She shook the can until we could hear the little ball bouncing around and sprayed inside the pillowcase until it was stained bloody brown. After that she bunched it up, pressed it to her lips, and took a deep breath. I'd never seen a huffer use a pillowcase. For that matter I'd never known a junkie who huffed. Life was full of happy surprises. Nora mega-inhaled a few more times, dropped the pillowcase, and gave me a bleary grin. Red spray circled her mouth. She looked like a woman who'd put her lipstick on drunk, if her lipstick came out of an industrial spray can and stopped oxidation. The stuff stank so much I could feel my own brain cells dying. I'd sniffed glue as a kid; the high was like being hit in the head with a brick. Rust-Oleum was similar, if you traded the brick for a monster truck tire, and it backed up over your skull.

Nora seemed weirdly unaffected. She wasn't one of the users who changed when she used. She didn't slur. She didn't dumb up. Neither did I, normally. But those fumes weren't normal. I had to focus just to lift up my words and set them down in a remotely coherent row, to even remember what words were, let alone what you were supposed to do with them. "*Why . . . are . . . you . . . doing . . . this?*"

"I told you before. That guy fucked me."

"Wait . . . the guy who—that guy? What does this have to do with him?"

Between the Rust-Oleum clown mouth and her still-glistening slit, that gulch in the rainforest, which she stroked idly as she aimed a blurry half smile my way, I was not focusing. Then she dropped her hands to her sides. Stopped smiling and sighed so deeply she seemed to slump.

"He really raped me, Lloyd."

This was one of the rare times she used my name. "You mean he raped you . . . when he stole your ideas?"

"Does it look like I'm talking about ideas?" Exasperated, she ran her hands over her belly, where she'd X'd in the Axiron. "Are you blind? I'm pregnant."

"Are you serious?"

My first thought, insanely, was that we hadn't been together long enough for this to be mine. But then, she didn't say it was, so why was I instantly obsessing? (Sometimes it was impossible to tell guilt from wish-fulfillment.) Would all of this be made more heinous, or less, knowing the baby whose health and well-being she was massively jeopardizing had sprung from my seed. Narcissism or martyrdom—you be the judge!

"See it?" she asked again.

I couldn't, but if I squinted, and thought about it, I could almost imagine the tiniest of baby bumps swelling her belly.

"I do. Sort of. Well, y'know . . . almost. So, uh . . . what are you going to do?"

"I told you. I'm going to fuck him up."

"I was talking about the baby."

"So am I."

"But why would you . . . I mean . . . you're sure it's a boy?" I asked idiotically.

"Are you that out of it? I'm talking about the father."

Maybe the problem was not just those rust-fighter fumes.

Some ideas are too cosmically wrong to contemplate on the first take. You need time to let them manifest. Then you can claw out your brainpan, douse it in lighter fluid, and strike a match. But Nora was not even discussing an idea. She'd left "idea" behind. She'd crossed from conceptual to actual. The proof, apparently, was right there in her pudding.

Real life. The ultimate performance!

Not until she reached for the Roundup and lay down on her back did the obvious sink in. The vision still scalds my eyeballs. Picture it: Nora on the floor, legs spread in the air, aiming the nozzle and spraying Roundup directly into her vagina. What in nature, what in life, what in religion, TV, Tumblr, or Japanese pornography prepares you for such a sight?

I stood over her, reeling, and watched while she squirted. She tossed the empty Roundup onto the carpet. Then, still holding open the shiny-with-poison lips of her pussy, she asked if I wanted to fuck her.

She whispered hoarsely, "We could do it now. It's nice and wet." Now?

Why, having witnessed what I just witnessed, would I even ask? Plus which, who was I kidding? I'd offed a man in a bus station because the woman who'd just aimed weed killer into her birth canal had suggested it. At the time I barely knew her—which was completely crazy. Now I *did* know her, and I was still here. So what did that make me? Besides even crazier?

Nora's eyes glazed over, the way they did when dope first came on. Her voice grew huskier. "Sperm is the best delivery system. The poison will get there faster."

"Get where?" My own voice was cracking, but not from lust. Or not so I could admit. "There are easier ways to abort, if you don't want to have the thing."

"Who said I don't want to have it?" She spread her labia even wider, easing her right hand halfway in, fisting herself, and trembling her clit on top with her left thumb. "I want to have the baby, then I want to tell everybody it's his. And I want to give it to him."

"Wait, you want to . . . to do all this, to use all these products to—tell me I'm wrong, please!—to give your baby birth defects? That's your revenge?"

"No. Yes. You don't get it," she said. "You think small. That's your problem. *One* of your problems."

I must have sulked.

"This isn't about you, okay? Listen. Do I want to make the man who did this to me miserable? Make him want to hang himself? Absolutely.

"But that's too easy."

Her face had grown red, her eyes with some internal chemical fire. "You ever read about the monk who burned himself in Saigon during the Vietnam War? Or the ones in Tibet who lit themselves up to protest China chasing out the Dalai Lama?"

"Of course. But they burned themselves. They didn't destroy a baby."

"I'm not destroying. I'm creating."

"Creating what? A little deformed metaphor?"

"You don't know anything," Nora said, the sex-glaze gone right out of her eyes, replaced by something I didn't recognize.

TWENTY-NINE

The Final Solution, Horizontal

Now I'd offended her. A woman sprawled on her back with a pea-sized fetus in her belly and a full can of Roundup aimed up her uterus. But instead of lashing out, as I'd expected, she went the opposite way. Grew quiet. Subdued. Testament, undoubtedly, to the serious thought she'd given the endeavor. I'd bet anything, I thought moronically, that no one in this motel room, probably any motel room, has discussed deliberately mutating an unborn child to make a point. Let alone to save the world.

"It's nothing new," she said, still low-key.

"What isn't?" Just having a conversation, any conversation, in the middle of this travesty, made me feel like an accomplice. Mengele's towel-boy. But here I was. So I listened.

"Deforming babies. Deliberately. The government's been doing it forever. Talk to the downwinders, in southern Utah. May 25, 1953, we tested Grable, a nuclear bomb."

"We?"

"The United States. The Defense Department, asshole. For months afterward southern Utah was showered with nuclear grit. Everybody pretended the government was testing the power of the blast, to intimidate the Russians. But it was never about megatonnage, or kill capacity, or any of that. It was about the birth defects. We pretended during the Cold War, that we were going to pulverize their people to dust. But that wasn't the real message. The real message was, 'Hey, Khrushchev, forget the little commies we're going to obliterate. The ones who don't get obliterated are going to be born with cleft palates, limb deformities, brains the size of pigeon eggs, rampant myeloma . . . The works! I'm talking about babies born with bones so brittle Mom and Dad would have to take them back and forth to the hospital wrapped in foam rubber."

"Did they have foam rubber then?"

"Lloyd, are you listening to me? I'm talking about Dow, Monsanto, the Koch Brothers, General Electric . . ."

"General Electric," I recited out of habit. "We bring good things to life."

"Lloyd! The whole point of everything is not what they want you to think. Even liberals, even *progressives*, they're all wrong. The point is not that birth defects are a side effect of rampant capitalism. The point is, birth defects *are* the point! Disease is the point! You think deregulation is just to make sure it's easier to make a profit? Wrong. It's so the general population can stay gene-raped, from conception on."

Nora grabbed another item from her bag, chartreuse nail polish, and began artfully painting her already painted toe- and fingernails, making sure to inhale huge, chest-filling gusts of the shellacky fumes.

"Why do you think the Supreme Court ruled against those

poor farmers in Utah whose babies grew up with spleens attached to their femurs, and God knows what else? Not that God even gives a shit. Why do you think there are PCBs in kid's pajamas, in couches, even in nursing pillows? This guy, Nicholas Kristof, wrote a column about it in the *New York Times*. And that shit is *nothing*." She stopped to bite her freshly painted pinkie nail, then kept going. "By now it's corny to even mention corporations polluting rivers, destroying mountaintops. All business does is eat the resources and shit out death. From the hollers of West Virginia to the dead fish of Love Canal, from the Amazon River Basin to Exxon in Nigeria. Woody Guthrie could write a song. You name it, and it's tainted!"

I had a feeling she'd given this rant before. Her speech, gone a little slurry after huffing aerosol rust proofer, sharpened right back up when she picked up a pipe and fired up what, from the acrid stink of it—and it had to be very acrid to cut through Rust-Oleum and nail polish—had to be bathtub crank.

"Now you're tweaking?"

"Everybody's tweaking. We live in a great big tweakiverse."

"Nice. Just be careful you don't blow yourself up with all those fumes you've got floating around."

As she smoked she fished in the bag and came out with a can of floor wax. She smeared the stuff on her hands like moisturizer, taking big whiffs off her palms. "It's almost funny. All these so-called prog types going on about depleted uranium turning a generation of newborn Iraqis and Afghanis into nerve-damaged, brain-fucked little leukemia bundles. Meanwhile, it's nothing, nothing compared to what we've got going on right here."

She paused to take a can of Glade out of her bag—

Cleansing Rain scent—and splooshed a few puffs between her legs and in front of her face.

"Toluene and phthalate. Look them up. Tests on spider monkeys showed infants born with gender abnormalities, including external ovaries and doubled testicles. You believe people spray this in their own homes? It's like, 'Oooh, we're Americans! We don't mind malignancy as long as we can breathe fake nature smells instead of our stink.' Not that there's nature anymore, right? You ever listen to Helen Caldicott? She says you can't even find an apple in Europe that isn't irradiated. Especially in France. Jerry Lewis and nuclear reactors. That's culture."

"I get it, I get it," I snapped. "Don't eat the French fruit."

Pacing above her as she lay naked on the motel carpet, breathing what she was breathing, I felt my own gorge rising, felt myself begin to sway. Not just from the bouquet of industrial death vapors she'd unleashed, but from the fact that she was unleashing them. That this was her *thing*.

I tried to stay calm. "Nora, baby, do you know how hard this is, watching you douse yourself? Stashing a chemical smorgasbord up your hole? The worst part is, I know what you're doing. I know the side effects. I know what might happen to you."

"Not me, I told you. It's not about me." Here she cupped her hands over her barely discernible belly. Speaking softly. "It's about my baby. My precious little American mutant."

She touched her stomach tenderly and raised her shining face to mine—exultant—while I gulped back vomit. "Nora" was about all I could manage without clunking down hard on the floor. "I mean . . . we're talking about an innocent child." That sounded tinny even to me, but I kept going. "It's all so fucking *Holocausty.* Is that what you want, to be a portable Holocaust?"

"Why not?"

"Nora," was all I could think to say to that, "Nora, what did this guy do to you? And don't insult me with the thing about stealing greeting card ideas, okay?"

For a long time she didn't say anything. When she did start talking, she had that "faraway look." Like she wasn't talking to me at all. Like she was talking to herself, telling herself a story she'd been telling herself for a very long time. Gone was the buxom bad-attitude pixie who sneered when I sat beside her on the bus. In her place, right now, I saw the face of a true believer. My naked, passionate schizoid, my delusional beauty, my insane, and insanely hot, wanna-martyr. Who deep down, I was beginning to think, just wanted to be some kind of dangerous saint. That, or she was just a chick who liked to lie on her back, get fucked up, and touch herself while she described her plan for becoming Genetic Apoca-Mom.

At some point, I just had to ask, "How can you do this stuff?" Her answer, like everything else about Nora, was not what I expected.

"When you love yourself, you can do anything."

It was one of those moments, with Nora, where I didn't know if she was insane (door number one) or just had a very dark sense of humor (door number two). Door number three: *you have no fucking idea where this door is going to take you.* Which is the one I followed her through. But you pretty much know you are never walking back out of it.

Listen to her:

"It's one thing when you read about their horror, what they

do, in the abstract. Like, okay, Dow Chemical makes napalm, phosphorus bombs, and PCB-dusted flame retardant that ends up in couches. I *get* it . . . Or like, in the photo of that burned little girl running naked down the street in Vietnam. You think, like, 'Okay, I get *that*. America may have deployed them. But Dow made the chemicals that burned her skin off. Shit that didn't just kill, it maimed and tortured. Got it.' But imagine meeting, in person, the man responsible, more than anyone, for all this death, this suffering. All right, maybe not the man responsible, but the fucker who makes the most money off it, the CEO . . . and in person he's just so . . ."

She stopped talking and zoned, the silence going on so long it got awkward, so I barged in.

"So arrogant? So piggish? So rich?"

"What?"

She looked startled, as if she'd forgotten she was talking, forgotten I was in the room. "No," she said finally, "that's the thing. He was so . . . *nice*."

"The CEO of Dow?"

Again, I don't think she heard me. She just kept going. "He was a *really* nice guy. At first. I know, right? It's like, when you watch *Sophie's Choice*. You see these prisoners in Auschwitz, dragging themselves around like starved, diseased ghosts, then one guard opens the gates and leads her into the Kommandant's private quarters. Suddenly, flowers are blooming, children are laughing, his lovely wife is serving a happy, laughing family a meal . . . This was the world the Kommandant was in. This is the world all those CEOs are in. The rest of us are in the camp."

"How'd you meet him?"

"How do you think? I was an escort. But I could talk. I was studying communications in college. In fact, that's how I was paying my tuition."

"So—" I hated myself, but I had to ask. "The whole greeting card thing?"

"That's actually true. Sort of. You know . . . Dow had made an acquisition, Taupe and Timely Accents. They made decoratives. For home and office."

"Decoratives. Taupe."

"Taupe's kind of light brown. Taint-colored. Decoratives are, you know, decorative: candles, pillows, doilies, inspirational plaques, and cards, that kind of shit."

"He told you all this?"

"Men like to talk about their business."

"After they bring you to the Kommandant's quarters."

"More or less."

Another little silence, but this time she ended it.

"I know what you think, if I was a sex worker, how could he rape me?"

"I wasn't thinking that, Nora. Give me some fucking credit."

"There's that," she said. "What actually happened is I became his 'girlfriend' when he wasn't with his wife. He thought I was clever, so he got me a job, or he said he got me a job. He wanted me to come up with something for their 'inspiration' line. It had to be good. So one night, after we had some shitty coke and champagne, I did. I came up with something." She paused, her gaze going inward again, and recited dramatically: "*The fearless man lives forever; the fearful man dies every minute.*"

"Wow. How'd you come up with that?"

"It came to me in a dream."

"I'm impressed."

"So was he. He liked it so much he had his products division head put it on greeting cards, on plates, on nine-by-twelve plaques. Even needlepoint. For one fiscal year it was a bigger seller than *You want it when?* and *Hang in there, baby.* You remember, with the cat holding on to the branch?"

"I remember. You mentioned it on the bus."

"It was such a phenom, the Society of Decorative Manufacturers gave it their ISY Award. In that world, it's a huge deal. He actually invited me to the banquet. Bought me a gown. The whole nine yards."

"So?"

"Wait. When it came time to give out the award, they read my quotation, and then the presenter said that, for his money, this was more than something you put on a china plate, or on a card, this was a—don't puke—'a transformative idea,' worthy of the highest ideals of man. He said he was 'sniffing a TED talk.'"

"He did not!"

"He did. Then he said he was proud to introduce the great mind behind this concept, and right when I was about to stand up, the Dow CEO—his name was Elliot, but he liked me to call him Mumpy—leans over, puts his hand on my shoulder, and kisses me. Just like that. A little peck on the cheek. A peck. Then he winks. That's when I knew the MC wasn't going to be pronouncing my name, he was going to be pronouncing his. I had to sit there, while the cheesedick bastard who banged my head off the marble floor of a Four Seasons bathroom—*after* he bounced his balls off my face, shoved his fat cock inside me bareback, and called me a filthy cum-bucket—made a twenty-minute speech about the nobility of man."

"No wonder you want to kill him."

"Not kill him. Necessarily. Wait . . . He also said he was going to give me fifty thousand dollars for my 'contribution to the company,' and he didn't give me a dime. P.S., he got a bonus that year of 4.7 million. But that wasn't the worst part. The worst part, I found out after I started doing research on him, is that Dow is probably responsible for destroying, murdering, fouling, poisoning, and generally future-fucking more of the planet than just about any company you can imagine, outside of Monsanto. And I made that lying psychopathic zillionaire sack of shit look enlightened. It makes me want to start purging again just thinking about it."

Done talking, she took a deep breath and began to backstroke naked across the skanky carpet. She stopped in front of an outlet, popped in a Febreze plug-in, turned around, and positioned her feet high and flat on the wall so the chemical fragrance from the device—something called Berry Bunch, though it smelled more like cough syrup—would flow directly inside her.

"The man raped you?"

"They're all rapists," she said.

"Who?"

Her voice went flat as she recited. "Dow, Monsanto, Johnson and Johnson, GlaxoSmithKline, all of them."

"I get it. But come on."

"Come on, what? Like corporations can't rape? They're human, aren't they?"

As she spoke, she continued to work that fumy, mutagenic

cloud into her sex. She might as well have douched with slime from Love Canal . . . She closed her eyes and continued dreamily. "They rape everybody."

"Maybe," I said, playing along. "But somehow I doubt I'm going to get pregnant."

She stopped slathering and regarded me. "Oh, you will."

Dead serious now, she reached up and touched my belly. "Only you won't be having a baby. Maybe you'll have a little tumor. A nice little brainstem glioma. Or a schwannoma. Doesn't that sound cute? Schwannoma. Kind of ethnic . . . like stuffed grape leaves. This could be the moment, right now, when you start growing your own brain-baby. Who knows? You might even have triplets . . ."

She giggled and moved her hand down to my balls, then up to my chest, and then farther north, to where my brain is supposed to be. Nora was not, normally, this playful. "Sometimes, I think of the defect as a little creature with a baby around it. And sometimes I think, Maybe the baby is the defect!"

I looked at her, and I saw her face the way it must have been *before* . . . I remembered my first glimpse of her, this tough little bus stray with the sullen pout and the attitude and the outsize breasts she seemed intent on hiding under her ratty army jacket, like concealed weapons. It seemed to me like she'd been five different people since then: the hard-ass chick, the victim, the junkie (well, all junkies are victims, until they steal your checkbook and make you one), the criminal (ditto), and, now, the R-PEA: the Radical Pregnant Environmental Activist.

"The child I'm carrying? Just one of millions of citizens of earth who've been exposed and never had a chance, never had a goddamn say in the matter."

"I get it, N. The Dow guy fucked you in the flesh. The other ones are genocidal criminals who did you—and are still doing everybody else—from their country clubs, or wherever, without even knowing what they've done. It's a little shrill, but I get it."

"Shrill? Fuck you. When's the last time you watched somebody die from something you did? Probably never. These guys do it nonstop and it never even affects them."

The base reek of the motel room combined with the industrial sprays and "air freshener" she'd unleashed. It smelled like some perfumed farm animal being burned on a stake, fur and all, three inches in front of me. She placed her hands on her rounded-if-you-squint belly, the way pregnant women do, and gave me a look so single-minded it was like having a laser aimed directly through my unibrow.

"You know what I'm going to do. I'm going to have the baby. And then, you know . . ."

"No, I don't know."

A rare and beautiful smile. "I'm going to make it an event. I'm going to show it off."

"To who?"

"His creators. If this were NASCAR, I could have a sponsor's patch on every deformity, one per tumor. Monsanto. Johnson and Johnson. Merck, Bayer, Kellogg's . . ."

I had to interrupt. "Kellogg's? Now you're telling me Corn Flakes will kill you?"

"Well, they're processed, but that's a different issue. FDA doctors found mold on them. Aflatoxins."

"Mmm. I bet the kids love 'em."

"You think this is funny?"

"Okay, okay . . . So then what?"

She reached in the bag again, felt around, pulled out a cherry Nutri-Grain bar and ripped off the wrapper. Shoved it in her mouth and kept talking. "What do you think? FDA crushed the research. It spends most of its resources spying on whistle-blowers. Hard to get a lot done when your resources are expended reading real-time e-mails. *Mmmm!*" She licked her lips and smiled. "My favorite flavor, Red Dye Number Two. But hey . . ." She dabbed a splodge of jelly from her lip. "I like the taste of cancer."

THIRTY

Almost Like Happiness

After a month or two Nora started to show. We were like a regular little family, or would be until little Mothra was born. After that, Nora's plans veered macro: into global techno-chemical reform and worldwide notoriety, among other things. Though she was never absolutely specific about how she was going to bring the world's attention to young Mutando. She just believed.

Thanks to network TV employment I was able to rent us a little house in Echo Park. CBS wanted more "extreme stories." I said, "Cool." It was like being paid to think up fucked-up shit, the one skill I'd acquired cranking out pharma-copy. Because, really, what else did mainstream old-time network-watching America want on a Thursday at 9 p.m.? No problem at all, provided I didn't bring Nora back to the set, and risk her reverting back to klepto-adolescence again and ganking another prop. For better or worse, no possible episodes of the shock-the-masses Vegas murder series compared to what was happening, in real life, at home.

It's funny, really, how you can get used to anything. How quickly the unutterable becomes ho-hum. But maybe that's just "acceptance." Like they say in the twelve steps and all. I'd climbed them once. Before I'd slid back down. And made my way back up again. Then slipped, then—you get the picture. In the end, I acquired a deep and abiding understanding of the immortal words of Jonathan Swift: "Climbing is performed in the same position as crawling."

The first thing we did, after slapping a mattress down on the bedroom floor, was ring it with as many appliances as possible. (Somehow the gesture felt oddly empowering, like heating the pool before you drown in it.) Electric blankets, a pair of microwave ovens, a WiFi router, a cordless phone and cordless phone base, both our laptops (recently "borrowed"), both our BlackBerrys (ditto), and a gaggle of old-school cells, iPhones, and Androids we'd been up able to pick up here and there. Of all the women in the world, I'd ended up with the one who slathered on sunscreen before she went to bed. (Sometimes my own luck scared me!) It was disorienting, at first, but she wanted that retinyl palmitate and oxybenzone to soak through her epidermis overnight, into her system. "Total hormone disruptor," she said—excited about it—when she saw me watching.

You know about this stuff, right? Don't tell me you still sleep with a digital clock? Electric blankets? With your computer and an iPhone charging next to the bed? Might as well camp out at Three Mile Island. And that's just radiation and electromagnetic node scrambling! There's so much EMF exposure in the average American home that boatloads of citizens stagger through their lives nauseous and dizzy and don't even know why. (That's how it feels to be us!) Even as we speak, the Pentagon is allocating entire wings to the development of an airborne microwave crowd-control weapon code-named "Active Denial"! (Perfect! Who thinks up these names? Who gets *that* job?) And I'm not even talking about the lung-destroying aluminum silicate dispensed by unmarked jets crisscrossing United States skies like white icing on a coffee cake. You don't believe me, go outside and look up. Check out the chemtrails.

I didn't know any of this stuff until Nora told me. I wasn't in active denial, I just didn't care. Didn't Lenny Bruce say, "No self-respecting junkie lives long enough to die of anything legal"? Or was that early American opium fan Ben Franklin?

But now it wasn't about us. It was about new life! The new life Nora was bent on creating. Whose origins, despite her explanations (or justifications) remained as cryptic and miserable as her intentions were "noble."

This, by which I mean Nora's pregnancy and her attendant efforts to, for lack of a better word, "influence"—though the better word may be "mutate"—it had crossed the line from possible side effects to probable monstrosity. And, like I say, after the initial shock, the revulsion—not for *her*, okay, but for the very idea of what she was trying to do—the whole thing began to feel like some kind of sick, if visionary, semi-credible science project.

Because I was writing for TV, I got into the Writers Guild. This meant health insurance. I actually wrote four more episodes after "King Baby," the mogul-in-diapers story. My favorite was "Fancy Pants," about a sex change that goes bad when the surgeon has an epileptic fit and leaves the job half done. This motivated the patient, forever doomed to limbo between pre-op and post-op, to take up the scalpel against successful transsexuals, for whom he/she harbored deep and unsettling jealousy. *They made me a sex monster instead of a woman, which is what I am.*

Years ago I read an interview with Samuel Jackson in which he confided how he'd learned to be an actor: "I used to be a drug addict." (I'm paraphrasing.) "Being an addict teaches you to say what you need to say to get what you need to get."

I explained to the (partly intrigued, partly creeped) staff how fly-by-night sex-changers sometimes used storage lockers to perform the operation. How these "surgeons" stuff the "female portal" with a toothpaste tube and suture it with piano wire "for shaping" while it heals. Then, after five days or so, the "mangina" is unsutured, the wires removed, and voila! Ernest, meet Ernestine! (Fun fact: Time of death—always important—was determined by the dead he/she's pubic hair. People think your beard grows after you die. Actually, your skin contracts, pushing the follicles out. Fresh-shaved pubes make it easy as pie for the CSIs to calculate time of death. One wonders how many future murderers will try to foil the investigators with high-end merkins. Look it up.)

Wannabe gender-flippers who couldn't afford the full enchilada—man-to-woman variety—had to settle for injecting silicone into their cheeks and buttocks; the ones who couldn't afford silicone would shoot motor oil. That's one of the things I loved about the show: you always learned something. It was rewarding to write dialogue that would stand the test of time. Like this one (not to brag) for Billy Petersen: *So how'd your fingerprint end up on a three-day-old vagina?* Not everybody can grow up to be Nicholas Sparks.

The WGA insurance only covered spouses, not girlfriends. A term, naturally, that Nora hated. She preferred "unmarried humans." Or something. It depended on the day and the drug. (What didn't?)

I was ready to pull the trigger. Get hitched. It seemed so wrong I couldn't stop myself. But Nora wasn't having it. Marriage wasn't part of the game plan. She was adamant: "I am not going to end up like some fanny pack with tits."

The woman could turn a phrase.

We were actually on our way to an OB/GYN in the Valley she had found online. Nora wanted to stop at Pink's, on La Brea. The famous hot dog stand. She was vegetarian, but Pink's chili cheese dogs constituted a necessary violation. You probably know of the potential health dangers associated with MSG. I had to learn. In wieners monosodium glutamate is used as a flavoring and labeled as an excitotoxin, meaning that it stimulates sensitive neurons. Ever the nutritional pollutant expert, Nora laid it out: "That's what makes MSG so headachy. It's like your brain is so buzzed it wants to vomit."

We'd just scored, so we both felt loose. It was always an "up," visiting Luz, the Mexican lady who sold us dope. She dealt out of the two-room apartment near USC she shared with her mother, her grandmother, three sons, and a cousin from Guatemala, who served us frijoles. Maybe it was the family feeling, but Luz's dope was always a soporific. No rush, but relaxing as a massage from Jesus.

It was hard to worry about hot dog toxins, standing on the corner of LaBrea and Melrose and breathing in face-blasting gusts of hot bus exhaust, Nora being the only Pink's patron who stepped to the curb to breathe fresh diesel. I had to pull her back, discreetly, in case she got gas-dizzy and staggered in front of a Mercedes crossover. (Speaking of mutants.) They were showing up all over Los Angeles.

"Sir, are you a sex offender? Stop harassing that woman!"

I'd know that voice anywhere. Sure enough, I turned around to face Jay, my fellow Christian Swingler. I hadn't seen him since Tulsa, when his cop boyfriend, Dusty, managed to extract me from the back of that police car. Jay looked exactly the same, except for missing an arm.

THIRTY-ONE

Nugger

Jay wore a blue blazer, the cuff of the left sleeve pinned over his heart, as though pledging eternal devotion. The weird thing wasn't his missing arm. It was the fact that he was wearing a sport coat. It was 101 in LA. Global toasting.

Jay saw me clocking him and smiled.

"Pastor Bobb caught me with my hand in the till."

"What about Riegle?"

"I was holding the till," a voice said.

I turned and there was Riegle. He too seemed exactly the same.

"But you've got both arms!"

This from Nora, sinking her teeth into her chili dog. I saw her the way my old friends must have seen her: a no-nonsense twentyish box of sauce in black bangs and office clothes. She was dressed for the first appointment with the ob-gyn. All drugsters figure coming off straight will get them more pills.

"Long story," Riegle said, waggling both arms. "I found a photo of the pastor. With a young Christian girl."

"How young?" Nora wanted to know.

"Young enough for the pastor. Old enough to need the money."

Nora nodded, conceding a little half smile. "Been there."

She fit right in.

We retired to eat our dogs and catch up in Jay's car. (A Saturn, of all things.) The encounter seemed entirely random. In retrospect . . . well, what good is retrospect?

Jay managed fine with one hand. "All worth it for the handicap sticker," he said. "Plus, nobody wants a Saturn. They stopped making them in what, '09? Parts rare as dinosaur bones."

"That and the fact we 'produced' an accident report." Riegle made air quotes. The only person I knew who could do them and not look lame. It's like we'd seen each other yesterday. "In the database, it turned out this Saturn had been in a flood. Completely immersed. They would have given it away."

Once they were satisfied Nora was bent—I couldn't have been prouder—Jay pulled down the visor, behind which he'd stashed a row of loaded syringes. "Look at Lloyd, all wifed up!" He stopped and shook his head. "Who'da thunk it? Good thing there's par-tay supplies."

"One place they never look," Riegle shrugged. "Behind the visor."

Nobody was going to look twice at four well-dressed white people in a beige sedan. No paranoia about getting off while mobile. Jay asked us to look away while he loosened his belt and fixed somewhere that required lowering his pants. There were public shooters, and there were privates. Jay's privates were private private.

When we were all nice—well, Nora and I were already nice, but we got nicer—Jay parked the Saturn in an alley behind a storefront synagogue, near Fairfax, and told Nora how much he liked her. A sentiment I took to be only partly opiate-fueled. "And he does not like a lot of women," Riegle was quick to add. The upshot of all this let's-catch-up smack-lubricated bonhomie was that Jay and Riegle offered to get us a marriage license. All we had to do was find a Kinko's. They'd handle the rest.

"WiFi and a printer," Jay said. "You don't even need two hands."

Nora's sneer was amiable. "But just in case, you have an extra one, right?"

I thought Jay was going to slap her. His face went purplish-red. Riegle stayed blank. I noticed a pair of Hasidim who had to be melting under their fur hats and fur-collared overcoats in equatorial West Hollywood. They didn't notice us and kept walking, fully engaged in the Talmudic puzzler of the day.

Nora reached into Jay's jacket and around his back. She didn't pull out his hand when she found it. (Taped ingeniously over his tailbone.) Not at first. She just looked him in the eye.

"What are you, some kind of nugger?"

"Helps with the suits," Jay said. "Everybody likes a veteran."

"Live every day like it's your second-to-last," Riegle added. "Maybe I've only got one wing, but I get 'er done! Folks appreciate that."

I was the only one who didn't know what a "nugger" was.

"Slang for amputee," Jay explained. "If you happen to live in a hobo camp."

Nora just smiled.

It took me a while to get back into Christian con man humor. But Nora kept right up.

Jay and Riegle claimed they were here, in LA, to make some kind of deal. A reality show. Based on Swingles. My alma mater. "Simple concept," Riegle told me. "We follow six clients: three men, three women. From filling out the form online, to face-to-face chat, to first date, to picking a restaurant, to—"

"Sodomy," Jay intoned, going full silver-tongue. "For the righteous few."

THIRTY-TWO

Agenesis

Hollywood Kinko's packed its own kind of inky desperation. "Half the people here are running scams," Riegle told us, under his breath. "The ones who aren't are printing band flyers. Or programs for one-man shows."

Jay went right into it. "Listen, people, I had a really dysfunctional family . . ."

Meanwhile Nora stooped beside each machine and breathed. "Positive ions," Riegle said when he saw her doing it. "Weird high."

Nora gave him a little you-have-no-idea-who-you're-dealing-with smile. "You want a high," she told him, "get down on the carpet, take a breath. There's chemicals in those fibers that give babies glow-in-the-dark transgender genitalia. Tiny hermaphrodite night-lights."

I waited for her to march out the good news—she was going to be a mom. I wondered if she'd also mention the target she'd painted on her womb. *I'm not just having a baby, I'm harvesting birth defects for my mutant chemical-bred capitalism love-child.* But Jay had his own surprise. Before he told us, he checked out a tall Asian man with a slight stoop browsing inspirational business books, then lowered his voice. "I got you guys a present."

Every three feet there was another poster of Larry the Cable Guy, leering like an inbred pedophile over his trademark slogan: GET 'ER DONE. It made me miss the *Hang in there, baby!* cat.

Still looking around, Jay slipped Nora a copy of Og Mandino's *The Greatest Salesman in the World*—the same tome the Asian man was browsing—except this copy had an envelope sticking out of it.

"You're giving me this book?"

"Jesus was a closer," Riegle said, then rolled his eyes like a fourteen-year-old girl.

"Weird tick in a straight middle-aged guy, huh?" Jay whispered, sotto voce, when he noticed me noticing. (It was true; I didn't remember Riegle eye-rolling move back in Tulsa.) "Our friend's gone a little Clarabelle."

Riegle ignored him. "The book you have to pay for. We're giving you the envelope inside it."

The Asian man was joined by an even taller older woman with striking white hair, dressed all in black, down to shiny patent leather heels. Possibly his mother. Or an elderly dominatrix. She appeared to be buying inspirational books for him. He had to be forty. The world felt so full of unspoken mystery, I wanted to lie down, but that was probably just my blood sugar. Or the brown sugar Riegle and Jay's dope was cut with. I could taste it in my mouth after we geezed. It was like shooting up a Cinnabon. At least shooting up sugar didn't give you cavities. It's all about the silver lining.

I wanted to know more about the reality show. If they'd hired writers yet. Reality shows needed a lot of scripting. If the subject was

Christian Swingles, who better than a former Christian Swingler?

Riegle feigned shock. Though mercifully, he eschewed the pre-pube eye-rolling move. "Why, I believe this man is asking for a job!"

"You've been disgraced," Jay said. "We all did some soul-searching, after your pharmacy trouble. You'd have to change your name."

The idea seemed to make Riegle happy. "We can do that. State papers are nothing. What would you say to Chad? Or maybe Melvin."

"I don't know. I don't feel Chaddy or Melvinish."

"That's the idea, son. Keep them guessing. Anyway, Pastor Bobb won't be any the wiser unless he comes to visit, and he doesn't travel much now."

"Why not?"

"Ankle bracelet. Disagreement with the authorities."

"Should I ask?"

"Oldest beef in the book. Pastor B thought the child was over seventeen."

"He also thought said child was a boy," Jay added happily.

"Sounds like somebody set him up."

"Now why would anybody do that?"

Riegle's girly eye-rolling returned. By now I was getting used to it. (God knows what new tics I might have acquired since last we met.) "Sometimes you're a little slow, aren't you, buddy?"

"I'm an addict. I'm professionally impaired. So how's your wife? Any better?"

"She passed." For a second, he reverted to the distant, hang-dog manner I'd remembered from our time together on the job. "The bone cancer. Tumors ate her for breakfast. Started with her jaw."

"Was she taking Vidaza?" Nora chimed in.

After this I half-expected her to ask if there were any leftovers in the medicine cabinet. Riegle studied her.

"My mother had cancer," Nora explained, before he could ask. I wondered, again, if she was going to share the news about our little science project. Deliver her fetal manifesto. Surprisingly, or not, she didn't.

Riegle ran a pink tongue over his upper lip and went on with his story. "We had a neighbor girl, Suze, come in and help out. Turns out she was pregnant. She was feeding Marie—my better half—the pills when I was at work and she was too weak to unscrew the bottle. Suze even gave her baths. Cleaned her."

I knew where this was going. But Nora couldn't wait to get there. "How's her baby?"

"That poor squib. Its legs alone . . ." Riegle stopped and sighed. He stared at a poster of a middle-aged white man in a short-pants Kinko's uniform. *Let Kinko's rock YOUR website!* Then stared back at me again. "Suze was Pentecostal. Foursquare Gospel Republican. Thought prenatal care was satanic. When I finally read the side effects on her cancer meds, my stomach sunk. I didn't know whether to tell the girl or not. Dreaded it. I thought she'd cry, or come at me. But I had to let her know."

"Know what?" Nora was enthralled. Though I had a feeling she already knew the answer.

"Know that just touching those meds could taint her baby's DNA. Malform the little thing. Make her special needs. But guess what? Suze was calm as toast when I told her. She just smiled. Got all peaceful and inside her self. "God's will be done." That's what she said. And sure enough . . . He sighed.

"Sure enough what?" I said.

"Sure enough, you couldn't really call the legs on that unfortunate little fella legs. They were more like cocktail shrimps, sort of veined and pinkish, curled under. One had a shell on the end. You ever see Turtle Boy? Kind of like that."

"Agenesis." Nora pronounced the word like it was common as ketchup. "Fetal limb anomalies." I could see she was excited. One more defect to hang on the mutant baby tree.

(And yes, I know how callous this sounds. All I can say, in my defense, is that, while I knew, logically, that this baby was on the way, that it was real, that it was, as they say, in the mail—it just never felt that way. The notion of an actual baby remained abstract. The pregnancy, on the other hand, was vivid.)

Jay came back over with a small stack of stapled documents. "Could have gotten her Blue Cross. Right, Riegle?"

"Could have, if her brother and father weren't law enforcement."

"Wow," I said, "I don't remember you two being such cyberpirates."

"When the wife went into hospice, it was just me and the computer."

That's when I remembered his daughter. Her palsy. He must have seen the hesitation in my eyes. Wanting to ask, but not to know. "She's gone too," he said, in a kindly way, as if trying to spare me any awkwardness. He said the words, then began staring off. I could tell he wasn't at Kinko's anymore. His body might have been sitting at the rental PC nook. But he was back in the dark days, with his dying wife. He took a slow deep breath, as if smelling the sickroom again. In five minutes he'd said more about his family than he had the entire time we'd worked in Tulsa.

Riegle was just one of those guys. Old-school.

THIRTY-THREE

IHOP Men

"You've got some tricky friends," Nora said, when we were back home, setting up our bedroom appliances for the night.

After the business at Kinko's, the four of us made plans to meet up for a pancake dinner. Both Jay and Riegle were IHOP men. The envelope Jay gave us was stuffed with gift cards: a bunch from Pep Boys, Walgreens, American Apparel, Trader Joe's, even two from urgent care facilities, for $500 apiece, which impressed Nora to no end.

"A gift certificate to the emergency room. Awesome."

Once Nora was safely under my WGA insurance umbrella, she could get an MRI a day, sometimes three, and plenty of X-rays. She didn't want diagnoses; she craved radiation. And doctors were only too happy (the ones who didn't throw her out of their offices). Between appointments there were tanning salons. And psychiatrists. "If I take more antidepressants will I get more antidepressed?" She wanted to lay in what she could before she started to show.

She loved to share her research: "Paxil babies had holes in their hearts. It was almost poetic."

At home, after a day in Santa Clarita discussing murder by neo-Nazi twin experiments, including involuntary scrotal implants (Is that a turtle in your bag or are you glad to see me?) by sexual misadventure while wearing a Winnie the Pooh suit (at a plushy and furry convention), or fatally sabotaging a pair of "Smother me, Elmo" panties . . . our ongoing natal experiment began to seem—how else can I put it?—reasonable. I knew enough about perversion to milk it. But Nora! *Nora!* A whole other side of her emerged as she prepared to become a mother. Even a chemically challenged one.

In the beginning, the idea of deliberately ruining a child, sight unseen, baby unborn, made my stomach churn. But more and more, the whole thing began to make sense. And more than that, it began to seem meaningful, necessary!

For a Side-Effects Man, this was heady stuff. Inhuman as it may sound. (Though, to see it as Nora saw it, what she and I were doing would save lives, shock the world into some kind of sensibility.) *Normally*—and this was part of the P.R. I was working on—*normally, the drug's efficiency was the point and the side effects the unavoidable price you paid for it. Now, my friends, the side effects are the point!*

There was more, about how she obviously wasn't taking testerone for increased muscle mass or to stay virile after seventy. She was taking them to demonstrate, for all the mothers and fathers out there, the genital havoc these products might wreak on the offspring of any female unfortunate enough to come in contact with them. In other words, for her, the side effects weren't on the side. They were the main dish. *Pharmaceutical-wise, you might say, the journey was the destination.* (On second thought, I'd probably cut that line.)

Whenever we got high, she'd give me the details all over again.

Regardless of how conflicted and uncomfortable I was about aiding and abetting a mother-to-be's drug use, by now she'd already done half the sprays and solvents in the household cleaning aisle, along with enough of the *Physicians' Desk Reference* to fill the trunk of a Buick, and God knows what else, so there was no point being squeamish.

To hear her tell it, which she did, like I say, every time we got loaded, there would be cameras standing by to document the birth, media representatives of every stripe, all on hand to record the epic little monstrosity she was going to deliver as part protest, part living guerilla theater and performance art, part beyond-anything-the-world-has-ever-conceived fuck Amerika anticorporate statement.

Designed—this is Nora, in imaginary press release mode—*to wake the country up to the dangers which we breathe, absorb, consume, and ultimately pay for with our money, our lives, and the well-being of our unborn children.*

I'm not making a statement, I'm making a baby. (That was my kicker.)

Baby Mutando would spring forth as the logical outcome of glandular capitalism. *Except the system isn't amok at all: It's all perfectly controlled. Pollution, illness, defects, deformity, and despair are not the accidental fallout of corporate America, they are the deliberate product.*

Sound bites are us.

If she was high enough, we'd rehearse.

THIRTY-FOUR

We Only Want What God Wants

Yes!

Nora was obsessed with the ribbon of juvenile pituitary adenomas that lay across the southwest like a Miss America sash.

It amazed me, after a while, how one puff of tar off a sheet of tinfoil could send her to Rachel Maddow Town. One measly shot transformed her into the anticorporate, household-toxins-centric Angela Davis of her generation. Except that Angela Davis was (justly) famous and celebrated. And nobody (at least so far) had heard of Nora but me.

Once Nora got insurance and began seeing doctors for a living, we decided to mix shooting with smoking. Chasing the proverbial dragon left her just as voluble as fixing. Our fave new spot to get off was medical building parking lots. A rolled-up straw in her mouth forced her to pensive silence. She'd fire the Bic, run it under the tinfoil, and watch the tar run like a black teardrop while she filled her lungs. Begin talking as she emptied them.

"Every disease"—SMOKE IN—"deserves a treatment"—

SMOKE OUT—"and every treatment deserves a profit. I mean, there's the military-industrial complex, right? Arms makers"—SMOKE IN—"collude with governments to start wars so they can"—SMOKE OUT—"sell arms. Same with Halliburton and"—SMOKE IN—"Blackwater or Xe or Academi or whatever the fuck it's called now. Start another war"—SMOKE OUT—"charge for the mercenaries."—SMOKE IN—"Why should the medical-industrial complex be any different? Generate a disease, mop up on treatment and pharmaceuticals. Like Monsanto. Developing Roundup to protect soybeans from pests. Then developing Roundup-resistant strains of soybeans. Then coming out with a stronger, faster Roundup—which everyone who grows soy now absolutely needs—to deal with that. Fucking"—SMOKE OUT—"capitalism. Create a need, then sell the solution. Then create a bigger need, then jack up the cost of dying from it. Kiss me!" SMOKE IN.

The impressive thing was how she could turn it on and off. With me, Nora was who she was. All ten versions. But she could walk into a waiting room full of moms in Burbank and fit right in. We found a Catholic hospital where they didn't do the testing we'd had done at Cedars-Sinai. Nora had major chameleon skills. "We only want what God wants," she told the nun who took our forms. Sister Mary Carrie. (Really.) Nora asked if they got to pick their own nun names. She said she'd have picked the same one. Then drifted lightly off.

"We have to go in now, darling. When we're done with Dr. Nelson we've got Dr. Cornfeld."

"Yes, Lloydy."

Lloydy? This was as happy as I'd ever seen her. Unless the sap was an act, pregnancy agreed with her. I don't think it was just the thought that she was carrying a deformed little corporate Antichrist. I think she enjoyed it.

"One more hit."

Big inhale. Then she's off again.

"The thing is"—SMOKE IN—"in case there's any disease we don't cause with our own consumption, or get from eating and drinking, or from using all the shit we buy that we think we can't live without, the government is happy to help out. I'm talking chemtrails."—SMOKE OUT. (I never saw anybody who could hold smoke in her lungs as long as Nora. She said it was from hiding from her father in the bubble bath when she was little. By the time she was ten she was a regular little Criss Angel.) SMOKE IN—"You can see them up there, blasting from jets. Spraying barium and aluminum salts, polymer fibers, thorium, and silicon carbide out of their ass into the atmosphere. Into our lungs, our skin. Government-made, to make living Americans sick and unborn Americans defective."

COUGH, COUGH.

Kiss.

"I know what you're thinking, Lloyd."

"What?"

"How can I invest in some of THAT?"

Nora humor! And more to come: "From each according to their disabilities, to each according to their disease."

Nora got more bombastic, the bigger (and more multiply polluted) she got. She was morphing into an industrial-strength incarnation of herself. Doing insane combinations, like bath salts and oxys—Florida speedballs. It was all very *Geek Love*. But I admit, the bath salts scared me, after the Miami face-eating thing. (It wasn't that I loved my face. I just have a fear of teeth.) This jolted me out of baby obsession. Instead I stayed up all night worried she might go love-cannibal. But all she did was sweat, then freeze; her incisors started chattering, then she dropped to the floor, where I realized it wasn't chattering teeth. She was convulsing. Going full floppy-fish. I used to get that when I over-smoked crack. One minute you're rushing, enjoying your heart attack, the next you're bouncing on the bathroom floor, trying to reach the heroin-streaked tinfoil on the sink, flick the lighter.

Hold the tinfoil tube in your mouth, hold lighter steady. SMOKE IN. Don't die. SMOKE OUT. Breathe.

Is . . . that . . . a . . . crumb in a corner?

Euphoria is the best side effect in the world. You're still you. But you're happy about it. Comfortable in your own clammy skin.

After I blew tar in her mouth, I waited till she calmed down to take her temperature. All her thermometers were rectal. (First time at the new girlfriend's place? Take a thermo tour!) When I asked Nora about it—never mind the snooping—she was blithe as Audrey Hepburn. If Audrey had had rectal fever issues but was totally okay about it. "But darling, why shouldn't everything be fun?")

For one bad moment, I was afraid Nora'd convulse and snap the glass off. But I managed. 104.2. Which had to be great for the baby.

I sat up with her. Waiting. What goes up, must go sideways. But no matter what, even in mid-convulsion, her palms never left her belly, stroking and patting (well, *drumming*) during the seizure, as if signaling her victim. Pretty soon she added to her stew of street drugs, toxic pharmaceuticals, and industrial by-products, deciding to include an extra ingredient: my sperm.

Festivities ensued . . . I began taking drugs, but not the kind we'd been taking. See, this entire time, and for decades earlier, I had been "suffering" with hepatitis C. I say suffering advisedly, because it wasn't bad. It wasn't AIDS. That's how most junkies viewed it. We'd dodged the big one. A little crushing fatigue, uncontrollable anger, some mood swings, your basic brain fog—look it up, "brain fog" is an actual medically indicated symptom. Like waking up every day with a brutal hangover, without getting drunk. (Saves on a bar tab.) But then I heard about this trial, at St. John's. An all-new cocktail was on the way! And I could be the first to belly up to the bar.

Pharma-sidebar: For years interferon was the treatment of choice for hepatitis C. The stuff was debilitating, causing suicidally depression, hair loss, daily nausea, and skin-clawingly itchy rashes. Plus, you had to inject it—and when isn't it a good idea to put needles in the hands of a recovering junkie?

The trial took ten weeks and did away with the interferon. That was the big news. No needles, no debilitation, no nausea, no hair loss. The experimental regimen consisted of Ribavirin—a staple of the modern-day AIDS cocktail—and a protease inhibitor called telaprevir. (And yes, I'd love to meet the genius who came up with the idea of calling a punishing drug regimen a "cocktail.") The other pills in the trial just had numbers:

the super-secret ABT 450 and ABT 333, as well as the vaguely menacing Z-10. They weren't sure what the side effects would be for the guinea pigs taking it. (Maybe I'd get the gig writing them!) They suspected we'd still get that party rash, and there'd be some OMD, occasional mental displacement. Also known as "profound spaciness." What they were certain about was the impact on the unborn. Which was very, very bad. You wouldn't want to be a fetus and go anywhere near this shit.

Talk about synchronicity! Or as they used to say at Christian Swingles, "Coincidences are Jesus's way of staying anonymous." Now I was the one packing all-new fetal-defect batter, an armory of pharma-financed, cutting-edge weapons to mutate an innocent baby. Fate had tossed my testes into Nora's wheelhouse.

THIRTY-FIVE

The Non-Interferon Treatment

So. The first thing you're told, when they accept you into Phase Two of the Abbott-financed non-interferon Hepatitis C trial, is that you must have no contact with pregnant women. The doctor who gives you this news is tall and athletic, Eric Cantor-y. He can't hide his contempt for the subjects of his own trial, mainly LA drug addicts. Maybe he'd rather have been administering placenta-based skin rejuvenation therapies. But he was a hepatologist. And right now a drug company was paying him to administer a trial to a room full of low-life livers. Six of us, on folding chairs in a fluorescent-lit room at St. John's. The other five—all guys—still looked fiendy. Or had some kind of residual prison vibe. Slouched in their chairs: legs apart, arms spread crucifix wide on the backs of the chairs to the left and right, taking up as much space as possible. The *What are you lookin' at, bitch?* pose. Not even showing ink; wearing long sleeves, to hide it, so you knew there was something interesting under there: like the Viking riding the SS thunderbolt on the hand of my Aryan neighbor to the right. Something you might not want Dr. Joel Weinstein to see.

Along with the possibility of curing you, the drug company was paying six hundred dollars for the privilege of plying us with untested antivirals and drawing blood once a week. (Rich people didn't need to join a study. They could get the stuff off-market.)

(The funny thing is I actually did get cured. Which can be disconcerting. It's so much easier when you have an excuse for feeling like shit and wanting to strangle people. *You mean I'm cured and I still feel this way? That all along it was me? I feel sick!*)

By now, I'd cleaned up and begun paddling around town in TV-writer drag: button-down shirt, good-boy khakis, New Balance running shoes. (On the inside, I felt like I was wearing a unitard.) There was no doubt, sitting with all these hard cases, that I was the lame one in the room. The square. Even though, I did not have to remind myself, I was the one participating in a crime so transgressive, so—when accompanied with the manifesto Nora was working up—real-life potentially world-changing, it was hard not to feel Dostoyevskian. If they only knew!

THIRTY-SIX

Tumor Daddy

Weeks turned into months. Our crime became grander, the more Nora and I discussed it. The real shock was not that she willingly did this to her own fetus. The real shock was that millions of women did the same thing *unwillingly*. And Nora would be their symbol. She'd be the Helen of Troy of corporate irresponsibility, of capitalism unconstrained by human consequences. Of profit made on the tiny, malformed spines of fetal-deregulation monsters. A one-woman corpo *Guernica*, with real womb and real blood. I felt like I was writing copy for a pregnant Revelations.

We had no doubt the video would go viral. From there—well, we had a long to-do list. (Her cause, as you can see, had become our cause.) Tumblr, Twitter, Pinterest, Vimeo, Facebook, Boing Boing, Gawker, Reddit, BuzzFeed. And those were just the beginning. The press releases, the event . . . It was the Kony campaign without the resources and the guy running naked through the street. (When rich people are filmed naked in the streets, they're suffering from fatigue. When poor people crack and go clothesless it's bath salts or *Cops*.) In free moments, when we thought about it, I'd jot down blobs of talk-show take-away, FAQs to give to interviewers. I reassured her that nothing went viral faster than hate—and some people were really, really going to hate her. Until I brought it up, she hadn't even considered a safe house. There was no guarantee the baby would even live. But if it did, there was no way social services would let it live with her. Or that righteous hordes would not want her hide. Look at Tanning Mom! I got it out of Nora that her real dream—mind you, this was somebody who carried a picture of Emma Goldman in her wallet—was to be the subject of her very own Lifetime special. *Because mothers watch Lifetime*, as I wrote for her to say when interviewed, *and mothers are the hearts and minds of this country.*

We had stacks of handwritten notes, since we had no printer and hadn't been to Kinko's since Jay and Riegle forged our insurance. Some nails to hit on talk-show pre-interviews: *We always knew we were going to go viral, Rachel, and we also knew they'd want to eradicate us. But you can't eradicate the truth . . . This isn't even about me, Charlie. The chemicals that did this to my baby are out there, unregulated, and the longer we go without acknowledging this quiet apocalypse, the more we're going to see what happened to my child happen to other children . . . I know what I did was controversial, Amy, I know some people are even calling it sick. Fair enough. People can think what they need to think. What we're thinking about are how many other babies, and how many families, are going to have to get sick at the hands of these capitalist monsters before this country changes its laws and begins to care more about the health of its children than lining the pockets of the chemical companies, the pharmaceutical companies, and all the lobbyists, politicians, and pundits—no offense—who are in the tank with them . . . Thanks to a bought-and-paid-for* Congress, *we are exposing an entire generation to unspeakable disease. These companies—like Monsanto, like Dow, like DuPont—are literally allowed to kill and maim with complete impunity. And they do it with something far more insidious than guns or bombs, Chris. They do it with the very products you buy yourself. Sunblock, sofas, soy milk, chewing gum, blueberries, deodorant. We are talking about the most commonplace items in your life killing you and dooming your unborn children . . .*

I could crank this stuff out by the yard. It felt empowering. Applying all my powers for good. Did the fact that I used the same skills trying to save the world as I did pimping fake testosterone cream make the effort any less meaningful?

Sometimes, we'd shoot up and do *The View*. I'd pose a question as, say, Elisabeth Hasselbeck, and then Nora would answer off the notes I'd given her.

Me (as Elisabeth Hasselbeck): "*Nora, how do you handle all the haters? So many in our audience have already tweeted . . . well, I don't have to tell you about the public reaction to what you've done.*"

Then Nora would read, or try and recite, from the words I'd given her: "*I'll take the hate, ladies. I'll take the name-calling and the death threats if, thanks to what we've done, other children can be spared the horrors to which we subjected our child deliberately . . .*"

Other times I'd shoot up and imagine myself on *The 700 Club*, fellowshipping with Pat Robertson. It was so realistic, my shins tickled from the little Prayer Partner contribution number crawling across them at the bottom of the screen. "*Did God ask me to do this? Well, Reverend, I'm not going to sit here and tell you that the Almighty came to us personally, like God telling Abraham to kill him a son, and said, 'Sacrifice your sweet unborn darling so that other sweet unborn darlings will live . . .' We're doing this for all the other darlings, born and unborn, who are victims of these capitalist monsters. Of course not. What I'm saying is, if there is a God, then God is working through my little girl . . . The Lord has chosen her to suffer the deformities and birth defects so that others can come into this world free of deformity and defect. . . ."*

There were times when I didn't think Nora was insane, and I really thought she had a chance to change the system. Until, eventually, I came to see the obvious. If she had a chance at saving the world, it was precisely because she *was* insane.

Meanwhile, we were still in the hep C drug trial doctor's office, where the doctor, obviously the drug company's man in Havana, was so concerned about what he was saying that he kept repeating himself. Abbott clearly had liability concerns. The upshot, in every version, was that we understood that if we so much as touched a pill and then touched the skin of a mother-to-be, there was the chance—let's not kid ourselves, the *probability*—of vascular and neurological defects. Your baby will be deformed. Not that the dozen other bad livers in the house had any grave concerns in that direction. "You mean *her* baby," one of the slouching wags muttered, to general snickering and some fist-bump-finger-touch yuk-yuk penitentiary handshake with the ambassador of goodwill next to him. But the doctor ignored them and moved on to a danger even closer to home. Our sperm would now be poison. Actually, he said "teratogenic." *Then* he said poison, explaining for the non-vocabulary-builders. Nobody smirked at this one. Personally, all I could think was that my ejaculate was now a lethal weapon.

We had to sign a form, in triplicate, in which we declared that we understood the risks—which, I discovered when I read the fine print, also included death and frequent nosebleeds.

Later, when the RN was drawing blood, I asked about the whole pregnancy-danger thing, and she put down her phlebotomy needle. "What I always say is, you and your lady be in bed together, and she expecting?" I caught a whiff of lunchtime Burgundy as she rolled her chair closer, so the doctor couldn't hear through the walls. "She so much as roll over in your sweat, that baby gonna be neurologically janky. At least. More likely, your shit will be seriously deformed. You ever hear of thalidomide?"

"I've seen pictures."

"Okay, compared to this, them babies was styling. They advise refraining from sexual relations for the length of the study. But we know that ain't gonna happen. So what you gotta do, you gotta wear two condoms. Sperm is what they call a volatile delivery system. It brings the bad stuff right up in there."

There it was. Nora was already pregnant, so it wouldn't be my little dumpling. I wouldn't be father to the child, just its defects. Thanks to my newfound trial-monkey status.

Call me Tumor Daddy.

When I told Nora about my toxic sperm, her eyes went wide. Knowing that sex was so dangerous did something for her. Some women got off on bad boys. Nora got off on bad sperm. Our lovemaking was never better. We took it next-level. This was the golden period of our relationship. And not just with each other. With, if I may sound so Buttercup Junction, the whole world.

Once she really began to show, everybody loved us. We were suddenly mainstream. Pregnancy was the great leveler: the universal acceptance magnet. Everybody loves a mommy-to-be.

Only I knew what was going on inside her. That what was coming would not be on the label of a Gerber baby food jar. Walking down the aisle at Trader Joe's, strangers would smile at us. Women with children exchanged knowing looks. Dads shot me thumbs-ups and winks. Happy citizens of a happy world. We always smiled back. If they only knew. It was like going out with a suicide bomber.

At three months I understood something: the universality of family. Until you're there, you just don't know. You can't. Black, white, Latino, Asian, homeless, or leaning out the window of a still-dealer-stickered BMW 760Li. Now it was more than smiles and nods. We would end up having coffee with other pregnant couples we ran into. Total strangers became new-mommy friends. Sometimes, after the couples left, Nora liked to pull out her short dog of Old Mr. Boston and pour a slug into her Starbucks. I could tell how much she would have liked to do it in front of people. I never could decipher her motivation for these displays. Except that the part of her that wanted to pass was always a little smaller than the part that was dying to say *Fuck you.*

Mostly, though, from the outside we were the perfect parents to be. Once, at *CSI*, when I was brought in again because they'd run out of perversions, I told them about shrimping. Bea always wanted to know what kind of life I led that I'd know about this. For once, instead of marching out an old girlfriend who worked at a bondage parlor, I told them something interesting: the first time I heard about toe-sucking it was under Clinton. "He did that, too?" Bea sounded more impressed than surprised. But I told them no, it wasn't Bill. His consultant, Dick Morris, broke his tooth on a hooker's toenail. There was an S beside his name in the Mayflower Madam's little book, which no one at the FBI could figure out. Until one bright young agent came up with shrimper. "Bingo," as they say in TV shows and movies. But never, in my experience, in real life.

Basically, the plan was, when Nora went into labor, to alert the media—new and old. To get the ball rolling fast and hard. But it had to be done right. She was using her own womb to make the statement. One wrong move and Nora would make Octomom look like Michelle Obama.

But we were ready. Once we had the photo and videos, Nora would provide her detailed list of all the products she'd been exposed to or taken. Everything USDA-approved safe for home and garden. (We didn't mention the narcotics—or that paint products are generally deemed "safe when used properly." Which, technically, did not include huffing them. But why niggle?) Nora insisted she didn't have a criminal record, when I told her how they'd be coming after her after Baby Mutando was born. The powers that be would want to make her bipolar, felonious, or otherwise unhinged and untrustworthy in order to dilute her message. "Look at Sandra Fluke," I said. "All she did was stand up for government-funded birth control, and Rush Limbaugh went foamy and called her a ho bag."

"I would love that," Nora said, staring dreamily off over the glass stem in her hand, features softened by crack smoke into something very Madonna-esque. (Not Madonna, the venerable performer, but Madonna, the mother of another celebrity freak-baby, Jesus Christ.)

Thanks to my newly reminted pals Jay and Riegle, we had everything media ready. (Or so they claimed.) We discussed the whole thing over pills and caffeine at Chico's, a Mexican joint in Highland Park where the pair spent a large part of the day imbibing Horchata and, as Riegle always used to say, "doing what we do." It was eight in the morning. Nora'd been up all night vomiting. Which, the doctors assured us, was normal for pregnant women. I'd sat with her, watching a very Barney Rubble-y Joe Scarborough, on *Morning Joe*, swapping fun political chit-chat with his perky sparring partner Mika Brzezinski.

By now Nora'd begun vomiting for hours at a time, but it never seemed to bother her. "You know," she remarked, coming back from the toilet as she was wiping her mouth, "Mika's father, Zbigniew Brzezinski, is the one who recruited Obama to be the Trilateral Commission's puppet."

"The Black Manchurian," Riegle two-centsed.

"As in 'Candidate,'" Jay explained. They'd taken to finishing each other's sentences like a married couple.

Riegle got a seemingly endless number of pills off the Internet. He still made the same joke he made when we'd grab a bite before going to work at Christian Swingles, back in the day: "Opiates and caffeine, breakfast of champions." After we got good and well, the pair started in about erecting a platform on YouTube. Or something. With the oxys, it was all pleasantly incomprehensible. I forgot how hillbilly heroin made your ears ring. (Speaking of Rush, how much did it take to make a fat man go deaf in one ear?) Jay and Riegle promised they'd get her "out there" Gangnam style.

"Being a con man ain't that different from being a promoter," Jay opined. "Look at Colonel Tom!"

Neither ever seemed overconcerned about what we were doing, or even what Nora was doing. Both these guys had a way of smiling like they knew something you didn't. Of course they knew that Nora wanted to make a statement with the baby. But, oddly, I think they both just liked the idea of becoming uncles.

"That little fucker's gonna be a world-shaker" was all Jay said about it. "A regular little X-Man."

Oxycodone made his voice deeper than heroin. It sounded like he was croaking from beyond the grave. Which could be disconcerting, and startled the other patrons of Chico's, who'd look away and mutter low to each other in Spanish. (I thought I heard *diablo*, but maybe not.)

I was as close to a techno-peasant as you could be and still know how to text. So when Riegle went on about how "Tumblr's configurable post queue can automatically publish your posts at designated intervals," my eyes glazed over even more than they already had. In my world electronic devices were to be procured and traded. Generally for an illicit product . . . I was whatever you call the opposite of cutting-edge. I owned a

BlackBerry, the world's most un-trendy paperweight, and lived guiltily as a bill-paying member of Verizon's union-busting network.

When I tuned back in, having spilled coffee on my lap—I was either sleepy or becoming palsied—Nora was declaiming her intentions yet again. The waitress, a plump Colombian mother of five named Daisy, forgave all at the sight of Nora's belly. But didn't stay to listen after she wiped up.

"This is the core of the message, guys. My baby is one hundred percent USDA and AMA approved."

This was, indeed what Nora wanted to get out there.

"That's cute," Jay said.

We hadn't told them that cute might not be a part of the package. By unspoken agreement we just didn't explain why we wanted to document and publicize the event. This was the A-bomb, and we were our own Manhattan Project.

Nora had—disturbingly—found photographs of birth defects that no Calcutta sideshow would have seen fit to display. But once—she deeply believed, and endlessly repeated—once people see, once they really see what the products that surround us do to us, to our sweet, innocent, lovely, never-had-a-say-in-the-matter children . . . Well, "We Are the World."

THIRTY-SEVEN

Secret Bible

Did we love the child? Did we even care about the child, or was the child just collateral damage?

These are the questions I imagined people asking later. (Was it, as we coke-projected some artsy pundit later observing, as if, instead of painting *Guernica*, Picasso had just built a bomb and blown up a child, to show what bombs can do? I didn't think so, but that's me.) Knowing what we had subjected our little princess to. Princess, yes: Nora decided it was going to be a girl—that is, if it even had a sex or, anyway, if it had just one.

Toward the end of the second trimester, if she had smoked enough crack, Nora claimed she could hear the child talking. There were eerie moments, sitting in the backyard of our termite-infested Echo Park bungalow at night, or the time, deep in bed at some pitch-black-curtains-closed three in the afternoon, when she grabbed my arm and eased me sideways, so I was ear to belly, and made me listen. "Do you hear that? What she's saying? She's saying she wants to be here. She knows she's been selected . . . She sounds just like Nina Simone."

"Nina Simone. Huh. That would be so odd, in a baby."

"She's not a baby," Nora corrected me. "She's unborn. The unborn are an entirely different species. We can't even be sure how many there are . . . Listen. Can you hear?"

"Um . . . not really."

Nora closed her eyes, altered her voice like an eighties trance channeler. Ramtha! " 'Mommy, please, don't worry about me. I want to help all the other mommies.' "

This spoken in her fetal Nina Simone voice.

I know how this sounds. It's just, I had so many feelings when I was with Nora. Fear being just one, at this particular moment. Which she seemed to sense, before she slowly guided her hand back to me, before easing her face south and planting it between my legs, before taking me inside her mouth. It was, I sensed, a gesture. But what wasn't? She wanted me with her; I wanted to be there. We'd come so far together, down this strange road, I could barely remember not being on it.

"Relax," she said, forgetting to switch out of her fetal Nina. It was disturbing, but not *that* disturbing.

As she mouthed me, massaging and sucking all at once, I heard the skittering of raccoons who lived under the house. I wondered, insanely, if they *knew*, and a thought occurred in the midst of my transport. Is there such a thing as a maternal Messiah complex, when a woman believes, not that she's the Messiah, but that she'll be giving birth to one? A Mary Jones?

"Mmmm," Nora moaned, "pop it out and fuck me. Call me a dirty virgin."

Then she burst out laughing. A habit with Nora that, mysteriously, didn't make sex less hot. It was somewhere between role-playing and parody. But I was too close to my appointment with destiny to appreciate it. I had that old premonitory quiver. What got Nora genuinely excited, what pretty much comprised her porn of the moment, was the thought of the toxins roiling out of my testicles.

Her thumb stayed in my mouth while she pulled her lips off my cock, semi-moaning, mumbling—mostly, I suspected, to herself. "*Mary knows what Joseph needs. It's in the Secret Bible . . .*" She ran her tongue up my stomach, to my mouth; with her other hand, now mumbling below coherence, she parted herself, under her clit, and brushed upward with her ring finger. "You know what I want . . . Fill me." So I did. I had to. (Some men, I know, from the months I put in writing and answering fake questions at *Penthouse* Forum, have issues with women who masturbate during sex with them. As if it's a competition. A comment on their ability to please. As opposed—at the other end of the self-pleasuring spectrum—to an act of unselfish, unself-conscious naked appetite. But not on the Internet. In real life. I couldn't hold out, and filled her with my thrilling, AMA-condemned, poison sperm.

This may be counterintuitive, but knowing what we'd done—what we were going to do—made us love the mutant munchkin more. Knowing the world of pain to which we had possibly condemned it—and knowing *why* we'd condemned it—only made us cherish her more. Does that make sense? This baby—can I say this too many times? Have I?—this baby would be a message, a global warning, a kind of toxic inoculation of the entire species. Our baby, the little Mutando, would by her example protect legions of future babies. At least that was the plan.

"John 3:16." Nora surprises me with her recitation. "For God so loved the world, that he gave his only begotten Son, that whosoever believeth in him should not perish, but have everlasting life."

"How do you even know that?"

That badass shrug. "I've done a lot of motel time."

In any event, that's what we were doing—giving our only begotten child, so that others wouldn't perish. Not for their sins—but for the sins of Monsanto and Dow and Squibb and Pfizer, etc. . . . (Not to mention Abbott, who more or less saved my life. Ironies abound . . .) People don't realize the torments even our staples can wreak. (Thank you, Diet Coke, for aspartame, bringer of stroke and brain cancer.) But after the birth of our child, after the artfully planned full-bore assault accompanying it, they would see with their own eyes.

Nora and my erstwhile Christian Swingles pals were spending more and more time together, cooking up the social media afterbirth, to make sure of it.

You see where this is going, right? *You want to make God laugh, make a plan, etc.* . . . Five weeks before the due date we'd been given, Nora jerked up out of deep sleep to find her sheets soaked. She threw back the blankets, like Jack Woltz in *The Godfather* before he saw his Arabian horse head gushing blood on his pajamas. Khartoum. She'd broken water and she wanted to unbreak it.

All the experts tell you to have a hospital bag packed and waiting by the door. But we weren't expecting a hospital trip for another month. We couldn't find the car keys, and I noticed burn holes in her T-shirt—technically, my T-shirt—right where you'd expect to get burn holes if you were holding a crackpipe to your lips and the hot rocks kept popping out. She hadn't showered in a while, either, and there was a trace of brownish gold around her mouth where she must have huffed something without turpentining her face afterward. "Honey," I said, as gently as possible, "you have to at least wash your face and change into something else. You don't want some ER nurse to get suspicious."

"Fuck that!" Nora was hysterical. Then I realized it wasn't hysteria, it was anger. She was furious she was going to have the baby and nobody would be there to see. All that planning! All the prepared remarks! All the high-impact photo ops! It was not supposed to be this way. What if a monstrous and deliberately deformed tree falls in the forest, and no one is there to tweet?

The baby is getting its revenge. That's what I thought but didn't say. Nora was already beside herself, throwing shit around the bedroom. She banged her hairbrush off the mirror and cracked it, so her face stared back splintered, like an old horror movie poster.

"We need Jay! We need Riegle! This ruins everything!

"I can video with my phone," I said.

She pounded her fist on the dresser, hard enough to knock out a few loose mirror shards. "That's not the plan! You know what we wanted!"

The plan. Right.

Here we were, relieving the 1974 Larry Cohen classic *It's Alive*. You've seen the poster. A stark black-and-white of a baby carriage below the cutline "There's only ONE thing wrong with the Davis baby . . . IT'S ALIVE!"

Mom-to-be was such a wreck she decided a little Mexican tar would help. It made me nervous. But everything made me nervous where Nora was concerned. "I'm not criticizing, baby, but are you sure you want to be gowed when you're having your baby?"

"I need to be gowed. It'll kick in the epidural. And don't look at me like that!"

"Like what?"

"Like you're Mister Fucking Rogers and I'm some fucking degenerate junkie whore."

Oddly, she'd asked me to call her that, when we were fucking. (Odder, I kind of wanted her to call me Mister Rogers, but this did not seem like the time to bring it up.) Nor did I bring up my fave fact about everyone's favorite kiddie host, that his real name—or maybe his middle name—was McFeely. *Mister McFeely's Neighborhood.* That's a whole different show.

Her contractions had kicked in hard. From none at all to under two a minute. Zero to red zone. Not normal. The last thing I wanted to do was fight, but she needed a target.

"It's like," she went on, "you think you're better than me. Don't forget, you're my accomplice, motherfucker. They come after me, you're going down too."

"I'll keep that in mind," I said. With the payload of mutagens she'd been feeding her fetus, Mommy was bound to be out of sorts. But, as zero-hour drew near, that's not what had me freaked. I'd been in denial about my own culpability. But how could I be? If Nora was Mama Frankenstein, then I was Fritz, the lurching, hunchbacked creepy assistant.

I threw a bag together with an extra T-shirt. Literally, a paper bag, like Nora's, from Vons supermarket. (Where, at the height of low-end junkiedom, I used to work my champion can scam: shoplifting that fifteen-ounce Dinty Moore beef stew, banging it on the curb to put a dent in it, and then returning it for a quick $1.99. Such was my life of crime. Not exactly *Goodfellas*, but you have to start somewhere. The art of it was maintaining dignity and conveying the muted indignation of a solid citizen appalled by shoddy shelf-stocking. Tough to do when you haven't changed your pants in a year.) The one suitcase we had was full of Rust-Oleum and Roundup cans. Nora wanted to keep the poison flowing till the bitter end. I threw her T-shirt in the Vons bag along with her Aveeno Active Naturals Positively Radiant tinted moisturizer. *(Dying for beauty!)* A product so natural, she explained, that it was shown to cause thyroid and brain-signal problems in lab animals.

The spoon was stained brown after we shot up all the dope. Shoe polish will do that. Lately the tar we copped on Alvarado was cut with the stuff. I don't know what studies had been done on the subject of IV Scuff Kote abuse, but it had to be as noxious as skin cream. At least there was enough left to spruce up our boots.

"You'll need a change of underwear, too," I said, fishing around on the floor and sniffing for something fresh. Nora saw me with the panties in my face and sneered. "Do we really have time for that, *now*? This is a catastrophe!"

"Nora," I said, thinking to throw her back one of her own pitches, "when Dow killed eight hundred seventeen people in one day at Bhopal, *that* was a catastrophe."

"What that fucking CEO did to me was a catastrophe, too."

Have I mentioned I already had doubts? Nascent. Not that she had (or hadn't) been raped. Molested. Tortured by a family member. Any and all. You rarely meet a hard-core addict who doesn't have some kind of hard-core abuse in their closet. Or not even in the closet. More like all over the room. That was a given. Then again, before Nora, I never knew one who grew up to be . . . Nora. I'm talking about the big-time CEO end of things. Her claim—and I suppose, using the word "claim," I am telegraphing my evolving attitude about her veracity. (Not to sound political spokespersony.) I can't tell you when they started—my doubts—but there, I said it. I sat there, among the toner cartridges, microwaves, paint thinner, and all their toxic friends—and reality curled its fingers around my throat. My mouth went dry.

As the big moment approached, I began to feel ambivalent. But it was too late.

I helped her cook up a shot and then slid a needle full of questionable Mexican between her big toe and the next one—her fore-toe?—despite the imminent trip to the hospital. I didn't mention that New Jersey charged a half dozen mothers with aggravated assault for giving birth to drug-addicted babies. What kind of case would you catch if your child was born rust-proofed? Happily, we weren't in Jersey.

By now Nora was groaning in pain. And fighting me. On her back, in bed, squeezing her legs together.

"This *mmmmph* this baby is not *mmmmphh* this baby is not coming out!"

Forget the labor pains. She did not want to go to the hospital. It was all wrong! She'd come so far. Endured so much. For the chance to record her attack on the plague of capitalism, on what America was doing to itself, on who we are and what we consume and what it does to the most innocent among us. We never even talked about what she was risking personally. Her body, her future, her soul. No question, a woman who uses the health—no, the sickness—of her child to make a point is going to pay for it. Turn your uterus into a fetal test kitchen, folks are bound to have opinions.

We made it to the door, Nora doubled over, clutching her stomach, walking with her legs jammed together in tiny, mincing steps. I had one arm around her, holding the overstuffed Vons bag with the other, car keys in my teeth. I don't even remember the drive. Just that the last thing she grabbed going out the door was a Bible. I didn't even know we had one, or why she kept it in the oven.

"It will be good for the nuns to see," she managed, between clenched teeth.

"Maybe," I said, "unless they find out you've circled all the bad acid shit in Revelations."

At this hospital, it all happened fast. Intake. Then—whoosh—right to the ob-gyn. The RN had to snatch the BlackBerry out of Nora's hand. The plan called for cameras, a news feed, national outrage, international attention, and—at least in Nora's wish-fulfilling mind—fury-driven and (thanks to her) enlightened global policy change.

"Are you the husband?"

Nora was now vibrating on the gurney. They were shoving

an IV in her arm. I handled the paperwork. Watched them prepare to whisk her off.

"Are you the father?" the nurse asked again.

"No," I said. (Awkward.) "Just a friend. I'm not the father. We live near each other. She needed a ride."

I spoke in a lowered voice, concerned. Though mostly my voice was low because I did not want Nora to hear. Did I love her? Of course I did. Do. Though that moment feels like the proverbial lifetime ago. I have done some very bad things for her, and with her, and—even though I was acquiescing, not initiating—*to* her.

But never mind.

I saw the RN consulting with a doctor at the elevator. Imagined, in that way you do when you're high, that what I thought they were saying they were really saying. Nurse: "Doctor, there's something here I think you should see." I watched the man in the white coat lean over, and then raise his face gravely: "What is this, *Citizen Ruth*? She's *huffing*."

Of course, this was just in my head. For all her aspirational toxicity, Nora looked like a healthy mom-to-be.

In truth, probably nothing of what I thought was said was said. Still, I had to wonder. *Had* I wiped off the gold smudgering around her mouth? Paranoia is just heightened awareness of possibly unlikely, possibly inevitable consequences. Or leaky adrenaline, depending. This was no longer about capitalist fallout. This was about not getting arrested. She was too far along to turn away, and the sourpuss admitting nurse did not hide her opinion on the matter.

THIRTY-EIGHT

Let's Review!

Okay. Breathe.

For the second time: Did we think about the child?

Of course. We both wanted her to be comfortable. And yes, I know how that sounds.

We weren't delusional. We knew what people would say. (As I've said.) What they would accuse us of. But the backlash was part of it. The more blowback, the better. The louder they—they being everyone: media, preachers, lawmakers, moms—screamed about what we'd done, the louder we'd scream that it was being done to us. We wanted editorials, hate mail, talk-radio rants, ultimate recognition for the sheer horrific rightness of the point we were making. However horrific the means of making it.

THIRTY-NINE

End Times

The birth itself is a blur. *It all happened so fast.* Isn't that what people say? That or *Time just stopped.* Actually, time did not stop. Time disappeared altogether. Everything happened at once, as if the event collapsed in on itself. One second we were in our humble domicile, consuming baby defectors, the next we were in the car, the ER, the elevator, the delivery room. The baby wanted out. Early. I can't say I blamed it.

Maybe, unlike Mom, the little polluted thing had some instinct for survival. I don't know. I do know that once Nora had her feet up in stirrups, and the nurse handed me pale-blue scrubs and booties, I barely had time to blink before the doctor shouted for Betadine and a second RN, gripping Nora's shoulders at the head of the bed, started chanting. I saw her momentary hesitation, eyes Velcroed to Nora's German shepherd Daddy tattoo. The dripping fangs. She willed herself to look away. Cleared her throat. "Okay, now, push . . . go ahead. It's like making a bowel movement. Push . . . Go ahead . . . PUSH!"

So vast and nurturing was the nurse's charisma, under those hospital fluorescents, that for one fleeting instant the whole process seemed somehow . . . wholesome. Normal. Even *life-affirming.* (Not a word I've ever used.)

Nora's screams I knew—I was the *only* one who knew—did not come from the traditional and well-documented searing pain of childbirth. Or not just. As the baby was crowning, and seconds later when the doctor eased the baby out, I saw, with shock, the same thing she saw. Her little girl had been born. Alive.

It was perfect.

FORTY

New Life

The horror.

The doctor pulled out the newborn, still attached to the umbilical cord like a Macy's Day float attached to a guide wire, and held her up. Red-faced, bloody, what turned out—after they snipped the cord and weighed her—to be six pounds, six ounces of squiggling, placenta-soaked mohawk. "Lanugo?" Nora asked hopefully, eyeing the mini Wendy O. Williams look-alike. The born-with-mega-hair syndrome was one Nora anticipated with fondness. "Nope," the RN replied. "Some babies are just born with a big do. Lanugo's when they actually have fur on their back."

"You mean . . ." I could see the words stick in her throat like sticks. "You mean, she's normal?"

Nora turned to me, stricken, as the new nurse, a tiny red-head, lifted the tiny creature and placed her on Nora's full and plangent right breast, to suckle. This was when I noticed the milky drop oopling from her nipple. Oddly indistinguishable from sperm and, inappropriate as I sensed the sensation was the instant I felt it, insanely hot. Here was Nora, devastated and suckling, her all-but-cleaved vagina just now being cleaned of blood and feces, and all I wanted to do was fuck her. Out of nowhere I remembered my late mother's favorite insult, yelped incessantly at me and my long-since OD'd brothers: "What were you, raised in a barn?"

There was one hopeful second, after the initial shock, when little Nico's outsized genitals gave us hope. (Did I mention that Nico was now her designated name? Nico Mutando. We both thought it had a ring.) Her girl lips swelled with the pink, protuberant shock of orangutan ass. "Oh my God!" Nora exclaimed. She tugged at her hair and wrenched her head from side to side, barely able to contain what I knew to be joy. At least this part of her mission was accomplished. The coverage could commence later.

Misinterpreting the New Mom's relief for torment, the doctor reassured her: "Oh, her lady parts? What you're seeing is completely normal. They'll go down in a day." In other words, temporary mutation.

And that was that. Nora wept. For the first time since I'd met her. After this, she was inconsolable.

So that's what happened. The thing we never expected. A perfect baby.

Nora was carried out screaming.

An hour later, a policewoman stood guard outside the door, doing a word find. Apparently, after Nora's outburst, the doctor decided to test her. And contacted the law enforcement liaison about the magic ingredients they found in her blood system. By chance I heard part of the call, which she made from the nurses' station, when I was coming back from the men's room. Apparently,

Nora's state of extreme inebriation constituted a violation in and of itself. Depraved indifference . . . Reckless endangerment . . .

All this I overheard in snatches, pretending to tie my shoe.

I knew, then, that we needed to make a statement about our intent to make a statement. Something on the order of *The child you see here is suffering, not from the action of her parents, but from the inaction of our government, which has subjected her—and millions of others, born and unborn, just like her—to unchecked chemical and pharmaceutical pollution from time of conception. And before.*

The problem was, she wasn't suffering. The baby was fine (except for those temporarily eye-popping genitalia), and the only pollution the medical and law enforcement people cared about was the individual kind: drugs and booze. Institutional poisons didn't count.

At the moment, when by all rights I should have been falling on my sword, protecting my beloved, my junkie instincts took over. I became what I always was: a survivor, not a martyr.

I knew it the second another cop, a brush-cut, gym-muscled sergeant named Muskie, grabbed me by the arm and asked me what I knew. At which point my true nature, displaying all the nobility of a rat in a basement corner, revealed itself anew.

"Me, *Officer*? I don't know a thing. I just drove her here. We're neighbors. I'm just a friend . . ." And so on.

Did I feel bad? Of course! I knew they were going to take her away. But what good would come of them taking *me* away?

I know it looks cold, I know it looks like betrayal. But really, how can I help her if I'm inside, too? It's like how they tell you on airplanes to put the oxygen over your own mouth first, so you can then help your child. Nora will have plenty of time to write while she's in there. Perhaps this was the best outcome of all.

I wanted to whisper to Nora, to tell her all this. But with the cops there, and the doctor and nurses all milling around with crossed arms and talking in low voices, I needed to pretty much stand out in the hall and act sad and perplexed. (That first policewoman, I later learned, wasn't even there for her. They were posted to the maternity ward—*every* maternity ward because of the prevalence of baby-snatchers in the past five years. Only two months before, a twenty-three-year-old Christian lady, distraught that her own child had been lost in a miscarriage, had showed up at this very hospital and tried to grab a newborn. Which explained why, as soon as they snipped the umbilical and wiped the blood off, they snapped a little ankle bracelet around the baby. As if she were a tiny felon. If someone so much as carried the creature within five feet of an exit or elevator, an alarm would sound. Talk about your Nanny State.)

So much about this would have made Nora indignant, fired her up. But she was still trying to make a bigger point, the one we'd wanted to make all along, the one, because of the baby's premature arrival—and its unnaturally non-mutant condition—we would now not be able to document and distribute, and inflict upon the world. I could hear her through the closed door of the hospital room. Yelling. For me. Her voice cracked with desperation.

"Tell them, Lloyd, tell them!"

This prompts the lady uniform to regard me, again, with

naked suspicion. Unless I'm off my game, perception-wise, and it's simple disgust. Interrupted by brush-cut Muskie, who steps out to tear open a spearmint Chiclets, pop a few in his mouth, and snort at the lady uniform, "Honest to Christ, you wouldn't believe what I just found."

He offers her a Chiclet. They keep staring at me.

"She's just a friend," I repeat. "I drove her over."

Knowing, even as I say it, how much Nora needs me. How much, right now, more than anything, I need some heroin to obliterate the reality of what I'm doing, that very moment, to stay free and do more heroin. To blot out awareness of my own betrayal. Needless to say, I'm fooling no one. "I just drove her over. She okay?"

"Lloyd!" Nora screams again. This time Muskie and the policewoman turn toward me. The policewoman nods toward the door. The others watch to see how I'll respond. I manage a shrug and open the door enough to pop my head in. I try to look contrite. "I'm sorry, Norma, I really am."

"It's Nora, you shit!"

I shrug. It's all theater now, designed to just get me out of there.

"I think she's hysterical," I say, with as much compassion as I can.

I walked halfway down the hall without looking back and could still hear her screams.

I didn't know, in that moment, what they were going to do with the baby . . . The—this was finally confirmed—beautiful, healthy, bright-eyed, squalling baby. Cute enough for Gerber. Who wasn't mine. Wasn't the Dow Chemical CEO's, either.

Who was, if the letter I received some months later from Nora is to be believed, her stepfather's.

I'm not proud of myself. I'm not going to lie. I'm no sociopath. That's the problem. I have a conscience. I may have walked free. But I feel very, very bad about it.

And the baby? I had Jay make inquiries. Discreetly. She's still okay. No word that she glows in the dark. Seriously, she's fine. (And if, ten years from now, it turns out she can repel fleas, is that so bad?)

The worst side effects are the ones we don't see. Some people don't acknowledge their own feelings. They don't cry when their mothers die. They just drive into utility poles for a few years. Become heroin addicts. (But maybe that second thing is because they like heroin. You can't blame Mommy and Daddy for everything.)

I don't know if what I felt for Nora was love. But it's as close as I've ever gotten. We were crime partners. And we made love a lot. (Or something like it, just a little more chemically depraved.) A tiny butter knife slices more skin off my heart every time I think about her. I guess you could say she made me hate myself on a higher level.

As they say in the rooms of everything Anonymous, if you want self-esteem, commit estimable acts. And vice versa.

For better or worse, some of us wash up more familiar with the vice than the versa.

Epilogue

I visited Nora before she died. Up at Lartewell, in Walla Walla, the hospital for the criminally insane. The leukemia would have been enough. There was also the pituitary adenoma, and the Cushing's syndrome, a metabolic disorder caused by overproduction of corticosteroids by the adrenal cortex. Plus the alopecia. The Parkinson's, the pancreatic neoplasm. There was more than that wrong with her, to tell you the truth. Things in her brain.

And all of it, all of it, in the end, testament to how ironically—if futilely—heroic this woman was. Every impactful disease she had worked to protect future children from—by attempting to induce it in her own child—she acquired herself. Thereby protecting her own child. Saving it, effectively, from *her.* A staggering gesture for the nine people who heard about it. Of course, there are websites; you can find some Nora stuff out there, if you poke around . . . You can find the *SCUM Manifesto*, too. But that hasn't exactly made Valerie Solanas a household word, despite the biopic.

Did I mention I found out her last name? Nora *Hoylits*! Funk was fake.

Even now, sometimes, the copy pours out, by itself, like vaguely embarrassing fever sweat coming off an engorged carny barker. *Was she satanic? Was she a saint? Meet the woman who willingly absorbed our national effluvium—the toxic givens that the rest of us absorb unknowingly, unwillingly—to save us all. A profound gesture! Profoundly unnoticed, beyond the delivery room where she birthed her polluted child.*

(And so on . . . Just listen to that prose! *Grandiosity—side effect of inner tininess?*)

The joke? Ultimately the menu of national poisons in Nora's nervous system was of less concern than the tracks on her feet. What Officer Muskie'd stepped out to tell the policewoman about, when I was skulking in the hall playing Concerned Neighbor. Shooting between the toes, it turns out, fools no one.

Jay, Riegle, and I met again, in Calvary Way, a Christian recovery center. Founded and run by Pastor Bobb. The dating thing was history; now that shopping and Facebook were as rehab-worthy as meth and bourbon, the big money was back in rehabs.

We are all good Americans. In permanent re-recovery, freer than we deserve, with lifetimes of savage, happy amends ahead of us.

Acknowledgments

The author would like to express special gratitude to editor/page-artist Michael Signorelli for his killer eye, Zennish patience, and unbridled enthusiasm for all things questionable. In the immortal (if suspiciously attributed) words of Dashiell Hammett, "*If writing were easy, I wouldn't be dead.*"

ALSO BY JERRY STAHL

PAIN KILLERS

A Novel

Available in Paperback and eBook

Down-and-out ex-cop and not-quite-reformed addict Manny Rupert accepts an undercover job to find out if a California prison inmate is who he claims to be: Josef Mengele, aka the Angel of Death. Suddenly Manny finds himself in the middle of a conspiracy involving genocide, drugs, eugenics, human experiments, and America's secret history of collusion with the Nazis.

PLAINCLOTHES NAKED

Available in Paperback and eBook

In a wildly careening plot that can only be described as crack noir, two pipeheads accidentally steal a photo of George W. Bush's presidential package and decide to blackmail the Republican Party. Before the crack-crazed thieves can follow through, however, gorgeous, whip-smart Nurse Tina, who's just offed her husband with a bowl of Drano-laced Lucky Charms, absconds with the goods. When Manny Rubert, a scarred ex-junkie turned codeine-popping detective, is called in to investigate the "foamer" hubby's untimely demise, love hits him like a wrench to the head.

PERV—A LOVE STORY

Available in Paperback

Set in 1970—the last, dark days of hippiedom—*PERV* is the story of Bobby Stark, a 16-year-old batch of angst and hormones whose "coming of age" takes him from private boarding school to his mother's condo, then down the hitch-hikers' road to San Francisco . . . with plenty of adventures along the way.

"*PERV* never lets up until its death-rattling, orgasmic climax."—*Paper Magazine*

"[Stahl's] brilliantly demented riffs beg to be read—or screamed—aloud." —*Entertainment Weekly*

***I, Fatty*, Stahl's faux-memoir of silent actor Fatty Arbuckle, has been optioned by Johnny Depp.**